Her Reluctant Bear

Weres & Witches of Silver Lake
Book 5

Vella Day

White tiger shifter, Jillian Garner, would know the scent of the shifter who killed her father anywhere. When she gets a slight whiff of him years after her father's death, all the old trauma and fear come roaring to the surface. Now more than ever, she's determined to track him down and get her vengeance.

Encountering Brian Stanley, Jillian knows instantly that he's her mate, and that he just might be the man to help her. However, leery of people and mistrustful of others, Brian wants nothing to do with Jillian—despite how incredibly beautiful and persuasive she is. Jillian knows Brian more than he knows himself, and she'll stop at nothing until he realizes his true potential. It's up to her to convince him of their future while they're both fighting the pain of their pasts.

But when Jillian's history comes back for her, Brian must find the strength and courage to help save her. The only problem is: he doesn't believe in himself. Can Jillian find a way to show him the power of his love or will her enemy destroy her once and for all?

Beneath the calm and shimmering surface lie intrigue, power, magic, and danger.
Welcome to Silver Lake—where appearances can be deceiving, and what you see isn't truly what lies below.

Chapter One

To learn about Vella Day's other new releases, contests, and find new
authors, subscribe to her newsletter and get three free books!
http://smarturl.it/o4cz93?IQid=MLite

An Unexpected Diversion (book 1 of Hidden Hills Shifters)
Bare Instincts (book 2 of Hidden Hills Shifters)
Montana Desire (book 1 of Rock Hard, Montana)

WHEN HIRED STRIPPER Sergeant McDirty swiveled his hips in front of the dark-haired bride-to-be, his rotating pelvis failed to match the beat of the sensual music. Given how far the other women's tongues and eyeballs were hanging out, Jillian Garner was pretty sure none of the women even noticed.

She just shook her head. Sure, the hunk was hot. Not only did he have a nice smile, he possessed slim hips and had shoulders packed with muscles, but he did nothing for her inner tiger—not that this was about her. Her college roommate and fellow coworker at the law firm, Renee Williams, was getting married, and Jillian couldn't be happier for her.

As Renee stuck dollar bill after dollar bill down the man's G-string, her older sister, Camille who worked Vice at the Los Angeles Police Department shouted, "Go Renee!"

It was good to see the defense attorney loosen up, something Renee hadn't done in the last few years. It wasn't until Richie had entered her life that she'd decided to slow down and smell the roses, so to speak.

As for Jillian, Los Angeles had wound her tighter than any Swiss watch, but she wasn't looking for someone to help her slow down. She was fine the way she was.

"Jillian," Camille said, nudging her arm. While Renee wore her dark hair short, Camille preferred her light brown hair shoulder length. She claimed it softened her appearance and made it easier for witnesses to relate to her.

When Jillian glanced up, Sergeant McDirty was thrusting his tiny maroon pouch at her. Oh my. The women, who were packed into Camille's tiny, modern living room apartment, clapped and cheered, waiting for Jillian to deposit the two dollars she'd been clutching for the last half hour into his *package*. She was thirty-two, much too old to be doing this sort of thing, especially with a guy who didn't look old enough to drink. For Renee's sake though, Jillian tossed him her best smile and jammed the bills inside, careful not to let her fingers touch his skin while at the same time not dislodging the mass of bills already crammed into the tiny space.

"Thank you!" He graced her with his perfect smile and thankfully moved on.

Camille leaned over. "Dalia would have loved all the fanfare."

"She absolutely would have." During college, Dalia had been the wild one of the three, but ironically, she was living her dream, studying nature in Oregon. Nature, she claimed, calmed her down. Jillian sucked in a breath. "Oh, shit. I told her I'd take pictures, but I forgot. I've been distracted."

"Haven't we all?" Camille winked.

Jillian chuckled then whipped out her cell. Pressing the camera's video button, she recorded the stripper gyrating and thrusting hips in front of his next victim. Jillian made sure to include the three egg tempera paintings above the teal blue sofa that Camille had painted. One of the smaller ones was of a richly colored iguana feasting on a plump red fruit. The one below it was the face of a wolf whose eyes glowed yellow. The delicate interweaving of gray, tan, white, and black in his fur blended together to create a striking image. The last picture was as tall as the two together. It was a magnificent scene of a white polar bear with her two cubs floating on a slab of ice.

Jillian continued her slow pan to include several women who Dalia had never met, but hopefully would. Even as she recorded the festivities, Jillian felt guilty coming to the party when Dalia had flown all the way in from Portland to attend Renee's bachelorette party, only to have come down with the flu.

Jillian gladly would have stayed home and played nursemaid, but Dalia insisted she attend—if for no other reason than to take pictures.

"She'll appreciate seeing Renee so happy," Camille said.

"Definitely." Renee, Dalia, and Jillian had roomed together freshman and sophomore year. "Dalia's here for another few days, so the three of us will have time to get together."

"Renee would love that. She was so disappointed when she found out Dalia couldn't make it."

One of the ladies approached them, or rather staggered toward them, with a big bottle of champagne and refreshed each of their glasses. Good thing Jillian's shifter metabolism could handle this massive influx of alcohol. Otherwise, she'd have to call a cab to drive her home.

Mercifully, around one a.m., the hired hunk said his farewells. While Jillian had enjoyed watching the drunken women paw over Sergeant McDirty, she was increasingly worried about Dalia. Her friend hadn't texted even once to ask about the party. Dalia's fever had come down to almost normal before Jillian had left, but those kinds of things could change in a heartbeat.

Just as she was about to tell Camille she was heading out, her friend jumped up and rushed over to Renee whose eyes had rolled back in her head. Clearly, the bride-to-be had partied way too hard. Good for her, though she'd be sorry tomorrow when the hangover hit.

Convinced no one would even remember she'd been the first to leave the festivities she'd helped organize, Jillian slipped out.

Fortunately, her house was only a fifteen-minute drive from there. As Jillian entered her neighborhood, she had to smile at how wonderful the get together had been. Camille, who dealt with crime all day, had been more relaxed than Jillian had seen her in months. Several of the other women at the party also worked in her same law office. Seeing another side of their uptight and ambitious personalities was something she would not soon forget.

As Jillian rounded the corner to her house, what sounded like gunshots came from her street! What the fuck? Even though she lived on the outskirts of Los Angeles, crime was rare in her upscale neighborhood.

Pressing hard on the accelerator, she sped toward her driveway. As she neared, a man wearing a ski mask dashed out of her house through the front door. He looked straight at her before turning and charging fifty feet down the road. He then disappeared into a maroon sedan and peeled out of there, leaving burnt rubber in his wake.

Her heart raced so hard, she thought she'd shift—something she hadn't done or considered doing in years. She couldn't afford for anyone to find out what kind of freak she was. Hell, the world wasn't ready to learn about shifters, especially her very rare kind of white tiger.

Her focus returned to her sick friend asleep in the house. Dalia! Oh my goddess. Had she been shot? That was the only plausible conclusion, but logic had failed her before.

Decision time: Follow him or check on her friend?

What am I thinking? It's a no brainer. Dalia comes first.

Jillian could only hope he'd left enough evidence for the cops to find the bastard. If he harmed her friend, she'd do whatever it took to find him and make him pay.

After cutting the engine, she jumped out of her Mercedes, not even bothering to pull into her driveway. Because it was so late, she used her Wendayan talent to sprint to the front door, moving almost as fast as a speeding bullet. She hoped no one would notice the super human feat.

The front door sat open, and acid burned in her stomach.

"Dalia?" Jillian yelled as she rushed in. When she received no response, her legs nearly gave way. Mouth dry and pulse soaring, her stomach performed a million somersaults as she ran to Dalia's bedroom. The stench from that man's scent permeated the air and, for a moment, blocked her brain from working. Memories came flooding back even though she tried to force them away. Something other than his scent overpowered her—something terrible. It was blood!

The door to the guest room sat wide open, and while the light was off, enough moonlight streamed in through the window to show the devastation.

"No!" Jillian screamed then choked out a sob.

As much as she didn't want to turn on the light, she had to see the extent of the injury. When she flicked on the lamp, Jillian gasped as one knee hit the floor. The side of Dalia's skull had a hole in it, the blood staining her long blonde hair. Jillian's heart stopped for a few seconds. While it appeared as if her friend was dead, Jillian checked for a pulse anyway. Unfortunately, her own heartbeat was near to bursting, preventing her from detecting any signs of life.

Her instincts clicked in, and she fumbled in her purse for her cell to call 911. The words to describe what happened barely formed on her lips, but the operator assured her help was on the way.

This couldn't be happening. Jillian's front door had been locked, and she doubted Dalia would have answered if someone had knocked. Had he busted in? Or was he more sophisticated than that and had picked the lock?

Grief rocked her as tears streamed down her face. It was déjà vu all over again. Twenty-six years ago, an unwanted shifter had broken into her home and shot and killed her father. She'd seen the killer then, and she'd sort of seen him now—or rather she'd smelled him again. The stress of both murders made her whole body feel as if a ten-ton truck was sitting on her, breaking her bones into tiny pieces.

The image of the man with the crescent-shaped scar that she'd seen this afternoon at the police station appeared in her mind's eye. Jillian had spotted him when she'd stopped in to see Camille. Because Jillian had helped with the party preparations, she needed to discuss some last-minute details with her friend. Halfway through her conversation, the same stench that permeated her house had registered. It had come from the man who'd killed her father. She'd been sure of it. Working hard not to let Camille know what was happening, Jillian had glanced around. Big mistake. The second she spotted the man's crescent-shaped scar on his jaw, she'd almost shifted. Then reason intruded. The man was a cop for goddess sake.

It is the same man, her tiger warned, angry at the quick dismissal.

It can't be him, she argued.

She didn't have to be a lawyer to know that memories of a six-year old were never reliable. Because scars weren't unique, she dismissed the thought that it was the same man.

You're wrong, her tiger screamed. *You never forget a scent.*

Her tiger might be right. His smell was identical to what she remembered all those years ago. Or had spotting the scar brought up that memory and was fooling her now?

FRANK WHITLAW SLAMMED his palm against the steering wheel. Seconds ago, he'd been gloating that he'd finally tied up that loose end and that he wouldn't have to worry again about a six-year-old's memory returning.

He'd jammed the key into the ignition and floored his souped-up car. A quick glance in the rear view mirror assured him that Jillian hadn't shifted. Even if she had chanced coming after him, she would have never been able to catch him.

How had he been so careless? For years, Frank had watched Jillian Garner—carefully. He knew where she lived, where she worked, who her friends were, and even where her relatives lived.

Nothing escaped him. Then this afternoon when Jillian was visiting her friend Camille at the station, he'd walked near. The moment she'd glanced his way, recognition crossed her face. Even though barely a muscle moved, hatred had filled her eyes.

That mistake on his part sped up his decision to kill her. When he'd picked the lock to Jillian's house, he'd made enough noise to waken any shifter. He'd expected her to come out and investigate. His plan was to then shift into his wolf and attack. Even though he didn't know her species, it didn't matter. He'd trained his whole life to be a fighter. Jillian was destined to die.

He should have questioned why the blonde woman in the bed hadn't stirred. Even more careless of him was the fact he hadn't detected a shifter signature, yet he didn't stop to think why that was so. He was slipping, and that really pissed him off.

The next time, he wouldn't fail. His thoughts jumped back to the night he'd broken into the Garner house. He wouldn't have had to kill her father if the straight ass cop hadn't suspected him of pilfering weapons and drugs from the evidence locker where he worked. Garner had said he was going to turn Frank in to Internal Affairs. No way he'd let that happen. The money was too addicting.

As he cleared Jillian's neighborhood, his shaking hands stilled. He'd fucked up tonight. Hopefully, the mask prevented Jillian from figuring out who he was. While he might have botched this first attempt, it wouldn't happen the next time. That was a promise he'd be sure to keep.

"MA'AM?" A MALE voice asked as he placed a hand on her shoulder. Jillian looked up to find two paramedics in navy blue uniforms standing next to her.

She hadn't even heard them come in. Jillian must be losing it since noises never escaped her notice. And how come their faces were so blurry? "Yes?"

"We need to check on your friend," the guy with the long face said.

Even though she was still holding her phone, she'd forgotten for a moment that she'd called for help. When she didn't move, the second paramedic helped her up.

Pull yourself together, her tiger demanded.

I'm trying, but it's so damned hard, she retorted.

Both men checked Dalia, and then the one with the long face stepped over to her. "I'm sorry for your loss."

So she was dead. Why would anyone want to kill her? "Thank you."

Jillian's heart nearly cracked. Or were those her bones, readying her to shift into her tiger?

I want to find the bastard, her animal growled.

Stand down, she demanded. The last thing she needed was for her caged animal to go off half-cocked. Jillian had spent years steeling her human, making her strong enough to fight her tiger's urges. Right now, she was losing the battle.

Jillian wasn't sure how long she'd stood there, but sirens sounded outside and then the paramedics moved out of the room, leaving Dalia in her resting position. No sooner had they left the bedroom than two police officers came in. One was a shifter; the other was not.

"Ma'am."

Her eyes took a moment to focus through the tears. When the man's face became clear, a giant claw ripped at her gut. No! No! No! The evil person who'd killed Dalia and her father—or so she believed—stood before her.

I have to be wrong, her logical side screamed.

No you aren't, her pushy tiger countered.

His foul scent once more seeped in through her nose and triggered that horrible memory along with the more recent one. Her tiger demanded that she shift and kill him right there, but she couldn't give in. As much as she wanted to rip him apart, she refused to let her anger take over. She'd have to find a way to prove he was the killer first. Then she'd bring him down legally.

Jillian drew on her lawyer calm and studied him. The man was tall, maybe six feet and had weathered skin, close-set eyes, and a weak chin. He also had that two-inch scar on his right jaw.

The instinct to flee was strong, but Jillian had to act as if she had no idea he'd committed this heinous act. Because alcohol tainted her breath, she believed she could use that to her advantage, and pretend she'd seen nothing—or almost nothing.

"We'd like to ask you a few questions," the man with the crescent-shaped scar said. He turned to his female partner. "Can you take her statement? I need to call the crime scene unit."

"Sure."

He sounds so professional. Could he be the killer? her human side questioned.

Yes, her tiger immediately responded as she scraped her nails along the lining of Jillian's stomach, probably to show the strength of her conviction.

Focus. Jillian had been introduced to many of Camille's coworkers, but she'd never seen this woman before. Her nametag read Rodriguez. She was human and stood about five foot five, the same height as Jillian. The officer's skin was a warm honey color, and thankfully, her dark brown eyes exuded sympathy. Concentrating on putting one foot in front of the other, Jillian followed her out to the living room.

"Please, have a seat," the officer said. "Can you tell me what happened?"

Jillian decided to mix truth with fiction, all the while pretending to possess only human traits—that is, someone who didn't have exceptional hearing or fantastic eyesight. She sure as hell wasn't about to mention how fast she'd rushed into the house. The only stroke of luck was that the killer hadn't been the one to interrogate her.

"I was at a bachelorette party all night. I probably shouldn't have been driving home after drinking, but it wasn't far." Jillian waved a hand, wanting to keep talking before she received a lecture about drinking and driving. "Anyway, as I drove up, I saw a masked man charge out of my front door." She slurred a few of her words for effect. "He ran down the street and drove off."

"Did you see what kind of car he was driving?" the officer asked with no signs of disgust.

Jillian shook her head. "It was dark, and when I saw him come out of my house, my heart beat so fast I couldn't catch my breath, let alone register what was happening." She'd never be able to explain how she'd caught the first three digits of the license plate, as no human would have been able to see them from so far away. The fast beating heart, however, wasn't a lie. Otherwise, she would have memorized the entire license plate number. "I do remember that it wasn't a truck or a van."

The officer jotted down the information. "What time was this?"

"I can't be sure exactly, but I think I left the party around one, so maybe it was 1:15 before I arrived home." That was the truth.

All throughout the questioning, Jillian wondered what the man was doing in the spare bedroom. Was he making sure he hadn't left any evidence? It wasn't like she could mention to the female officer that her partner had killed her friend because he smelled the same as her intruder. Humans didn't have a keen sense of smell.

"Can you describe what he looked like?" she asked.

Jillian had said the man wore a mask. "He was maybe six feet tall. He might have been middle aged because his gait appeared stiff." That was all she was going to say. If the man believed she could identify him, he might come after her.

The officer kept asking her what seemed like the same questions over and over again. Even the ones about Dalia and her contact information were difficult. Eventually, two more people arrived with cameras and cases. Given they wore overalls and then slipped on disposable booties and head covers, they must be with the crime scene unit. Her house now a crime scene, Jillian figured it was a matter of time before they asked her to leave.

"I don't want to stay here tonight. I'd have nightmares. Would it be okay if I packed a few things and went over to a friend's house?" Her plan to escape town had evolved during the questioning.

"Absolutely. You can't remain here anyway. Where will you be staying so we can keep in touch?"

The first name that came to mind was Camille's. "Camille Williams. She works for the LAPD."

The officer wrote her name down. "That's perfect."

For effect, Jillian staggered as she left the living room. Unfortunately, she had to pass the guest room before reaching the master, so she forced herself not to look. As quickly as she could, she threw warm clothes into a suitcase. Tennessee, where her brother lived, would be cold in February. She picked that location in part because Jillian wanted to be as far away from Scarface as possible. Dalton also would be able to help her figure out what to do next. Her clients might revolt that she'd skipped town, but they would be more upset if she were murdered.

Something niggled at the back of her mind at that thought. Had the bullet that killed Dalia been meant for her?

Chapter Two

T HE LAST PLACE Brian Stanley wanted to be was in his dead
parents' house packing up their possessions, but his very
pregnant sister Elana had asked for his help and he couldn't say no.
Thankfully, she'd already done most of the furniture removal before
he'd moved to Silver Lake.

Two days ago, she'd told him it was time to put the house on the
market, and he was thrilled. He wasn't so crass to mention that she
could burn the old homestead down for all he cared. After all, he'd
found his parents murdered in the living room and sworn he'd never
step foot in this place again, yet here he was. That was how much he
wanted to reconnect with his baby sister. For as distant as he'd been
from them most of his life, even he agreed with his therapist that
unless he found closure to his parents' actions, he'd never heal. So
here he was—back in the town where it all started.

As calloused as it sounded, it wasn't holding his dying mother in
his arms that still haunted him; her rejection and total lack of love
still fucked with his head. Hell, it had taken him thirty years of
therapy to mostly come to grips with being tossed in an institution as
soon as he turned eight.

"The door leads to the attic," Elana said pointing to the ceiling
in the hallway outside their parents' bedroom. "Just yank on the
cord."

He was more than aware what was up there, but perhaps it
slipped her mind that he had lived in this house until she was born.

Many times he'd sneak up there when his parents weren't around—which was much of the time—and pretend he was a stowaway on a pirate ship headed for some Caribbean island where he could run free.

As much as he didn't want to touch anything that belonged to them, Elana was asking for his help. If he had any chance of experiencing what it was like to have a family, he couldn't blow it now. He'd already walked out on her once, and he was determined not to rebuff her again. In the short time he'd been in Silver Lake, Elana had proved to him that she was pure goodness.

He tugged on the cord, climbed up the steps, and then turned on the bare bulb that only faintly illuminated the attic. Heart pounding, memories assaulted him, and he had to squeeze his eyes shut to block out the images. Despite the precaution, he couldn't stop his mother's sharp voice from entering his mind. The sound bounced around like a pinball, slamming against his brain until it hurt. No sooner had that stopped than his father's pinched face came into view filled with disgust and disappointment that were heaped upon controlled anger.

Brian slipped his hand in his pocket looking for his meds, but they weren't there. Damn. Only then did he remember that he'd tossed the small pillbox in his glove compartment in case of emergency. Today might be the day that broke his streak of being one-month medication free.

"What do you see?" Elana called from below, immediately blocking his parents' grim faces.

"Ah, boxes."

"How many?"

Happy to take his mind off where he was and why, he swept his gaze across the two pieces of plywood that sat on top of the rafters. Pink insulation covered the rest of the area. "I'd say no more than eight."

"I'll have Kalan and some of his friends come over and bring them down."

If she'd planned on doing that, why ask him to help? "I can grab some of the smaller ones." He needed to be useful.

"Okay." The cheer in her voice bolstered him.

Ever since he'd come to Silver Lake a few months ago, something wonderful had happened to both his body and his attitude. Not only had he dropped the excess belly fat he'd been carrying for years, he'd been able to more or less wean himself off his bipolar meds. Even though Brian was thrilled to be mostly drug free, he still didn't understand why the change had happened, though he sensed it had something to do with his sister. Every time he visited her, it was as if his worries suddenly disappeared. However, it could be that the air was less polluted in Silver Lake than in Ohio, which helped suppress his allergies. Bottom line, something was affecting him— and in a good way.

Pushing his questions aside, he brought down the four lightest boxes one at a time.

Elana examined them. "I wonder why Mom didn't mark what was in them."

"Maybe she didn't want anyone to know what was in them. She was secretive that way. You could open them and find out."

Elana inhaled then ran her hands over her protruding belly. For a moment she looked like their mother, but he dismissed that unpleasant thought. Elana was much prettier and a hell of lot nicer. Maybe it was the pink top that cinched under her breasts and the pink bow that held back her thick hair that made her look so young and innocent. What he knew for sure was that his sister was happy, and that gave him hope he could be too.

"Yeah, I know, but I'm not ready to see what's inside just yet," she said with a bit of depression in her tone.

He wasn't ready to see their stuff ever. "I'll put these in the back of the truck then."

"Thanks."

The moment he finished loading them, Elana slipped into the front seat, and Brian couldn't wait to leave the property. The drive down the tree-lined driveway caused too many bad thoughts to jam his brain waves. He even had to force himself to loosen his grip on the wheel.

"Looks like it might snow," Brian said, wanting to take the focus off being in his parents' house.

"It does, but I don't mind the cold."

As much as he disliked the inconvenience of driving in the wet stuff, of late, things like slippery conditions and the wind cutting right through him, didn't seem to really bother him much anymore. Even the gunmetal sky, while dark and foreboding, couldn't dampen his overall mood—only thinking about how his parents had treated him could.

Ten minutes later, Brian parked in front of his sister's house. "Where do you want the boxes?" he asked.

She withdrew a remote from her purse and clicked it to open the garage door. "Just stack them on the right side."

"Can do. Why don't you head inside while I take care of it?" He didn't want her to push herself too hard. His nephew needed his rest.

"You have a moment to come in?" Elana asked.

He did, but he wanted some alone time. Who was he kidding? He needed his meds, and he didn't want to take them in front of her. "Can I have a rain check? I have a lot of chores to do. It's been a long day—and I bet the baby wants you to rest too."

Elana leaned over and gave him a peck on the cheek. That one action heated his cheeks, but it also lightened his heart. She pushed open the truck door and eased out. "Thanks for helping me. I know that was hard for you."

Brian had never been around anyone like Elana before. "It couldn't have been easy for you either."

Her thin smile told him she was working to hold it together. As soon as Elana waddled to the front of the house and let herself in, he placed the boxes inside the garage. Once done, he fished out his meds from his glove compartment and downed an anxiety pill. Disappointment washed through him. Fuck. Why was he so weak?

He knew. It was his parent's fault.

Stop blaming them for everything, that little voice in his head told him.

Shaking off his own self-loathing, he drove off. While he had every intention of heading straight to town, something made him turn toward the lake. He'd only seen the shimmering water through the trees one time when Elana had given him a brief tour of the area, but even that small glimpse had drawn him in like a rubbernecker to an accident.

It might be cold, but today he needed to explore the area. It was as if some siren was calling to him. After a two-minute drive, he reached a spot where car tires had rutted a stretch of land. He shut off the engine, zipped up his jacket, and headed down the path that led to the water.

As he neared, his step turned lighter and a strange joy seeped into him. He swore Silver Lake was emitting some kind of drug that created a surge of endorphins, or else the pill he'd just swallowed had kicked in already.

The pine trees were giving off a fresh scent that entombed the area in coziness. There was definitely something strange going on here. He could feel it, but what was *it*? What he wouldn't give to have this fleeting euphoria stay in his heart once he left this lake.

Brian walked around the shoreline, confused as to why his years of hatred toward his parents dissipated the longer he spent in the lake's presence. Perhaps he was crazy to attribute his happiness to a body of water. It didn't really matter. Contentment surrounded him.

It's the pills.

No, it isn't. He'd taken these pills for years, and they'd never worked this fast before or made him feel this way. Once his demons shut up, Brian returned to his car, determined to unravel the mystery of Silver Lake.

JILLIAN WAS EXHAUSTED. As soon as she'd flown the coop, she'd driven straight to the Los Angeles airport, praying the bastard didn't realize for a few weeks at least that she'd left the state. Because she'd given the female cop her cell phone number, Jillian had to turn it off, fearing *he* might be able to trace her location. Even if Camille called, she had to remain offline.

By the time she arrived at the airport, it was almost three in the morning, and unfortunately, the first plane to Knoxville, Tennessee didn't depart until six.

With her suitcase by her side, she slipped down onto one of the terminal airport seats. Twisting her long blonde hair into a knot at the back of her head, she tried to stretch out on the hard lounge chairs for the long wait, but she couldn't get comfortable. It might have been because with each passing minute, not only did her mood head south, her anger at the injustice of Dalia's death caused her stomach to turn into a cauldron of acid.

Believing she was safe in the airport, she closed her eyes. Seconds later that horrible man's smell floated toward her, and she jackknifed into an upright position. Jillian twisted around, expecting to see the cop with the scarred face, but no one was there. Damn. The last thing she needed was an over active imagination to mess with her senses. Her tiger was already on high alert.

No sooner had Jillian pushed aside the heinous violation that had occurred in her home than she realized she'd have to call Dalia's parents and tell them how sorry she was. Hopefully, they wouldn't blame her for leaving their daughter to go to the party.

While Jillian tried to relax once more, a looming sense of doom prevented her from letting down her guard. She might not be psychic, but she'd always had a sense about people. It was what made her a successful lawyer. If that cop was involved in Dalia's murder, he might consider her a loose end. And loose ends needed to be eliminated.

BY THE TIME Jillian made it across the country, rented a car, and then drove the hour to her brother's place, it was a little after dinnertime. Thank goddess for the GPS system or she'd never have found Dalton's house.

The only good thing about arriving late was that her brother might be home from work. If not, she'd find the sheriff's office and ask for him there.

Her brother had lived in Silver Lake for nine months, yet she hadn't found the time to visit her only sibling before now. Jillian could see that had been shortsighted. Family had to come first. Clearly, her struggle for success had blinded her to what was important in life.

As she pulled in front of his one story brick house, his white SUV sat in the drive. Jillian smiled as she remembered how happy he'd been when he bought his new car. He'd added the black wheel well trim, joking that his car was more of a white tiger than he was. He had even kept his identity secret from his werebear partner, Kalan Murdoch. As far as Dalton knew, only wolf and bear shifters existed in this town, and he didn't want to be the odd man out ever again.

As soon as she cut power to the engine, the tension in her shoulders unknotted. She'd made it. *I'm safe, for now at least.*

Leaving her suitcase in the car, she stepped into the brutally cold air and shivered. Looking over her shoulder one last time, Jillian rushed to the front door and knocked. Shifting her weight back and forth to keep warm, she rubbed her arms. Voices sounded and then the door opened.

"Jillian?" her brother said with wide eyes. "What are you…doing here? Not that I'm not glad to see you. Never mind, come in, come in."

For a cop, he sure was tongue-tied. The moment he closed the door, he wrapped his arms around her in the best and warmest embrace ever.

"Someone killed Dalia," she blurted into his shoulder, her throat clogging at the words.

Dalton held her at arm's length, his brows pinched. "Your college roommate?" She nodded. "Come sit down." Dalton escorted her to the living room.

Just speaking those three terrible words unleashed the horror all over again. To make those images stop, she focused on his handsome face. Whereas she took after their mom with her fair skin and honey colored hair, Dalton had olive skin and medium brown hair like their dad. Their father had been way too handsome, and so was Dalton. "They call you Hollywood around here like they did back home?"

He grunted a response.

"Yup," someone chimed in with a smile.

Whoa. She hadn't even seen the other man there. Showed how stressed she was. While he wore the same sheriff's department uniform as Dalton, this man had shoulder length light brown hair. Unless he was working undercover, she was pretty sure he wouldn't have been able to keep that look at the LAPD.

Dalton squeezed her shoulder then let go, and the loss of support made her heart hitch.

"This is Kalan Murdoch, my partner at the department."

Shake his hand, her inner voice nudged her. "Nice to meet you," she said, finally remembering her manners. "Dalton has said nice things about you."

The men exchanged glances. Apparently, Kalan was surprised by that comment. "Good to know."

She was glad his partner was also a shifter. Even though she and Dalton had emailed back and forth every few weeks, he had never mentioned what kind of shifter Kalan was. That was most likely because Dalton had never mentioned his breed to Kalan.

"Can I get you something to drink?" Kalan asked, seemingly very comfortable in her brother's house.

"How about a glass of wine?"

"You got it." Kalan walked all of ten feet into the open kitchen situated on the wall opposite the front door. The living room was at the front of the house, and given there was a door on the west side of the room, she figured that was where the bedrooms were located.

Dalton told her he'd rented the place furnished, and it showed. The owner had to be over eighty. The place had white walls, a brown sofa, two brown chairs, and a brown and black rug. The kitchen counter top was beige Formica, and the appliances looked tired.

"Here ya go." Kalan handed her a glass of red wine.

"Thanks." She sat on the sofa while Dalton, who looked cute in his brown uniform, sat across from her. Kalan took the other chair.

"Tell me what you know," Dalton said, all evidence of compassion gone. He was in his cop mode—exactly where she needed him to be.

She went through the whole story about Dalia flying in for Renee's bachelorette party, but that once Dalia took ill, she decided to skip the party and sleep. "I drove home a little after one, and as I neared my place, a gunshot sounded. Seconds later, a man wearing a mask rushed out of my house."

"Did you notice anything distinctive about him?" Dalton asked, showing little emotion. He was, however, paying close attention to everything she said. Surprisingly, his attitude was comforting.

"He was a shifter, but he moved rather stiffly. At the time, I estimated him to be about fifty. As I followed him with my gaze, I was able to see the first three letters of his California license plate, but I didn't tell the cops that fact for obvious reasons."

"What were those letters?" Kalan asked as he slipped a pen and paper from his shirt pocket.

"RJC. The best I could tell, he was driving a maroon sedan. Sorry, I didn't see the model. My head was spinning." Dalton nodded while Kalan jotted down the information. "Here's the odd thing. I think I know who he is."

Kalan's pen stopped. "You said he wore a mask."

She inhaled, not really wanting to go through the horror of her father's death again, but for Dalia, she had to. Starting with when she was six, she detailed what she remembered about that night. "As you know, my being a shifter means I can remember a person's scent. When I smelled him again at the police department that morning, my heart jammed in my throat."

Dalton held up a hand. "Wait a minute. You're saying the man who murdered Dad was at the LAPD?"

"Yes. And he's a detective."

His brows pinched. "Are you sure?"

She couldn't blame him for asking. She'd asked herself the same thing a hundred times. "He had the same crescent-shaped scar on his jaw."

Dalton sat up straighter. "Do you think he knows you recognized him?"

At least her brother believed her. "I didn't give any indication that I knew anything. I make a living keeping my expression blank."

Kalan tossed down his pad. "I'm going to disagree that he doesn't know. Think about it. You see him at say noon and your friend is murdered *that* night. Can you even be sure he didn't think it was you? You said her back was to the door."

Acid burned in her throat, but she wasn't ready to believe that was true. "I can't be sure of anything, but Dalia and I have the same colored hair and are about the same size. She was in the guest room."

"He may not have realized that."

"True."

"You're positive it was the same man who killed your father?" Kalan was demanding in his questions but kind at the same time.

A tight band squeezed her chest. "Yes. So maybe he did recognize me." She guzzled half of her drink, and the smooth wine instantly helped calm her.

"You really haven't changed all that much since you were six," Dalton said.

Yes, she had. As Jillian was about to say she didn't look anything like her six-year old self, a horrible idea occurred to her. "Shit. Maybe he's kept tabs on me. If a six-year old were my only witness to murder, I'd want to know what she was up to." Her chest constricted, making it hard to breathe.

Her brother moved next to her on the sofa and clasped her hand.

"Don't worry. You're safe here."

"I can't stay here forever. I have a job. I'm here because I just couldn't bring myself to remain in Los Angeles in case that creep came after me."

"You were right to come here," Dalton said.

Kalan leaned forward. "Did you use your credit card to pay for your airline tickets and your car rental?"

Anger and dread collided. "Yes. It was after two in the morning. It wasn't like I could go to a bank and withdraw cash." She came off sounding too defensive. "Sorry. I didn't mean to snap."

"No problem. You've been through a lot, but I had to ask. If this man's a cop, he might trace your whereabouts."

Her fingers weakened, and she set down her glass before she dropped it. "He knows I'm here then." Neither man said anything. Sorting through her options, she discarded them one by one. "I couldn't go to Mom's house. If I were with her, he'd harm her too." Their mother only lived ten miles from Jillian.

Kalan looked at Dalton briefly then back at her. "While I've never discussed this with Dalton, there is a shifter compound on the other end of town. Maybe you could find a place there to stay for a while."

"Or she can stay here." Dalton faced her. "Realize though that I'll be gone all day and sometimes nights."

She didn't want to put anyone out. "I'll stay in a hotel."

"That isn't wise. You can stay with me and my mate," Kalan offered.

No way would she be a burden to anyone. "I wouldn't want to intrude."

"You wouldn't. Elana is pregnant, and I can't be home all the time to help her with things." He held up a finger. "But don't tell Elana I said that. She'd skin me alive. In the last few months, she's become rather feisty, shall I say." Kalan grinned.

Her pulse soared. Being able to help would take her mind off her worries, but she'd feel more at ease if his mate invited her. Having their first child was a highly personal thing. If she'd just mated, she wouldn't want some stranger seeking refuge in her house. "When is she due?"

"Since this is Elana's first child, we can't be sure. The doctors say two weeks."

She squeezed Dalton's hand. "What do you think?"

"I think it's a good idea, but relocating will only be part of your problem." He glanced back at Kalan. "Do you really want my sister to bring danger to your doorstep?"

He stabbed a hand through his hair. "No. You're right. Sorry, Jillian."

"Stay with me for a few days and we'll look at your options," Dalton said. "First thing though, you'll have to return your rental car. I'm sure we can hook you up with something to drive while you're here. And no using your credit card or your phone."

The phone part she'd already figured out. "I'll need money."

Having a big savings account didn't help if she couldn't access it.

"I'll lend you some. I know you're good for it."

"Unless I'm dead." In that case though, he'd get everything. She turned to Kalan. "I would like to meet your mate if she's up for it."

Kalan smiled. "I'll see if Elana wants to do a lunch in the next few days?"

Jillian could use a friend. "I'd like that." She finished her glass of wine. "What I need right now is some food, a shower, and a good night's sleep."

Dalton smiled. "That we can do."

Chapter Three

D URING HIS BREAK at the hardware store, Brian texted his sister, instructing her to let him know if she needed him to drive her to the hospital. Her due date was any day now, and if she couldn't reach Kalan, Brian had offered to take her. He had let his boss know that he might have to leave at a moment's notice, and to his delight, his boss was very understanding. He even told him to go whenever she called.

This store sure was nothing like where he used to work in Ohio. Then again that might have been because Brian hadn't attempted to interact with any of the customers like he was doing now. His boss at the Silver Lake Hardware store even told him a few people had commented on how helpful he'd been, and Brian's face had heated at the unexpected compliment. At the Ohio store, all he did was stack and retrieve lumber. Here in Silver Lake, he could cut, stack, and even order lumber for the store. Hell, his boss told him last week that he knew more about wood than any of his employees!

Brian attributed a lot of his new attitude to being around Elana. She'd provided unconditional support—something he'd never experienced in his life.

Now he could see that leaving Ohio had been the best thing he'd ever done. Being near the mental institution continually reminded him of his abandonment issues, which wasn't healthy. The only good thing he could say about living in Ohio was that he'd had access to the basement where he rented a room. The landlord seemed pleased that he'd turned her dingy space into a workshop. As long as Brian provided her with a handmade table or a custom bookcase every now and then, she was happy to let him make as much noise as he wanted.

Silver Lake was a different story. Not that he wasn't grateful to be living above where his sister worked, but the tiny apartment, and lack of a basement, made it hard for him to do his woodworking.

"Can you help me?" a customer asked, jarring Brian out of his reverie.

"Sure. What can I do for you?" For the first time in his life, he looked forward to chatting with people, especially when the topic revolved around building materials.

The young man explained he was building a go-cart for his four-year old son and needed some wood custom cut. For the next ten minutes, Brian was in his good zone—measuring and cutting. He refused to dwell on the fact his dad never made or bought him anything as exciting as a go-cart. Once done, he stacked the wood on the man's dolly. "Anything else I can help you with?"

"I hope so." He asked if Brian had any suggestions for the type of wheels and bearings he should use. While that wasn't in his job description, Brian loved working with his hands and was quite good with anything mechanical. His therapist had always encouraged him to express himself through his projects.

For the next few minutes they discussed the pros and cons of quality versus cost of the bearings and tires. After a few minutes of back and forth analysis, the customer left happy, and that made Brian smile.

It was now time to clock out and do a little of his own shopping. The cradle he was building for Elana's new baby was almost finished. All he needed was the motor to rock it gently, some paint, varnish, and brushes. Then he'd be done. He couldn't wait to give Elana the present. Knowing her, she'd love it.

As he exited the store with his purchases, his cell rang. When he saw the caller was Elana, his heart raced. Assuming the worst, a blast of anxiety ramped up his heartbeat. Tucking the shopping bag under his arm, he answered. "Is the baby coming?"

She chuckled. "No, I'm not due for another two weeks. I'm calling to invite you to a party this weekend."

Panic attack avoided. "Thanks, but I'm not the partying type." That might require a double dose of meds.

"You can't stay holed up in the apartment every night. You have to get out and meet people."

It's all he'd ever known. Moving here had been a huge enough step for him. "I appreciate the offer, but I'm good."

"No you aren't. You're a recluse. One of my best friends, Teagan Pompley, has a brother, Sam, who is leaving the service. She and her fiancée are throwing a party for him. I want you to meet my friends. You are an important part of my life, and I want you in it more often."

He was an important part of her life? It was what he'd yearned for—to belong. "Can I get back to you?"

"Sure, but make sure you say yes."

He chuckled. "You sure are bossy."

"Someone has to look out for you."

She knew how to push his buttons. "I'll give it some thought."

"You better."

As soon as he disconnected, he headed home. Brian had the next two days off, giving him confidence he could finish the cradle in time for the birth of his nephew.

After throwing a frozen dinner into the microwave and then scarfing it down, he plugged in his sander and went to work on polishing the sides he'd cut yesterday. Tomorrow, he'd cut and polish the bottom and then assemble it. The day after that, he'd paint it, and put on a coat of varnish.

After four hours of work, he was covered in sawdust, and even though he'd hung plastic to keep the dust from going everywhere, a thin film seemed to be on the walls and floor. He so needed a workshop. Despite wearing a mask, his lungs were coated in the stuff.

It was time to call it quits before he made a stupid mistake.

Brian spent another hour cleaning up then stacked the materials under the living room window, ready for the next stage tomorrow.

He showered and then turned on the television to take his mind off his work. Close to midnight, after having dozed once or twice, he shut off the set and hit the hay. He must have been more tired than he thought because he didn't wake up until a little after ten. Having a lot more to do on the cradle, he rose. After scrambling some eggs and brewing a pot of coffee, he went to work again. He only had to cut two more pieces and sand them before assembling it.

The pounding on his door didn't register until it was followed by a few shouts. Thinking Elana needed to go to the hospital, he shut off his saw and rushed to the door, not giving any thought to his attire.

He threw open the door to find Anna, his sister's assistant standing there, a scowl on her face. "Is Elana having her baby?" he asked, wiping his dirty palms on his jeans. Instead of being anxious, a wave of elation slammed into him.

"No. Elana asked me to let you know that we can barely hear what our customers are saying. Your power tools are making too much noise." Anna planted a hand on her hip. Between her tattoos and piercings, she looked mighty fierce. "You can't be doing that in here anyway."

"I'm really sorry. I wasn't thinking. I'll work after the shop closes."

"Elana will be happy to hear that, but if Mr. Berta finds out that you're spewing sawdust everywhere, he'll probably evict you."

His heart dropped to his stomach. "I thoroughly clean up every day."

She shrugged. "Just saying." She peaked around him. "What are you making anyway?"

He saw no harm in telling her. "I'm making a cradle for her baby, but don't tell my sister."

Her eyes widened. "Really? She'll love that."

"I hope so."

Anna tilted her head. "For all the trouble you've caused, you can make it up to her by going to Teagan's party this weekend."

A trickle of relief rushed through him. While his actions probably hadn't lost business for his sister, she decided to use that as leverage to get him to attend the gathering—or maybe it was Anna's doing. For his sister's sake, he'd go, but he wouldn't stay long. This time, he'd keep some meds with him in case things became too intense for him.

"Leave the address with me, and I'll try to make it."

She smiled. "Thank you."

He wasn't sure what he'd gotten himself into, but if it would make Elana happy, he'd go.

JILLIAN WAS ANXIOUS to meet Kalan's mate. Hell, she was anxious just to get out of her brother's house. He'd woken her up at six in the morning and then apologized for having to go into work. Before he left, he gave her a bunch of instructions about making sure the doors were locked, and why she shouldn't go out. Jillian swore she was more anxious after his little talk than before she'd left California.

Then, at eleven, Dalton had called to say that Elana had a free hour to meet for lunch. Somehow his rule of not stepping foot out of the house seemed to have evaporated. He did tell her that as soon as he got off work this evening, they needed to return her rental car to Knoxville. As much as she wanted her independence, she understood that having that particular car was a liability. Tracing her whereabouts would be too easy for the son of a bitch who killed Dalia.

At a quarter to twelve, Jillian left the house, but not before scoping out the area. Not detecting any shifters, she hopped in her car and followed her brother's directions to McKinnon's Pub and Pool. With a few minutes to spare, she parked as close to the entrance as possible.

From the outside, it looked to be in good shape and was actually better than she'd expected. Apparently, the name McKinnon was well-known in the shifter community, since Rye McKinnon was the Alpha. His father before him had been one too.

A twinge of jealousy surfaced. Because there were so few white tigers in the world, she'd never even met her Alpha—assuming there was one for her Clan. Being surrounded by those like her would have been so comforting.

Move on. You can't change your identity, her tiger said with a lot of distain.

Sheesh. Can't a girl feel sorry for herself? she retorted.

No.

It was times like these that she wondered if the cons outweighed the pros of being a shifter, especially with an animal who was so opinionated. Not wanting to be late for her lunch date, she dashed inside. It was rather dark and took a moment for her eyes to adjust, despite her shifter ability. A long bar with a huge mirror above it sat opposite the entrance, and peanut shells littered the floor. She spotted another room straight off to the left that held pool tables. Nice. She might have to come here to practice.

A flash of Kelly green caught her attention, and Jillian twisted to her right. A rather short pregnant woman eased out of a booth at the far end of the bar and stood. Given she had long dark hair, Jillian bet that was Elana.

Smiling, Jillian headed toward her. The pregnant woman's shifter signature was apparent, as were many others in the building. Hell, the whole place seemed to be swarming with them, and Jillian's blood pressure immediately dropped. She'd never been surrounded by so many before, and it gave her a sense of family.

She might not have been this comfortable had Dalton not mentioned that except for one group of mutated shifters called Changelings, the *Weres* in Silver Lake were awesome.

When she reached the back booth, she held out her hand. "Hi, I'm Jillian."

The young woman smiled and shook hers. "I'm Elana, Kalan's...ah mate." She whispered the last two words. There were some non-shifters in the bar, so she was smart to keep her voice low.

They both sat down. Seconds later, a waitress came over with a menu and handed it to Jillian. Not wanting to be rude, she offered hers to Elana. "You want to look first?"

Elana chuckled. "That's not necessary. I always have the same thing."

Normally, Jillian wasn't picky about what she ate, but today she had been craving meat. "I'll have a classic burger, medium rare, and an unsweetened iced tea."

"You got it," her server responded.

Elana readjusted herself in the seat. "Kalan told me what happened to your friend. I'm so sorry. I can't imagine what you're going through." She visibly shook.

"Thank you. I still can't believe it. Dalia and I roomed together in college. When I spoke with her parents, their grief made the horror all too real again."

Her brows furrowed, and Elana seemed to think about Jillian's situation. "Kalan mentioned you might know who did this and that he might come after you." Jillian appreciated her concern. Kalan must have mentioned his offer for her to stay with Elana and why Dalton thought it was a bad idea.

"Yes, and I don't know what I'm going to do. It's not like I can rush back to California. I'd be looking over my shoulder twenty-four seven."

"So what will you do?"

"I'll hang around here for a while. Having my brother and your mate close by brings me a sense of security I'd never have in California."

She nodded. "Can you get a job here?"

"I'll have to check if Tennessee honors my license, but even if they do, I want to return to California eventually. I have some savings, but I fear if I withdraw anything from my bank in California that cop will find me."

Elana hissed. "I know what it's like to have a target on your back." She explained about her parents being killed over a piece of stone. "When the Changelings thought I had what they wanted—which I did—they came after me. I was never so scared in my life. Fortunately, Kalan was assigned to protect me." Her face glowed when she said his name.

"At least something good came of the tragedy."

Elana smiled. "Totally true. I was this innocent human girl before I met Kalan, despite having had this mad crush on him for years. I sure did learn a lot in a short period of time."

"Did it come as a shock to learn about our kind?"

She shook her head. "My best friend, Izzy, who's mated to our Alpha, was a Wendayan. She told me all about shifters, but never let on that Kalan was one."

Hearing the name *Wendayan* bolstered her spirits. "My mom is Wendayan, which in turn, makes me one too."

"Really?" Elana looked like a kid in a candy store. "What can you do?"

She saw no reason to hide her talent from her. "I can move fast, whether I'm in my shifted or human form."

"Fast, as in fast like an Olympic runner?"

Jillian leaned forward. "More like a speeding bullet fast."

Her mouth dropped open. "That's really cool. Even Izzy can't do that, but she can control fire, wind, water, and earth. That's even after her powers were cut in half when she mated with Rye."

Jillian had never been around anyone that powerful before. "I'd love to meet her."

"You can. Tomorrow, another Wendayan friend of mine Teagan Pompley is throwing a welcome home party for her brother who just retired from the military. You should come and meet her and the other Wendayans. The shifters are pretty cool too."

Jillian was tempted. "I don't want to party crash."

Elana waved a hand. "Nonsense. Teagan would love to meet another one of her kind."

"Is Dalton going?" She should know as he was her brother, but he hadn't mentioned anything to her.

Her new friend looked off to the side. "I don't think so. He's not exactly open about being a shifter."

That was sad to hear. Ten bucks it was because he still thought of himself as an outsider. "I'll have to work on him."

"Please do. Kalan has always known your brother was a shifter, but your brother has always avoided talking about what he was. It wasn't until a newcomer—Ainsley Chancellor, who is part Wendayan and part wolf—told Kalan that Dalton was a white tiger shifter."

So the secret was out. She wondered if her brother knew. "Does that bother anyone?"

Elana's brows pinched. "Why would it?"

"Because we're different?"

She reached out and clasped Jillian's hand. "Absolutely not. I think the more diversity we have in Silver Lake the better."

"That's good to hear." Maybe coming to Silver Lake had been a good thing for more than one reason.

Chapter Four

JILLIAN TRIED ON, and then discarded, almost every outfit she'd brought with her. Why she'd packed such dressy attire, she didn't know. This was rural Tennessee, not the elite Los Angeles crowd she was used to. Elana said the party was casual, yet for some reason, Jillian wanted to impress those who were there.

That's stupid, her tiger said in a tone that implied Jillian was being shallow.

You're right, her human half said. *I need to be myself. Only how?*

Her tiger refused to answer. Now she shuts up? Sheesh.

In reality, it didn't matter what anyone thought of her. Unless Dalton figured out a way for her to access her bank account, she'd be returning to California just as soon as her funds ran out.

To her surprise, her stomach clenched at the thought of leaving. In the few days she'd been in Silver Lake, she'd only met Kalan and Elana, but they were two of the most kind, sincere, and generous people she had ever met, and they made her feel at home. Who would have guessed?

Perhaps her dismay stemmed from the fact she'd be leaving Dalton too. Jillian let out a big sigh, disgusted at how wishy-washy she was. One minute she would pretend she'd be returning to LA and pick up where she had left off, and the next she wanted to stay here and embrace them all.

In the end, Jillian tossed on a pair of jeans and a neon blue sweater. Because she looked washed out, she dabbed on some blush and let her long wavy hair do whatever it wanted since she didn't have the energy to fuss with it. In LA, her firm expected her to use her looks to sway jurors, which meant smoldering eyeliner and full red lips. From the little interaction she'd had with Dalton's friends, those tactics wouldn't work here.

Her cell rang, and she jumped. Not only had she returned her car, Dalton had insisted she use a burner phone. She rushed to the living room where she'd tossed her purse and located the new cell. It was Dalton, of course, since he was the only one with her number. "What's up?"

"I caught a case and won't be able to make it to Teagan's party tonight." He had said he'd try, which she considered a victory.

"That sucks." She couldn't tell if that was the truth, but if he didn't want to go to the party with her, she didn't need to pressure him. "If you finish up early, stop by. The only people I'll know are Elana and Kalan."

"You'll do fine. Just make sure to check your rear view mirror on the drive over."

"Way to ruin my day."

"Sorry. I can't help it. You're my sister, and I would blame myself for the rest of my life if anything happened to you."

Was he sweet or what? "You're the one who needs to be cautious. You have the dangerous job."

"I'm good. There have been times when I've moved so fast, the criminal couldn't even react quickly enough to run away."

Really? That alone was dangerous if anyone said something. They didn't need the world to know their talent. "Don't you fear he'll wonder how you suddenly appeared next to him?"

"I'm careful."

That was what Dalton always said. "You better be. I'll see you later tonight then."

After bundling up against the February cold, she slipped into her rather ancient loaner—a 2006 Toyota Rav 4. While there wasn't any snow on the ground this week, if it did precipitate, she'd be thankful for the four-wheel drive.

Elana had drawn a map for her and promised Jillian would only have to make two turns to reach Teagan Pompley's fiancé's house. They lived in a place called the Cove, and apparently, shifters and Wendayans knew that the area was strictly for the small group of witches, though how they kept others out was anyone's guess.

Because Jillian was arriving an hour late, she wasn't surprised to find a ton of cars lining the street. She parked behind the last one, locked her door, and hustled up to the party. Given the loud noise coming from the large two-story home, the festivities were in full swing. Good. Chances were many wouldn't even notice her arrival. She rang the bell and waited, and when no one answered, she figured it was okay to head on in.

The moment she pushed open the door and stepped into the foyer, the blast of shifter signatures squeezed her heart and ignited other parts of her body with such a force that she nearly turned around and left. These new sensations really threw her for a loop. Holy hell. Her tiger sure had woken up.

The inside air smelled sweet, kind of like a forest after a hard rain, yet she'd never known this to happen in a house before. Something strange was going on in this town, but she couldn't put her finger on it. Most likely it was because her nerves were frayed— so much so that she was having a hard time processing the events going on around her.

Inhale and let the tension go. She could hear her yoga instructor at her LA gym chanting that mantra.

Once her breathing calmed, she followed the laughs and cheers. About twenty people were either leaning against the island in the open concept kitchen or congregating in the living room. Most of the partygoers ranged in age from about thirty to early forties, but all were focused on the man in the middle of the living room.

Elana was seated on the sofa next to Kalan, and her gaze too was on a man in uniform who was tall and good-looking. In front of him stood a woman with long, red hair. Her eyes were open, but they seemed to be unfocused. Her pretty face suddenly relaxed.

"What do you see?" the man asked her.

She smiled. "A forest full of beautifully colored birds." She reached out as if to touch one.

He snapped his fingers, and when her eyes widened, she clasped a hand on her chest as she glanced around. Everyone clapped. Jillian had no idea what kind of parlor trick he'd pulled, but she had to assume this was Sam, the guest of honor.

"Jillian!" Elana called to her and waved.

Smiling, she headed toward her friend. Even though the two had met only a few days ago, the baby seemed to have grown. "Don't get up," Jillian said.

Elana laughed. "Without Kalan's help, I'm not sure I could if I wanted to."

Jillian took the empty seat next to Elana. "Thanks for inviting me." She leaned closer. "Is everyone here one of us?" Jillian had grown up cautious, rarely even saying the word *shifter* in public.

"Everyone except my brother Brian are shifters or Wendayans." Elana nodded toward the kitchen, but Jillian didn't know which one he was. It didn't matter. She'd figure it out sooner or later.

"He knows about our kind though, right?"

Elana's eyes widened. "No. He has no idea, though in a few years when Aiden learns to shift, he'll figure it out."

"Aiden?"

She patted her stomach. "Kalan and I decided to name our child after his grandfather."

Kalan looked over at her. "Loved that man. I'm sorry he's gone. He would have enjoyed having a great grandson."

"I'm sure he would have." She turned to Elana. "I know you said your brother had a trouble past. Is that why you're waiting before you break the news?"

"Yes. I don't want to be responsible for sending him back into therapy. I figure I'll break the news to him slowly."

"That makes semse."

Kalan nodded toward the kitchen then stood. "Can I get you something to drink?"

She didn't need to take up more of their time. Besides, her mission was to speak with as many people as possible since she didn't know how long she'd be staying in Tennessee. From experience, she'd learned that friends grounded her. "I'll grab something. May I ask if the woman in the middle of the room was Izzy?"

Elana smiled. "That was actually her sister, Missy." She nodded to the taller redhead with the handsome man. "That's Izzy with her mate, Rye. He's our Alpha."

So that was Rye. If she needed to stay for a prolonged period, she should ask about the Clan and their politics and whether they would consider letting her join them.

Ask him, her tiger urged.

For years, she'd promised her animal that she'd find a place to call home, where shifters were welcome, but somehow she'd never been willing to give up the glamorous life in LA.

Later, she responded.

Not wanting to think about the future, Jillian walked past several people who were engrossed in conversation. She headed toward the two coolers sitting on top of the kitchen island. Just as she reached in to grab a beer, an intriguing scent—musky and fresh—invaded her senses. Seconds later, her body was on fire from the rapid release of hormones. Holy hell. She glanced around. Some shifters were emitting waves of sexual vibes, and apparently, she'd been caught in the middle.

One man, who looked to be close to forty, was watching the group congregating around Sam, but from the way he was scraping the label off his beer bottle with his nail, he wasn't having a very good time. He was a shifter that much she could tell, though for some reason, his signature had dampened. Perhaps he hadn't shifted in a long time—kind of like her. A few feet away were two other men, but they weren't shifters. So where the hell was the rich scent coming from?

Mate, mate! her tiger roared.

Jillian almost laughed out loud at that ridiculous thought. There were many in the room who seemed to be mated, and together, they must be sending lustful signals to each other. Made sense to her, but what did she know? Her shifter father hadn't been alive long enough to explain the facts of shifter life to her, and it wasn't a topic she felt comfortable asking her brother. Her mom was a Wendayan and had explained a few things to her, but it wasn't enough to give her a clear picture. She did say that Jillian would experience some kind of blue glow when she was highly excited, but Jillian was pretty sure that was an old wives' tale because she'd never seen a hint of color shoot off her body.

"Need help opening the bottle?" the man who was standing by himself asked.

She had been trying to twist off the cap, but all she'd managed for her efforts were red fingers. "Thanks."

When she held out the beer, his fingers touched hers for a second before he lifted the bottle from her, and two blue sparks shot off her hand. Holy hell. "Did you see that?" she blurted.

"See what?" he said with total sincerity.

She wasn't about to say that blue points of light had darted off her skin. Apparently, he wasn't a Wendayan, meaning he wouldn't be aware what that meant anyway. "I thought I saw something out the kitchen window."

Lame, her tiger commented. *Press up against him,* her animal urged.

Jillian wasn't sure what had gotten into the tiger. In California, she rarely said a peep. Maybe it was time to go home.

You can't, her tiger reminded her. *Remember who's back there.*

Thanks for the mood killer.

The twist of the cap released a whooshing sound, jerking her back to the moment. "Here ya go," he said.

He handed her the beer, and she quickly took a long swig. "Thanks. Name's Jillian. I'm Dalton Garner's sister."

When he didn't react to the name, she guessed he didn't know who that was. "Brian Stanley, the pregnant lady's brother."

If she hadn't just swallowed her beer, he might be wearing it. Elana's brother was not supposed to be a *Were*, and yet here he was in all his shifter glory. It wasn't her place to break the news to her new friend however. Elana would be devastated to find out they weren't true siblings—but how had she not known Brian was a shifter?

"How long have you been in Silver Lake?" Jillian asked. It was a blatant excuse to get him to talk. Brian kept glancing around the room, acting as if he didn't want to be near her.

Mate, her tiger said once more.

He is not my mate. Sheesh. He was cute enough, and her body right now was pulsing and acting as if she'd just skipped through a field of flowers on a summer day, but the euphoria had to be from the collective group of shifters charging the area with their combined scents.

"A few months. Hey, I gotta go. Nice talking with you."

Brian set down his mangled beer bottle, stepped behind her, and then disappeared around the corner. What the hell? No man had ever had a ten-word conversation with her and then walked off. The scariest part came when the front door closed. The air in the room nearly smothered her and her blue sparks went into hibernation.

Told ya, the sassy shifter said. *He is your mate.*

Jillian wouldn't even answer that comment. Her tiger was dead wrong.

BRIAN COULDN'T BREATHE. His heart was pounding, and his blood pressure was rising. He'd been relatively calm when Sam was performing his act, and from what he'd overheard, the guest of honor was some kind of magician. Apparently, he could send thoughts into other people's minds and make them think they were seeing one thing, when in reality nothing was there. Of course, Brian didn't buy it, but it was a good parlor trick. Whoever that girl was doing the trick with him must have been in on it. It didn't matter she looked genuinely surprised when he clapped his hands.

Once Brian jumped in his truck, he had to do some tricky maneuvering to get out of his spot. Stupid people had parked too close. After a minute of easing in and out, he finally pulled out on the road. Christ. He never should have come here. His hands had started to shake and the pounding in his head had intensified the moment that woman walked into the party—Jillian something.

Sticking his hand in his pocket, he withdrew one of his anxiety pills and downed it without water since he couldn't wait until he arrived home.

He blamed this jittery feeling and tightening in his chest on the girl with the golden hair and luscious body. While he'd had some brief relationships, his body had never betrayed him like that before. Shit, she was probably laughing at him now—the man who could barely keep his erection in check. Good thing he'd had the good sense to leave. No telling what he'd be tempted to do with her if he'd spent more time in her presence.

I know. He'd want to kiss her, touch her tits, and then taste every inch of her.

Stop it! His body was out of control and that scared him. Even in one of his manic moods, it wasn't this bad.

Jillian's perfume had invaded his body and was trying to twist his insides into a Celtic knot. He sniffed the air and damned if he couldn't still smell her. She must have rubbed against him and left a trace. While he couldn't name the scent, it reminded him of spring flowers. Not a rose. More like honeysuckle.

A horn honked, and he returned his focus to the road. With quick reflexes, he swerved to avoid the car aimed straight at him. *Fuck me.* Somehow he'd drifted into the oncoming lane. That was it. He'd never accept an invitation to another party again. His sister's friends had the ability to do mind control—and they'd used him as the guinea pig.

Chapter Five

JILLIAN HAD NO idea what had caused Brian to rush out of the party. It wasn't as if she'd asked him some sensitive question about why his sister didn't know he was a shifter. Hell, Elana should have been able to sense he was one. It was possible she'd dismissed it because she didn't want to face what that meant—that Brian was only a half-brother or possibly a stepbrother. She'd be in for a rude awakening when she learned of it.

It was bad enough that Brian hadn't even told Elana that he was leaving the party. Elana was so open and sweet, yet Brian appeared rather distant. It always amazed her when siblings turned out so differently, though in Brian's case, she could see why he acted the way he did. While Elana hadn't filled her in on everything that had gone on when Brian was growing up, Jillian understood the gist. Certainly, if her mother had shoved her in a mental institution at a young age, she'd be distant too.

She thanked her lucky stars that Dalton and she had a lot in common and were rather close. It might be because their mother had to raised them alone.

"Where did Brian go?" Kalan asked, jerking her back to the present.

Crap. She hadn't even noticed he'd walked up to her. "Ah, he left."

Kalan glanced back at his mate. "Did he say why?"

She shook her head. "One minute we were talking—or rather I

was talking—and the next he excused himself and rushed out."

Before Kalan could ask any more questions, Elana let out a shriek, and Kalan's eyes widened. His chest caved, as if he felt his mate's pain. "Excuse me," Kalan said.

Face pale, he rushed to his mate's side. Before anyone could move, he scooped her up in his arms.

"Take her into the bedroom," a man with a beard and his hair pulled back said.

Both of them seemed to know what had happened. Rye, Izzy, and Izzy's sister followed. The party roar immediately quieted as the six of them disappeared down the hallway.

A pretty blonde woman sidled up next to her. "Hi, I'm Teagan. I don't think we've met. If you're wondering, the man who made that command was my fiancé, Kip."

Jillian should have guessed since this was his house. Teagan was Wendayan and wanted to ask her a lot of questions, but right now all Jillian could focus on was Elana's well-being. "Jillian Garner."

Teagan smiled. "You're Dalton's sister."

"Yes." Jillian wasn't in the mood for small talk right now. "Do you think Elana will really be okay?"

"I hope so. She had a midwife, but the woman was called out of town on an emergency. Elana didn't seem concerned as she wasn't due for another ten days."

Jillian nodded. Before she could discuss how the Wendayans were organized in this town, Kip rushed back out, and everyone faced him.

"Listen up. Elana's water broke, but don't worry, Missy is there to help. Elana has time to get to the hospital. She'll be fine, but just in case, we've called an ambulance."

From the tight lines around his eyes and mouth, he was just saying that so no one would panic. Poor Elana. Jillian wished there was something she could do.

Kip returned to the room, but it was a good minute before the buzz in the room slowly increased. All went silent again when Kalan rushed out. "Is the ambulance here yet? The baby's breech, and the umbilical cord appears to be wrapped around his neck." He darted over to the window and peered into the black of night.

Panic gripped her. A friend of hers had the same issue. If she hadn't lived so close to the hospital, the baby would have died.

Kip rushed from down the hallway and grabbed Kalan's arm. "Elana's not breathing."

While he spoke softly, Jillian heard what he'd said. She strained her ears for the sirens, but the ambulance must be far away. She excused herself from Teagan and stepped over to Kip and Kalan. "I'll take her to the hospital," she volunteered.

Without waiting for anyone to answer, she sped passed both of them and shot into the room where Elana was lying on the bed. Izzy and Missy were huddled around her. Rye was taking her pulse as Missy placed something under her head. Elana's eyes finally opened. "Is the baby—?"

Izzy grabbed her hand. "The baby is going to be fine."

Whatever it was that Missy put under Elana's head must have helped. The baby, however, might still be in jeopardy. "I can take her to the hospital if you tell me where it is." Both women looked at her, probably wondering who she was. "There's no time to explain. I move really fast."

Elana reached out. "Bullet fast." Then her eyes closed.

Those few words of support seemed to jumpstart them. Kalan rushed in. "I can't wait for the ambulance. I need to drive her myself."

"That'll take too long," Jillian said. "Where is the hospital?"

"It's north on Robin's Ridge and then left on Oak Avenue."

"Open the front door for me and then call the hospital to say we're on our way. The meet me there." She used her most authoritative tone with Kalan, though she'd be there before he'd taken his cell out of his pocket.

Izzy rushed out to hopefully open the door. No one had any idea just how fast she was capable of moving, and there wasn't time to explain. Not waiting one more minute, she scooped up Elana. Because the pregnant woman was totally dead weight, Jillian had to beg her tiger to help her hold on.

With the precious cargo in her arms, Jillian repeated the directions. Then she took off, but she doubted anyone saw her leave. Less than thirty seconds later, she arrived at the hospital. A row of hedges lined one side of the parking lot. Jillian slowed her speed then lumbered the last few feet to the Emergency Room door, trying to act as if she'd carried her friend from the car.

Once inside, she spotted a gurney by the front desk and placed Elana on it. "Can you help me?" she asked the admitting nurse. "Her water broke, and the baby's breech. She's really weak." Jillian's words rushed out.

Without saying a word, the nurse glanced at the very pregnant Elana and picked up a small radio. "Emergency at the front desk." Her voice boomed over the intercom.

As much as Jillian wanted to comment that Elana had briefly stopped breathing, possibly as a result of being connected with her unborn child, she didn't need her new friend to be subjected to a lot of tests. They'd never figure out the reason if it happened to be shifter related.

Two men in blue scrubs rushed out and went right to work, asking the duty nurse questions. Elana partially opened her eyes and reached out her hand. When Jillian clasped it, Elana gave it a squeeze. "Make sure Kalan finds me," she said, her voice weak and her skin pale.

"Don't worry. I will. You just relax. You're in good hands now."

Elana looked up at the doctors. "Can she come with me?"

They faced Jillian. "Are you a relative or her birth coach?"

As much as she wanted to be there for Elana, she'd never lie. "No."

"We'll let you know when the baby's born."

That was all she could ask for. She supposed she could race back to the party, but Kalan would be at the hospital soon, and he'd need support and probably some answers.

No sooner had they wheeled Elana away than she sensed several shifter signatures arriving. Jillian rushed up to them. Kalan had arrived with Izzy, Rye, and Missy. No doubt a lot more had wanted to come for support, but he'd probably explained that the waiting room would only hold so many.

Kalan looked around. "Where's Elana?"

"The doctors just took her. They said you can be with her, but the rest of us can't."

"Thank you. When this is over, I want to learn how you moved so fast."

"The same way I've heard Izzy can part water."

He huffed out a small laugh. "Wendayan power. Got it." He then rushed off.

Izzy held out her hand. "Hi, I'm Izzy by the way—the infamous parter of water."

Jillian's shoulders relaxed for the first time in minutes. Being around a Wendayan helped center her. "Nice to meet you."

THE NEXT HOUR was tense. The four of them chatted, but because clusters of people would come and go, they really couldn't discuss much. In one of the lulls, she explained that her mom was a Wendayan, and that Jillian had inherited her ability to move in the blink of an eye.

Rye shook his head. "Before I could even register how you were able to lift a pregnant woman, let alone carry her, you were gone."

"I wanted to explain, but there wasn't time."

"I understand."

Because they were the only four in the waiting room at the moment, she could tell them. "Both Dalton and I have always been super fast, but my mom cautioned us against using our talent except in emergencies. When I saw that Elana wasn't breathing and the baby might die, I didn't have a choice."

Rye nodded. "Did anyone see you?"

"Did you?"

"Good point."

She held up a hand. "Don't worry. I slowed down before I entered the Emergency Room. If anyone was watching, they would have seen a strong woman carrying a pregnant woman. Adrenaline can do amazing things."

Rushed footsteps sounded. It was Kalan, and the smile told it all. "Elana is doing well, and Aiden is fine, thanks to Jillian."

She blushed as the knots in her stomach loosened. "I did what I could. When can we see her?"

"Maybe in an hour, but I'd like to request each of you only stay a few minutes. She's really exhausted."

They chatted a bit about the baby, but it was clear Kalan was anxious to get back to his mate. "Thanks for everyone's help."

Kalan hadn't even reached the elevators when her body vibrated. The antiseptic smell of the hospital disappeared and was replaced with a strong sensual scent that reminded her of mountain streams. What was going on?

"How is she?" said a voice Jillian instantly recognized.

Her human half groaned, still stinging from the rebuff of earlier tonight while her inner animal was panting and making Jillian's heart beat way too fast.

She whipped around. "Brian. You're here." She shouldn't have had so much surprise in her voice, but he had ditched the party scene without having the courtesy of letting his sister know.

He was scared, her tiger rebutted.

What was she talking about? *Scared of what?*

"No sooner had I made it home than Kalan called and said Elana had gone into labor." He hugged the large teddy bear he'd carried in, acting as if he was the one who needed its comfort.

"She did. Congratulations, you have a healthy nephew."

His smile altered something inside her. "Really? The baby's okay? And Elana?"

"Both are doing just fine."

Rye clasped Brian's shoulder. "Since you're her brother, you can go up and see her. Kalan suggested we let her rest a bit before the we barge in, but you can go first."

"That's all right." He shoved the bear into Jillian's hands. "Can you give this to her?"

Was he kidding? Sure he'd only met his sister a few months ago, but that was no excuse not to visit. "I bet she'd like to see you herself." Hell, Elana would be upset if Brian didn't show up.

"She's tired, and I don't want to make things worse."

"Not seeing her will make things worse. Your visit will perk her up."

"You think?"

From the way Elana spoke about Brian, she was thrilled he was back in her life. Jillian returned the soft bear with the black eyes and light brown fur to him. The red heart attached to its chest was totally sweet. "Now go. You can ask at the desk what her room number is."

"Okay." Just like at the party, Brian took off. A woman could get a complex being around him.

When he disappeared, she turned to the remaining group. "When do you think he'll tell Elana that he's one of us?"

Rye's mouth turned downward. "What do you mean by *one of us?*"

Jillian glanced behind her. "Brian's a shifter of some sort."

He shook his head. "I never detected anything."

You know because he's your mate. He's so repressed, no one else can tell. Her tiger's voice held way too much glee.

Well damn. "Maybe I was mistaken."

GIVEN IT WAS already past midnight, Jillian decided it would be best if she came back the next day to speak with Elana. Visiting hours were definitely over. After Brian's visit, she had a lot of thinking to do. Had she been wrong about him? She'd never mistaken a human for a shifter before. Why now?

What have I been telling you? You need to do a better job of listening to me.

Shut up. Her animal was driving her crazy. Maybe she should go for a run to tire her out. The problem was finding a location where no one would see her. If anyone spotted a white tiger, it would be plastered all over the news. She knew all about that. It had happened about five years ago. Since then, she'd been cautious.

After saying her goodbyes, she headed to Dalton's house, hoping no one caught sight of her blur as she raced back. A wave of safety washed over her when she spotted her brother's vehicle in the drive. With the key he'd given her, she let herself in.

"Hey," she said.

Dalton was in the kitchen making eggs. "How was the party?"

"Bizarre, scary, and then wonderful." She slipped off her jacket and placed her purse on the arm of the sofa.

"Sounds interesting," he said as he transferred the eggs from the pan to his plate. "You hungry?"

"Actually, I'm starving. I had to use my magic to speed from the party to the hospital."

He froze then set down the spatula he'd been using to remove the eggs. "What? Start from the beginning."

"When I first arrived at the party, Teagan's brother Sam was doing some kind of mind control act with a woman named Missy."

He smiled. "He's quite the powerful Wendayan. From what bits and pieces Kalan told me, Sam can make people believe something is in front of them when it's not. He was instrumental in helping Kip and some others from McKinnon and Associates retrieve stolen Wendayan magic."

He'd written her about the theft. "I can see why. He's very impressive."

"What was the bizarre part?"

This would be hard to explain, but she needed a sounding board. "You're aware that Elana was human until she mated with Kalan, right?"

"Yes. She's now a bear. So?"

"That means her brother should be human."

He set the hot pan in the sink and the contact with the water made it sizzle. "Your point?"

She crossed her heart. "As goddess is my witness, Brian gave off a shifter signature, faint though it was."

He shook his head. "You probably sensed the other shifters in the room and became confused. Were you drinking?"

Her mouth dropped open. "No, I'd just arrived. And why would you doubt me?"

"I've met Brian. He's all human. No shifter blood in him."

He's your mate! Only you can tell. She wished her tiger would go to sleep, especially since her animal was being so freakin' horny with no basis for it. *Tell your brother how your body vibrated with intense need, and then how you could feel my claws dig into your belly because I was begging for my release.*

Ignoring her little inner demon, she conceded. "Fine. Maybe he's not a shifter, but I was curious about him. I asked him how long he'd been in Silver Lake, to which he promptly set down his drink, excused himself, and walked out of the party."

Dalton slid the plate of eggs in front of her. "Eat these. I'll make more."

"No, you take them. I'll fix myself a sandwich."

He pulled the plate back toward him. "Are you upset that he didn't fall for your siren ways?" Dalton asked, acting like the typical, smug big brother.

She waved a hand. "I don't have siren ways. All I wanted was to find out more about him. Between you and Elana, I've learned that he had a rough life."

Dalton shoveled a forkful of eggs in his mouth, chewed, and then swallowed. "True."

"Anyway, as soon as Brian left, Elana went into labor and stopped breathing."

Dalton dropped his fork, and it clanked against the edge of the plate. "Is she okay? Why didn't you tell me?"

"Both she and baby Aiden are fine. Sorry. I'm still a little dizzy from all that running." Even now, her muscles were shaking. "I had to carry her in my arms from the Cove to the hospital, but we made it in time. Rye said the baby had the umbilical cord wrapped around his neck. I think when Elana sensed her shifter baby choking, she lost her own air for a few seconds."

"That's some scary shit about the baby and about you having to run all that way. Did anyone see you?"

"I doubt it. If they did, they wouldn't know what the blur was. Besides, if anyone is going to get caught, it's you. I haven't used my Wendayan talents but a handful of times. Seems to me, you use yours more often."

He shook his head. "I use my talents sparingly. Hell, Kalan doesn't even know what I'm capable of."

"I think he'll figure it out now that he knows what I can do."

Dalton lowered his head and finished off his plate of eggs. "I thought you wanted a sandwich."

She had wanted something to eat, but now she'd lost her appetite. Dalton was a very private man, and she hoped she hadn't messed things up between her brother and Kalan.

Chapter Six

FOR THE LAST few hours, Brian had walked the aisles of the lumber department, making certain that all the pieces of wood were lined up perfectly. It was the only way to keep his mind off Jillian and how he'd almost screwed up with his sister. What had he been thinking tossing a near stranger the bear and then asking her to deliver the present to Elana?

Answer? He hadn't been. It was all Jillian's fault too, with her wide-set eyes the color of the sky on a cloudless day and hair the same hue as the richest golden oak. Her delicate face highlighted her perfectly formed pink lips and long lashes, so much so that no man could resist her. Being five inches shorter than him, made her even more perfect.

Why someone like her even bothered talking to him at the party was anyone's guess. No woman as beautiful and soft as she was ever had before.

Thankfully, after a decent night's sleep, he was calmer. Of course, having the anxiety pills kick in helped too. Though after the way his body reacted to her last night, he might need something stronger to take the edge off his racing mind.

A small smile lifted his lips as he remembered the look on his sister's face when he walked into her hospital room carrying the bear. Her eyes had sparkled. Buying the teddy bear had been the perfect present. He'd found it a few weeks ago and had to get it for her. The only thing he wished had turned out differently was for her son,

Aiden to have been there. Elana said the doctors were still checking him out.

Brian was already making plans to build his nephew a rocking horse for his first birthday. For sure, he'd have his own go-cart when he was ready. Aiden Murdoch would always know he was loved. Brian would see to it.

"WHEN DID THEY say you could go home?" Jillian asked Elana, who looked beautiful with her brown hair splayed over the pillow. Even her coloring was almost back to normal and her skin looked smoother than ever.

"Later this afternoon, assuming Aiden is good. I've been very pleased with how cautious they've been. I guess breech births can be tricky, and the cord around his neck scared them a bit."

Jillian was so happy for her. "You are going to stay home for a few weeks and rest, right?"

From their conversations, Elana was driven. She still had some loans she owed Izzy's dad, and she was determined to pay them off as quickly as possible. She'd refused to let Kalan take care of them for her, and Jillian admired her drive.

"I'll stay home for a few days. Being a shifter will help with the healing process, and while I'll have terrible separation anxiety leaving Aiden, Kalan's mom said she'd watch the baby during the day. I just can't leave Anna to fend for herself at the store. Valentine's Day is one of our busiest holidays."

"I can help out," Jillian blurted without even thinking.

Elana pushed up on her elbows. "You know something about being a florist?"

Jillian laughed. "Nothing. Okay, I can tell a rose from a petunia, but that's about all. I'm sure I can figure out how to use a cash register, and I'm wickedly good with a broom. Would that help?"

Elana smiled. "You're this big-time lawyer. Wouldn't you be bored doing a menial job?"

"Bored? Try sitting all day at Dalton's house doing nothing. No. I'm going crazy not being around people."

"Then it's a deal. I pay ten dollars an hour."

Jillian waved a hand. "Nonsense. I work for free. You'd be doing me a favor." While she could use the cash, she'd never accept payment. "Besides, I'm only a trainee."

"That would be fantastic. I really am looking forward to spending time with my baby. I'll call Anna now. When can I tell her to expect you?"

"I'll stop over right after lunch. How about that?"

"Perfect."

They chatted a bit more about how nervous Elana was raising a son, especially one who would be shifting by the time he was two or three. A few minutes later, the nurse came in carrying a fussy Aiden.

"Time to feed," the nurse said, handing Elana the baby.

He was such a beautiful child, and Jillian's mothering instincts kicked in. She'd always pushed aside the whole concept of having children, but after seeing Aiden's sweet face, she might have to reconsider.

That would require a mate, however, and the chances of that were slim to none.

Brian, Brian, her animal chanted.

Jillian wished she knew what she'd eaten to make her tiger so randy. It had to be the large number of shifters in this area that had woken her up.

"I'll let you two bond. Don't worry about your store." Jillian smiled and waved goodbye.

After she stopped at a fast food place and chowed down a rather good chicken sandwich, she drove over to the Blooms of Hope. When she walked in, a woman about twenty-five with an armful of tattoos was working quickly behind the counter helping a man. The aroma of flowers was pervasive, but nice.

She looked up. "I'll be with you in a moment."

"I'm Jillian, and I'm here to help."

"Oh, there is a God. If you're ready to help, can you go into the backroom and bring me two long boxes? There should be a few on the table."

There was nothing like jumping into the proverbial deep end without a life preserver to boost her spirits. Jillian stepped behind the counter and entered the back room. *Very nice.* Floor to ceiling shelves covering two of the opposite walls were filled with vases, stuffed animals, ribbon, and other assorted things one needed to make the perfect bouquet.

A large table in the middle took up most of the room. On top were several pre-made boxes. Some were long and thin, perfect for packing long-stemmed roses, and others were large cubes, just the right size for a stuffed animal. Jillian picked up two of the long boxes and carried them out.

"Are these the ones?"

Anna smiled. "Perfect." She placed half a dozen roses in the box and then cut pink ribbon to length. Once Anna wrapped it lengthwise and then widthwise, she looked up. "Can you place your finger here?"

"Sure." Images of wrapping Christmas presents with her mom flashed in her mind's eye, and a brief high washed over her, filled with contentment and joy. Being here in Silver Lake and helping out at the store was so much less stressful than reading motions and depositions.

Once Anna finished, she smiled and handed the man the gorgeous box. As she rang him up, Jillian watched how she swiped the man's card and what buttons she pressed on the register. "Thank you, Mr. Jenkins. I hope Mrs. Jenkins loves her gift."

"I'm sure she will." He smiled and then left.

When no one else came in, Anna sagged. "I am so happy you were willing to help. I've been swamped all day."

"My pleasure. It gives me something to do." While carrying in two boxes from the back and placing a finger on the ribbon wasn't a great feat, Jillian understood that just having help around gave a person a sense of hope that she'd get through the day.

"I can't believe I forgot to ask. How's Elana? When she called to tell me you'd volunteered, I was so excited that I didn't ask about the baby."

"She's doing great. While she's happy, I think Elana's a bit scared at the same time. First time mother jitters, I guess."

Anna grinned. "I can't wait to see the baby."

"I only saw Aiden for a few seconds, but he's a cute, chubby boy." Jillian glanced around. "What do you need me to do besides making arrangements? I'm willing to sweep floors, tidy up, or work the credit card machine."

"For starters, can you grab the red vase with the wild flowers from the second shelf and bring it over? I want show you how to use the helium machine to blow up balloons and how to attach them to the vases."

For the next three hours, Anna ran around like crazy, helping customers and directing Jillian to grab this or that. When there was a lull, she explained how to use the credit card machine.

It wasn't until close to five that things settled down. Just as Jillian allowed herself a pat on the back for surviving her first day, pounding feet sounded on the stairs causing Jillian's pulse to rise. It was immediately followed by a wave of lust that nearly made her drop the two vases she was holding.

Mate, mate, urged her tiger.

Damn. She had to shut up her animal. The only possible solution was to go for a run.

You promised that before and didn't deliver, her animal said.

I will just as soon as I ask Dalton where I can go and not be seen.

Jillian returned her attention to what had distracted her. "What is all that noise?"

Anna waved a hand. "That's Brian, Elana's brother. He lives in the apartment upstairs. If you think that's noisy, the other day was even worse. When I went up to see what was going on and to ask him to keep it down, he acted as if he had no idea that saws and drills made noise. Thankfully, he agreed not to work until after the shop closed, though once Mr. Berta gets wind of it, I bet he'll boot him out." She smiled. "Don't tell Elana, but Brian made a cradle for the baby."

Jillian's heart warmed at the idea of a man who was so uncomfortable in his skin, making something so personal for his sister's baby. "He has to work somewhere. I guess workshops are hard to find."

Anna chuckled. "I guess."

Anna flipped over the Closed sign on the front door and then finished with the last arrangement that needed to be ready early tomorrow morning for pickup. Jillian swept up the scraps and straightened some of the mess in the back room.

"Let's go home," Anna said as she grabbed her coat from the hook near the door. "In case something happens, and you ever need to come into the store to open up, the code is 93412."

Not wanting Anna to think she had a steel trap for a brain—which she did—Jillian pulled out her phone and put the code in her notes. "Got it."

Heads down against the chilling wind, they both returned to their cars. Even though Jillian slid into the driver's side and pretended she was making a call, she was waiting for Anna to leave.

As soon as she did, Jillian shut off her engine. Why she felt this urge to march up the back steps and demand answers from Brian, she didn't know.

The idea of your mate shutting you out scares you, her tiger claimed with an all too smug attitude.

Not true. Brian seems sweet but very lost, and I just want to help. Brian would be better off embracing his shifter side, and maybe even moving into the compound for more support. Sure, she'd told Dalton she might have made a mistake about Brian being a *Were,* but in her heart—and especially in her body—she knew she was right.

Inhaling deeply, Jillian slid out of her car and hurried to the back entrance. With one hand holding her jacket tight around her body, she punched in the code with the other. After pulling the door open, she stepped inside the dark hallway, happy for the warmth. The air was a bit stale, and the area closed in, but those were minor inconveniences. She was on a mission.

At her first step, her muscles froze. What exactly was she going to ask him? Or rather, how could she find out for sure that he was a *Were*? If he wasn't, and she discussed shifters in front of him, there could be bad consequences. His relationship with his sister might become more strained.

He's your mate.

Doesn't mean he's a Were, she countered.

He is.

She'd have to trust her instincts this time. The fact her pulse was fluttering and a dampness was pooling between her thighs gave some credence to the whole idea that Brian Stanley might be her mate, but she wasn't going to let her tiger know she might be a believer. All the more reason to find out who he was—or rather what he was.

Treading lightly on the steps so Brian wouldn't hear her coming, she made it to the top landing. Suddenly, the door opened and Brian filled the frame. Guess she wasn't as light on her feet as she thought, or else he had shifter hearing.

The man, or rather the *Were*, didn't look pleased. "Jillian? What are you doing here?" The harshness in his voice was then replaced with a softening around his mouth. "Is Elana okay?"

Brian clearly loved his sister. "She's fine. May I come in?"

He studied her as his body transformed from tense to almost rigid. Was he really considering not asking her in? If his body were vibrating half as much as hers, he would be freaking out right now, kind of like she was, and need to have her near. He lowered his gaze. "Sure."

She stepped inside. The apartment was tiny and smelled like wood shavings—sweet and rich. Then again, maybe it was Brian's scent doing some damage to her ability to distinguish smells. "This is cute."

The dark leather sofa and chairs suited him.

"Thanks." He cleared his throat. "You want a drink?"

She'd rather have answers, but a drink was better than him kicking her out. "Sure."

Brian walked over to the kitchen and grabbed two beers from the fridge. She slipped off her long coat and placed it across the back of the sofa to let him know she planned to stay for a while.

He handed her the bottle. "What do you want?" His tone came out rather harshly again. Damn. He wasn't making this easy, but she'd dealt with plenty of reluctant witnesses before. She could do this.

Most men wouldn't have been so abrupt, but Brian had been raised without parents so she'd give him a pass—this time. She sipped her beer, and it went down smoothly. Perhaps because he was upset, his shifter signature was pulsing so strongly there was no mistaking he was a *Were*. "Why have you never told Elana that she's your half sister?"

That came out way too angry, but Elana deserved to know.

"Excuse me?"

Her heart skipped a beat at the shock in his voice and the hardness around his eyes. Had her stupid tiger been trying to get the upper hand by somehow making her believe she smelled his shifter aura?

I'm never deceitful! her animal declared.

You better not be.

"Then how do you explain that Elana was fully human before she met Kalan, and since you're—"

"What?" He moved so close, his presence cut off her words. It wasn't until a few seconds had passed before he averted his intense glare. "What do you mean by *fully human*? As opposed to what?"

So he wanted to play the game of denial? That wouldn't fly with her. "As opposed to being a shifter." There. She'd said it.

"What's a shifter?"

Jillian had to hand it to him. He was a good actor, but she'd go along. He had to know what a shifter was. Hell, he was one. "A shifter is a person who is part animal."

Brian loomed over her, and she found it difficult to breathe. "Lady, I don't know who you are, but I do know you're crazier than I've ever been." He slipped the beer from her fingers. "Please leave."

For the first time in years, Jillian was at a loss for words. "Half the town of Silver Lake is made up of shifters. Why are you in denial?"

"Me? In denial? Denial is when you won't admit that something is true. I've spent the last thirty years in therapy revealing my deepest darkest secrets. I'm not in denial about anything. I'm willing to admit I was a shit to my sister when I walked away from her after we first met. I'm not ashamed to say that I was afraid to get close to her for fear she'd leave me—just like everyone else in my life."

"Elana would never—"

He poked her shoulder with her bottle. "You don't know anything about Elana. After I reread her texts and letters about a hundred times, I finally realized that she wanted to connect with me. Me." He tapped his chest with the same bottle. "Her *brother*. She's honest and good, so don't say she's not even human. As for myself, trust me, I'm fully human and all male." She half expected him to grab his crotch, but thankfully, he didn't. "While my mom said I acted like a wild animal as a child, I'm not one now."

Shit. She'd royally messed this up. *What to do? What to do?*

Prove it to him, her tiger screamed.

No. Maybe I'm wrong. The scar-faced man in LA might have messed with my head.

You're not wrong. What's his scent doing to you right now? You want Brian, right?

Wanting had nothing to do with him being a *Were*. "I'm sorry. May we sit?" she asked.

His breath came out way too fast and his lips thinned as his gaze bounced around the room. "I guess, but don't mention Elana again."

He set her bottle on the coffee table then dropped onto the chair. Jillian sat on the sofa across from him. She wasn't sure how to begin finding out if perhaps he was unaware of his animal heritage. His scent was indeed messing with her head, and there were way too many urges heating up her insides to deny he might be her mate, but it was still possible he wasn't a shifter.

He has the scent of a shifter, her tiger insisted.

"Can I ask whether when you were growing up, you felt this intense urge to be outside—especially at night? That sometimes the walls in your house felt like they were closing in on you?"

A quick flash of concern crossed his face, but then his stoic façade returned. "Every kid wants to be outside. If you had parents like mine, you'd consider running away on a daily basis. Why do you think I down so many pills? As far as running away, I was smart enough to know I wouldn't get far, so instead, I acted out."

That wasn't quite what she'd asked. Damn. This wasn't getting her anywhere. While she didn't know everything he'd gone through as a child, she suspected it might be worse than how he was portraying it. During his youth, with his animal hormones coursing through his system, he would want to claw at the earth, climb a tree, and run wild. Since he wouldn't understand why he had those urges, frustrations would continue to build. "It must have been pretty bad."

"You have no idea what it was like having parents who wanted nothing to do with me."

"Why do you suppose that was?"

He leaned back, his mouth slightly agape. "Lady, who the hell are you? Did my shrink send you to make sure I'm doing okay?"

"No one sent me."

He stood. "I think you should go."

Not liking that he was looking down at her, she stood too, but there was no way she was going to walk out of his apartment without proving to him that his parents might have decided he needed help because he was different. Being a shifter might explain some of their actions.

An overwhelming urge to give him comfort startled her. "I'll go, but not before I show you something."

"What's that?"

"This."

Chapter Seven

B RIAN SET DOWN his beer bottle and clenched his fists, waiting to see Jillian's next move before escorting her out. Strange things were happening to him. His body seemed to be heating up from the inside out, and something sharp was poking his insides, though that was probably stomach acid eating away at the lining.

His anxiety levels had been fine until he'd opened the door and found Jillian standing there in her sexy as hell black jeans and rose colored buttoned down shirt. Hell, his pulse rate had gone off the charts, and his first instinct was to throw all caution to the wind and drag her inside and kiss her. For a moment, he thought he was reliving his dream from last night, but he'd never act out those fantasies. The consequences would be too painful. He was damaged, and when she learned what kind of person he really was, she'd reject him, just like his parents had.

Suddenly shy, Jillian looked off to the side, her fingers playing with the buttons on her shirt. Her hair was a bit tangled, and it hung loosely around her shoulders. He flexed his fingers wanting to wrap his hand around each curl and then bring those thick strands to his nose to smell her delicious scent.

Jillian shook her head and refocused, taking Brian back to reality. A second later, she kicked off her shoes and unbuttoned her blouse. His throat tightened up and his cock turned rock hard. "Ah, Jillian. What are you doing?"

She tilted her chin upward. "I'm preparing for my demonstration. It's the only solution since you won't listen to reason."

She was certifiable. He'd have to warn Elana to stay away from her. He held up a hand, but he couldn't bring himself to move closer. "Just stop what you're doing."

Her brows pinched. "Why? I don't want to ruin my clothes."

"What the hell are you planning to do?" His mind spun with a myriad of possibilities, all of which would result in him losing his mind.

She slipped off her black pants and stood before him wearing only her sexy red bra and panties. Holy hell.

Take her, his crazy voice urged. Brian had spent his life working on shutting out his voices, but of late, this one had been very insistent.

All of a sudden, a low growl erupted from Jillian, and the protective part of his brain made him move forward to help. He froze the second white hair sprouted on her arms and legs, and he blinked rapidly to clear the crazy image. Had she doused his beer with some hallucinogen when he wasn't looking? He swore he'd had the bottle in his hand the whole time.

Fearing she had, he set his beer down. Fur flew and her blonde hair spun. What the fuck?

Before he could blink again, a tiger formed in front of him, and his breath caught in his throat. The room closed in on him, and his heart beat erratically. *I need my pills.* He patted his pocket, hoping he'd stashed some there, but he came up empty.

As if on the prowl, she stalked toward him. Oh, shit. Heart in throat, he backed up, only to run into the sofa arm. "Don't come any closer," he said, his voice wobbly.

The tiger, if that was what it really was, lowered its head and edged toward him, the brown and white striped tail wagging. The animal was maybe three feet tall with big white paws. She looked up at him as if to let him study her. What looked like a tree branch with brown leaves on either side was drawn from her brow to the top of her head. Except for some brown stripes around her mouth, her nose was all white. Whiskers sprouted from above her eyes and along the side of her mouth.

As if she was tired of posing, she moved closer. Brian only guessed the animal was a female because Jillian had been there one minute and gone the next. Where she'd stood only moments before lay a torn red bra and panties. If this was a real animal and she was in his bedroom, he'd have to hand it to her. She was a true magician.

The animal rubbed against his leg and then nudged his hand. He raised it out of the way. As if that was the wrong reaction, the animal lifted her paw and trapped his hand against his body.

Looking up at him, the tiger tilted her head as a soft mewing sound came out. The animal seemed to be asking for some loving. He couldn't resist that plea. Not now.

You can do this. Tentatively, Brian reached out and petted her head. "Nice tiger."

He didn't expect her to continue purring, but it helped reduce his anxiety a notch. At first, he thought the tiger would bite him, but after a few strokes, she licked his knuckles with a tongue that was akin to general purpose sand paper—rough but not destructive.

Not wanting to upset her, he sidled toward the door, thinking if he could get her to leave, he could then call some vet to trap her. He'd made it about three feet, when she seemed to sense his intention and blocked his path.

Before he could reach around the tiger to pull open the door, the animal disintegrated right before him. Seconds later, Jillian stood before him—naked.

Holy fuck. Jillian looked like she'd just been involved in some hard loving—the kind he wanted to participate in. Her blonde hair went every which way, and her nipples stood erect. As much as he wanted to soak in everything about her body and drown in those blue eyes, he couldn't afford to take the risk. His body was vibrating, and he found it difficult to breathe.

Brian turned his back. He'd never be able to think straight seeing her like that, and he needed answers. "Can you put something on, please?"

Most likely, her perfectly bow-shaped mouth was open since he'd bet no man had ever asked her to put her clothes on before.

Her delicate footsteps tapping against the floor exploded in his head, but he refrained from pressing his palms against his temples. It never quelled the noises anyway. He could detect the scraping of each foot along the inside of her pants followed by the clickety-clack of her zipper rising. The air whooshed through her top as she picked it up.

You need help, his inner voice said.

Yes, I do. Brian rushed into the kitchen, yanked open the kitchen drawer, and poured an anxiety pill onto his palm. Aw hell, why not? He added an anti-depressant. It was time to start building them up in his system again.

"You're not crazy," Jillian said. "I know seeing me change into a tiger was a shock."

It was a lot more than a shock. His world view had been turned upside down. Leaning over the sink, he filled his mouth with water and then downed the pills.

Letting them settle into his stomach, he turned around.

Her hard nipples protracted through her thin shirt. He glanced to her jacket on the back of the sofa and debated asking her to put it on, but she'd be too warm. "I have something you can wear."

Without waiting for her response, he charged into his room and routed through his closet. At the end of the rack, he found a clean, flannel shirt. While it would be huge on her, at least she'd be covered.

He returned and handed it to her. "How about putting this on?"

She slipped her hands in the sleeves and buttoned it up halfway. "Thanks."

Brian inhaled. "How about explaining what the hell happened? Or was it some kind of trick?" He hoped it was the latter.

"It wasn't a trick." She stepped around him and returned to the sofa. "Sit down, Brian. This may take awhile."

CLEARLY, JILLIAN HAD gone about this reveal all wrong. Elana should have been the one to break the news to him in a kinder, gentler way, but Jillian had been so convinced he'd been faking it that she'd taken the plunge and shifted.

And she'd been wrong. Brian didn't know he was a shifter. No one could fake that kind of shock, dismay, and fear. All she could figure was that somehow one of the parents, unbeknownst to them, had messed around with a shifter.

"I'm sorry you had to see that," she said.

"Sorry? How can you say that? From the moment you walked in my apartment, you were determined to get my attention. You wanted to prove something, but you failed."

Her defense mechanisms flared up. "I just wanted you to under-stand that you're more than you realize."

"What the hell does that mean?" He picked up his bottle, lifted it halfway to his lips, and then set it down.

"Whether you want to believe it or not, you have the ability to shift too." She would discuss his sister's new abilities later—much later.

Brian dipped back his head and laughed. "I have no idea what kind of drugs you're on, but maybe I should add them to the list of mine."

This was getting worse by the minute. "Listen, I'm a shifter—as you saw. I can sense when others are too, but I totally get why you don't believe me. I was raised by a shifter dad. From a young age, I watched my father transform from human to animal and back again. He told me to picture myself as a tiger, and one day when I was chasing a ball and laughing, I was suddenly on all fours."

Brian cocked a brow. "That's a nice story, but neither of my parents were shifters."

She would have considered maybe they didn't know, but then Kalan would have sensed Elana was one. "How about closing your eyes?"

"Why?"

The man was stubborn to the core. "Because I asked you to?"

He did. "Fine. Now what?"

"Don't look. I'm going to rub two things together and I want you to tell me what they are." He shrugged. Brian probably wasn't aware that his senses were better than most, especially his hearing—as well as his sight and his sense of smell. She picked up her jacket and rubbed it on the wooden table. "What does this sound like?"

He huffed out a breath. "Fabric against wood. That was easy."

"Good. What about this?" To challenge him, she ran her palm down her pants leg.

"Fabric scraping."

"Open your eyes." He did. "Shifters, whether they are wolves, bears, tigers, or whatever, have a heightened sense of smell too. I bet you can tell the difference between Oak and Maple."

"Any good craftsman can."

She stood and turned off all the lights. Except for the numbers on the microwave, the house was dark. Thankfully, he didn't question what she was trying to prove. "Face me." He did. In front of the dark flannel shirt, she held up three fingers. Only a shifter would be able to see in this dim light. "How many fingers am I holding up?"

"Three."

"Do you think many people could see in the dark?"

He looked off to the side, as if trying to remember when he'd been in the dark with someone else, how much they could see. "No, I guess not."

Jillian bounced over to the lamp next to the sofa and flicked it on. "Believe me now?"

"I believe that I have good eyesight and good hearing, but that doesn't prove anything."

"You opened the door before I was at the top of the steps. Did you hear me or smell me?"

His face paled. *Gotcha!*

"I smelled your perfume. Whatever kind you're wearing, I'd wish you'd stop. I think I'm allergic to it."

A smile lifted her lips. "I'm not wearing any." That almost clinched it, but she needed one more test. "Are you attracted to me?"

It was a little too soon to be asking him anything more specific, like did his heart race and his body go wild with need every time she was near? Just like hers was doing now.

"You're okay, why?"

Once more, Brian avoided answering her directly, so she stepped closer to him. Now that her tiger had been freed for a few minutes, she wanted more of Brian.

It's too soon, she cautioned. *He'll spook for sure.*

You might be right.

Really? I know your game. If you gave in that easily, you must be up to something.

Her tiger growled. Now that her mate was near, her animal was overly anxious, which meant it was Jillian's job to rein her in.

"Brian, have you ever heard of the expression soul mates?" Her palms dampened as she awaited his response. Jillian might be an experienced trial lawyer, good at determining when and how far to push a witness, but she had no confidence in her ability to draw Brian out.

"Yeah, what about it?"

His gaze didn't waver, and she didn't detect any erratic pulse at his throat or temple. Clearly, he wasn't experiencing this intense draw yet. He would, though, once he learned to shift and all of his new hormones flooded his system. "It's nothing. Look I think I've done enough damage to your mind for one night." She rushed over to her torn underwear and snatched the garments off the floor.

He held out his hand. "I can throw them in the trash for you if you like."

"Sure." Aha. So he wasn't immune. She handed them to him. Ten bucks said he'd keep them as a memory. Before things turned any weirder, she took off his flannel shirt and slipped on her jacket.

"If you have any questions, you know where to find me."

With that, she pulled open the door and rushed out, her heart lodged high in her throat. As she sped down the steps, heat raced up her face. She'd actually undressed in front of Brian, and then completely forgot about what would happen when she shifted back. The look on his face as he stared at her naked body was akin to horror. Dear goddess, if she could go back in time, she'd sell her soul.

Chapter Eight

J ILLIAN FELT TERRIBLE at having scared the crap out of Brian. The poor man had been traumatized growing up, and what she'd just done might make him relapse. If that happened, Elana would never forgive her.

How could he not know he was a shifter? One of his parents had to have been one. Only which one? And why hadn't they told him? As much as she needed to find the answers, she had to do it safely and gently.

Oh, crap. She'd forgotten to tell him not to say anything to anyone, though she doubted he would, especially to Elana. When she found out what Jillian had done though, her friend might not want to speak with her again. Jillian's only choice was to confess her sins and pray for forgiveness.

It was only a little past six, and most likely Elana would be home, assuming the hospital had released her as promised. The problem was that Jillian didn't know where her friend lived, but Dalton did.

As she rushed to her car, the chill went right to the bone, but she'd gladly stand naked for an hour in this weather if she could take back her bold move. Stripping then shifting had been stupid, but she'd been desperate. Hopefully, when she explained what happened, Elana could find a positive side to the reveal.

After Jillian started the car and turned up the heat, she called Dalton.

"Hey, I thought you'd be home for dinner by now," he said without preamble.

"Me too. Listen, I decided to have a talk with Brian about something, and I stayed longer than planned."

"I thought he didn't like you, which was why he kept running away from you."

Perhaps telling Dalton everything hadn't been smart either. "I wanted to change his mind, but then things got a little out of hand."

"You slept with him?" Anger laced his tone.

She wasn't going to take any of his shit. It didn't matter that her brother had been wonderful and let her stay at his place. "No, but even if I had, it would have been between consenting adults."

"You're right," Dalton admitted after a long pause.

"Besides, having sex wouldn't have caused this problem," she said.

"What did you do or rather say?" Now he sounded like the exasperated brother she was used to. "You didn't tell him Elana was a shifter did you?"

"Worse. I shifted in front of him."

"Oh, Jilly, why?"

Her pet name almost made her cry. "It's a long story. I need to explain a few things to Elana, and when I return to the house, I'll give you all the gritty details. Can you give me her address?"

"Do you want me to go with you?"

There was no way she'd be able to give any details about her being naked in front of Brian. However, since she had shifted, it kind of implied it. "No, thanks."

Once she had the directions, she headed for the shifter compound. Too bad, her stomach was tied up in knots. Normally, she would have called instead of just showing up at Elana's door, but explaining something like this over the phone wouldn't have been good.

Following Dalton's instructions, she found the home easily. It was situated on a nice piece of land. With the house lights on, it looked so cozy, like her home, but she refused to dwell on what she'd left behind. Unless Whitlaw was caught, Los Angeles would be too dangerous to be in right now. Not to mention that after what happened there, her house might never be cozy again.

Once she parked, Jillian figured both Kalan and Elana knew they had company. The borrowed car would not be given high marks for being quiet.

Kalan answered on the first knock. "Jillian, what's wrong?"

Why did everyone assume something bad had happened? Perhaps it was because the first time she'd met him, something had. That or she had the look of tragedy on her face. "I'm sorry to barge in, but I need to speak with Elana."

"Come in. She's in the back with Aiden. I'll get her."

Jillian should turn around and leave, but this was too important. "Thanks."

A minute later, Elana came out from the back wearing a maternity top with a clean diaper over her shoulder. She looked down and plucked it off. "Sorry."

"I just came from Brian's. We need to talk."

She stilled. "Is everything okay?"

"More or less. Can we sit and chat?"

"Sure." Elana took the lounge chair and propped up her feet while Jillian sat in the comfy leather chair across from her.

For some reason, Jillian was more nervous telling her tale to Elana than when she'd approached Brian. "There are a few things that I think you should know about your brother."

Jillian explained her theory as to why Brian had left the party at Teagan and Kip's house. "I'm not trying to be egotistical, but I think he was attracted to me and didn't know what to do about it."

"That's possible. I don't think he's dated a lot. Certainly not since he's moved here."

Elana didn't seem upset with the idea of Brian liking her, but Elana wasn't pleased either. "However, my reaction to your brother was much stronger. In fact, it was so intense that I'm convinced he's my mate."

Heavy footsteps sounded down the hallway. Kalan must have been listening. "Your mate?"

Great. Now she had a true disbeliever. "Yes. It wasn't planned. You know how it is." She glanced from Elana to Kalan. "When you first saw Elana, weren't you surprised when your body went haywire around her?"

He glanced away for a moment. "Yes. I really thought the goddess would have paired me with another shifter, but I thank her every day for giving me Elana."

At least they seemed to understand that mates were pre-destined. "You can imagine my surprise when I found out my mate was Brian. But here's the thing. Because I'm his mate, I could sense that he is also a shifter."

"What?" they said in unison.

Jillian held up her hand. "I sensed it, only I had no idea that Brian didn't know he was one."

"That's impossible," Elana said.

"Is it? Were your parents so in love that one of them couldn't have had an affair? Or perhaps they adopted Brian. Do you know the real story behind your brother's birth?"

Elana looked up at Kalan. "I guess not, but he looks like my mom. He has her nose."

That wasn't conclusive evidence. She explained about the hearing and sight tests she'd given him. "He passed with flying colors."

"Did you mention shifters to him?" Kalan asked.

Now came the hard part. "Worse. I showed him."

Their wide eyes said it all. Elana placed her hand over her heart. "How did he react?"

"About how you would expect. He was shocked, stunned, and disoriented, but he seemed to accept the reality, though it would have been kind of hard not to when I shifted into my tiger form and then turned back again right in front of him. The part he wouldn't accept was that he was a shifter too. He just laughed at me when I told him."

"That sounds like Brian. Maybe I should see how he is," Elana said, slipping her legs off the lounge looking as if she planned to drive over to his place right now.

Jillian raised a hand. "I think he needs time to sort through everything. Before I realized he didn't know about his heritage, I asked him why he hadn't told you he was your half-brother. Brian didn't like that question and tried to throw me out."

A small smile lifted her lips. "He's come a long way. The longer he's here, the more convinced I am that he really does care about me."

"He cares a lot. You're all he has. Since I was the one who poked the hornet's nest so to speak, what do you think I should do?"

"Are you positive Brian's a shifter?" Kalan asked. "I never sensed anything."

"Dalton said the same thing. I think his inner animal is hidden so deeply inside him that only a mate could sense it."

Elana reached out and clasped Kalan's hand. "I'll speak to him tomorrow," she said. "It's time I tell him the truth about us anyway. In a way, this might be a good thing. It's been hanging over my head for months, but I was afraid he'd become unglued and never recover."

Jillian hoped that wouldn't happen. "I'm not sure Brian will forgive me. If we really are mates, I'll have a steep hill to climb."

"Be careful," Elana said. "All he's known is disappointment. I hope he doesn't have a setback."

"Me too, but if he didn't realize he was a shifter, it might explain why he acted out growing up—or so he told me."

"How would knowing have helped him?"

"Without being aware of his heritage, he would have become increasingly frustrated by all the shifter hormones in his body. He'd have no idea how to handle the strange feelings."

"Jillian might be right," Kalan said. His support helped.

She faced Elana. "Do you know what really happened to him

growing up?"

"Not really. But it's Brian's story. He needs to tell you. I don't want to put any more strain on our relationship."

"I totally understand. I just need to find a way to reach him without doing any more damage."

Once she filled Dalton in on this conversation, she hoped he'd be able to offer sound advice.

DESPITE TAKING MORE medication, Brian couldn't fall asleep for the life of him. At least this time, he understood why he was so restless. It wasn't every day a person saw another human being change into a tiger then turn back again. His worldview had definitely been altered, and he wasn't sure for the better. What other crazy things hadn't he'd known about? If tomorrow Jillian came to him and proved that aliens existed, he just might have to dig a hole and hide in it for the rest of his life.

All night, he debated whether he should contact Dr. Patterson about changing his meds, but what would he say? *Doc, I think I need a different drug because I truly believe this woman I have the hots for is an animal in disguise?* Yeah, no. They'd come for him with a straight jacket, ASAP.

At first, Brian had dismissed everything Jillian had said about him being a shifter, but then some old memories came floating back that could prove her right. His only childhood friend, Danny Reverlo, and he loved to play hide and seek. Brian always won because Danny was noisier than ten squirrels fighting over a nut. They'd often play late into the evening and Brian could never believe his friend hid where everyone could see him. Looking back, Brian found Danny because of his excellent hearing and eyesight. But that alone didn't mean he was a different kind of freak—one who could shift.

Jillian was right about his ability to smell. The moment she'd arrived at Teagan's party, his interest had piqued—okay, his body had gone crazy—when her scent had seeped deeply into each and every pore. Even now, he could smell her lingering scent, but he wouldn't tell her that. She held enough power over him.

The big question that had him tossing and turning all night, was what was he supposed to do now? Jillian seemed interested in him, and it would be a shame not to see where that could lead. If she decided he wasn't the person she imagined, or rather the animal she believed him to be, at least he'd have spent time with her. He had no doubt that time would be highly enjoyable while it lasted.

He smiled. Dr. Patterson sure would be proud at his willingness to risk his emotions—to grab the ring as his therapist liked to say. Knowing how strong-willed Jillian was, she'd probably pester him over and over again to get him to shift. He wouldn't, of course—or rather, he couldn't because he was human—but it might be fun to try playing her little game. His whole life he'd been hesitant to go after a woman as beautiful as Jillian, but she'd been the one to put the moves on him. So why the hell not grab that brass ring?

WORK THE NEXT day was harder than usual since it took all of Brian's efforts to pay attention to what any of the customers asked him. Everything Jillian told him was bouncing around his head like a steel cylinder in a pinball machine, making it hard to concentrate. He couldn't take his mind off the concept that shifters existed. What was he going to tell Elana? *By the way, people can turn into animals, and worse, Jillian thinks I'm one. How about them apples, sister?*

Elana would probably suggest he return to Ohio and check in with Dr. Patterson, but Brian wasn't sure what his therapist could do. It wasn't like he could erase Brian's memory.

As the day progressed, Brian became more anxious. More images from the past flickered through his memory, but he never remembered seeing an animal, other than a dog or cat, anywhere near the house. His parents couldn't have been shifters.

From experience, he knew the best way to calm down was to get this off his chest. He needed to speak with Elana and tell her the truth: Jillian, a newcomer to town, wasn't who his sister thought her to be. That was a shame, since Elana really seemed to have bonded with her.

At five, he clocked out and went to the grocery store to pick up some oatmeal raisin cookies. Elana had briefly mentioned those were her favorite. Perhaps with some sweets in hand, she might find comfort after he spilled the beans about this alternate life form. Because he hadn't found the right time to take her the cradle, he carefully placed it in the front seat of his truck and headed over.

If he thought it would do any good, he'd pop one more anxiety pill.

Suck it up, Brian. Be a man.

His little pep talk didn't help. Ten minutes later, he pulled in front of his sister's house. He eased out and walked up the front walk, thankful the snow had melted. He rang the bell.

Kalan opened up. "Brian, come in."

Why didn't he sound surprised? That set him further on edge. "Is my sister here?"

"Hon?" Kalan called. "Brian's here."

He set the bag of cookies on the coffee table and placed the cradle next to the sofa. A minute later, Elana came out with the baby in her arms, breastfeeding Aiden. He should look away, but it was a rather beautiful sight. His sister looked so happy.

"I made you a baby gift." He picked up the cradle to show her. The sides he'd left varnished, but the two ends had the Murdoch tartan colors of green and blue.

"Oh, Brian, it's amazing. When did you make this?"

"After work. I thought you'd figure it out since I was making so much noise that day."

"Is that what you were doing?" she asked. He loved how her eyes shone with such joy.

"Yes."

"I'd give you a hug, but my arms are full. I hope you don't mind if I feed Aiden while we talk."

"Not at all." He put the cradle down then nodded to the bag on the coffee table. "I thought you might like some cookies. They're oatmeal raisin, your favorite, right?"

She smiled, just as he'd hoped. "They are, thank you."

While he'd rehearsed what he wanted to say, he wasn't sure now where to begin. His therapist said to just start talking. "Jillian stopped by my apartment last night."

"We know," Elana said. "She felt terrible about shifting in front of you."

Of all the things he expected her to say, that wasn't it. "She told you?"

"Yes."

"Weren't you shocked that she shifted in front of me?"

"Totally." Elana glanced up at Kalan. "Can you join us?"

"Sure." Kalan slid next to Elana, and the threesome warmed his heart. This was a family the way it should be.

"Brian, there is so much that we need to explain to you."

"What more could you tell me other than Jillian is a white tiger shifter?"

"Kalan and I are bear shifters."

"What the fuck?" His vision blurred, and he stuck his hand in his pocket hoping to find something to take, but he came up empty. A band tightened about his chest. When his hands began to shake, he fisted them.

Kalan jumped up. "Can I get you a beer or a whiskey?"

He shouldn't drink given how many pills he'd taken, but he needed something to take the edge off. "Whiskey would be great." He returned his gaze to his sister.

"I'll explain." She told him how Kalan, who'd been assigned to protect her after their parents were murdered, had turned out to be a bear shifter. Yes, she'd been shocked, but she had known about shifters from her friend Izzy. After she and Kalan agreed to be with each other, he bit her neck as a way to ensure a lasting bond between them. That action allowed her to inherit, if that was the right word, his abilities.

"So, you're saying a human can become a shifter if another shifter bites that person in the neck?"

"I guess you could put it that way, but it's way more than that. Love is involved."

Those details weren't important at the moment. "Does that mean you can shift like Jillian?" She nodded. "I can tell you this, I've never been bitten, so I know I'm not a freak. Crap. I didn't mean that I thought you were or anything."

"I understand."

Kalan stood. "You need to see what Elana found this evening. It might change your mind." He walked down the hallway and returned a minute later.

Brian recognized the box from the ones he'd removed from the attic. "You looked through Mom's things?"

"Yes." She adjusted Aiden so that he was feeding on the other side. "After Jillian came and said you were a shifter too, I was in a bit of denial, but her logic was sound."

"Are you saying Mom and Dad were shifters?"

"No. That's why I was human." She pulled out what looked like a diary.

"Why would Mom keep a log of her life, especially if there was something as revolutionary as shifters in it."

Elana held up a hand. "Just listen. *Dear Diary, I'm not sure if I should even be writing this. In fact, it's taken me days to have the courage to put my thoughts on paper, but I have to get this off my chest. While Richard is a wonderful man, he doesn't thrill me like he used to. However, that's no excuse for my actions. I didn't plan it. It just happened.*

Richard and I were in Bangkok buying artifacts, and he was spending an inordinate amount of time with our suppliers. Usually, he invites me along, but this time he thought it was safer if I stayed in the hotel.

One night, while having a drink in the restaurant, this tall, hand-

some man approached me. He looked at me as if I was the most beautiful woman in the world. Until then, I hadn't realized how much I missed having a man look at me like that. Now, I can see that he was merely using me, but at the time, I was desperate for affection."

"That doesn't sound like the mother who raised me. She was bitter and unaffectionate," Brian said.

"This might explain why she changed." Elana flipped to the next page. *"Darren, that was his name, was so sweet and charming. When Richard called to say he had to travel to a neighboring town to look at some merchandise, and that he wouldn't be returning until morning, I gave into Darren's charms."*

"So she had an affair with him?" The thought of his mother having sex sickened him.

Elana closed the book. "Yes. I won't read the rest since you don't need to hear the sordid details, but the bottom line is that you were the result of that dalliance."

"Did Richard know?" He could no longer call him Dad.

Elana shook her head. "No! Mom was too ashamed of her behavior to tell him. Apparently, Darren left in the middle of the night, but only after stealing all her money and some of her jewelry. The affair was bad enough, but she couldn't tell Dad that she'd been robbed."

Her priorities were so messed up. "This just gets better and better." Brian chugged half his scotch, and boy did he need that. "I'm not sure which is worse: being raised by an unfeeling asshole or having a thief for a father."

Kalan leaned forward. "This has nothing to do with you, Brian. Be thankful you didn't know your real father."

He doubted the thief could have been less affectionate than the dad he did have. "If you say so."

Elana readjusted herself before lifting Aiden over her shoulder to burp him. "The diary goes on to say that when she was pregnant she debated abortion, but Dad found out and was furious. He thought you were his child."

It wasn't because he wanted to be a father. "I wish she had terminated me."

"Don't say that," Elana said. "I don't think it's healthy for you to read her journal entries until you feel stronger and can handle everything. Basically, every time she looked at you, she saw her own mistake."

He didn't know whether to be happy that her wrongdoing had such dire consequences, or be angrier with the man who tried to take advantage of her. Could he have a more fucked up life or what?

Water under the bridge, as his therapist used to say. If Dr. Patterson were here, he'd tell Brian to spend some time absorbing the news and then move on. The past shouldn't define the future. Bullshit. He'd like to see how his therapist reacted if he learned all this about his heritage.

"Brian, I wouldn't be surprised," Kalan said, "to find that your mom told Elana's dad, and maybe even your therapist, some fabricated things you supposedly had done, but never actually committed, just to get you out of her life."

His hatred for his mother flared, causing him to run his palms down his legs, trying to block the images. "Does she say if my real dad was a shifter?"

"No, but it doesn't mean he wasn't. I doubt he'd break that news to her on their first and only date."

"True."

A knock sounded on the door and Kalan stood. "I'll get it."

That was bad timing. Brian hoped it wasn't Jillian. His head was spinning enough, and he sure as hell wasn't in the right state of mind to talk to her this soon after the stunt she'd pulled.

Kalan opened the door, and a blonde woman with a purple streak in her hair came in and hugged him. Brian had met her before at Elana's baby shower, but he couldn't remember her name.

"Brian, this is Ainsley. She's mated to my brother Jackson."

"Hi," he said, but he wasn't in the mood for someone else to learn about him.

She waved a hand. "I don't want to interrupt."

"No. We could use your expertise on something." He turned to Brian. "Ainsley is part wolf shifter and part witch, or what we call a Wendayan."

Witches? Mixed breeds? He wasn't sure he could absorb anymore. "Okay."

"She has a special gift. Tell him, Ainsley," Kalan demanded.

"You mean how I can become invisible?"

Invisible? He'd definitely been transported to another world.

"No, I mean about your ability to detect a person's shifter type."

"Oh that. Sure."

His stomach dropped. Brian didn't really want to know what he was—assuming he was a shifter. Right now, being all human seemed the best option. On the other hand, if he wanted to be part of the family, he'd fit in better if he were a shifter. God, how had his life become so messed up in such a short period of time?

Chapter Nine

AINSLEY GLANCED AT Kalan who nodded. "When I first met you, I didn't say anything to anyone because your signature was very weak, but I could tell you were a bear shifter, like your sister."

If he had to be a freak, being a bear was a good choice. "Better than an otter shifter."

They all laughed, and suddenly Brian felt like he was actually part of a group who accepted others, whether they were human, witch, or part animal.

"Are you okay with that?" Kalan asked.

Brian appreciated his concern. Kalan had probably asked because Brian had just let out a long breath and his leg was bouncing wildly. "I guess, though I don't see that I have much of a choice."

"You do in a way. You can always decide not to shift, though I know it can happen spontaneously if a person is angry enough."

Wonderful. "I guess I'll be making sure to take those anxiety pills regularly."

Elana didn't smile and that hurt. He suspected she wanted him to be comfortable enough with his thoughts not to have to use the medication.

Kalan shook his head. "I gotta hand it to you. I don't know how you've gone thirty-eight years and never shifted. It would have driven me bonkers. What with all those shifter hormones, I wouldn't know which way was up and which way was down."

He wondered if those hormones were what created the imbalance in his brain in the first place. "I didn't know I could shift. Rest assured, I've certainly been angry enough to induce it."

Ainsley piped up. "It's easiest on the white moon. You should try then."

White moon? That must be more fantasy mumbo jumbo. "Why would a white moon make a difference? If I believed the lore about wolves, I could understand it, but is it the same for bears?"

She looked to Kalan who shrugged. "It is, but I don't know the science behind it. I suspect only Naliana or James really know," she said. "The Changelings are different. They need a red moon. Then and only then can they touch someone and transform into that person for a few days."

"Jesus. Are you making this shit up just to scare me?"

Elana reached over and touched him arm. "I wish we were." She stood. "I need to put Aiden down. I'll be right back."

Brian looked at Kalan as soon as his sister disappeared. "So what's it like to shift?" If there was a possibility that this crap was true, he wanted to be prepared.

"What's it like?" Kalan repeated. "It is pure joy blended with total freedom. You'll love winter, especially when it snows, and you can roll around in the stuff. You'll have more power than you can ever imagine, but there won't be an urge to harm anyone with your enhanced strength if you're wondering."

Ainsley's eyes brightened. "As a wolf, I can run fast. I find shifting to be amazingly exhilarating and mind expanding. I spent years reining in my wolf because I feared my evil genes might force me to do something bad. But ever since I was cleansed, I've been going on crazy long runs."

"If being a wolf is so great, why don't you live as a wolf then?"

She shrugged. "Even in our shifted form, we're connected to our human side. We value our relationships and want true love, and I'm not talking about the animal kind."

That sounded too good to be true. "Will I hibernate if I'm in my bear form?" Never in his life did he expect to be asking that weird question.

"Not that I know of," Kalan said, "though I've never tried it. I have a job and people to protect. Disappearing for months on end would certainly raise questions. Besides, in Tennessee, we don't have the amount of snow to sustain a hibernation."

"Well hell, maybe I should have Jillian teach me to shift just to see if I like it." Assuming all this stuff about him being a shifter was true.

Jillian. Her name had slipped out, but he now understood what courage it had taken her to fill him in on what he'd been missing. He hadn't treated her well because of it, and he needed to make amends. There was definitely more to her than a hot woman. She seemed to want something from him, but she wasn't going to push him too hard for it. He admired that.

Kalan smiled. "Sounds like an excellent idea." He turned to Ainsley. "Now that you helped settle that, how's my brother? I haven't spoken to him in days."

"Jackson's rather bored, waiting for the other shoe to drop, so to speak. I think after the whooping we gave the Changelings a while back, they're now reluctant to make any bold moves. We both agree that they'll want some kind of revenge for that defeat though."

"They might be waiting for the red moon," Kalan said.

Brian felt as if once more he'd been dumped into the middle of a video game and no one had told him the rules. That was twice now that they'd mentioned these Changelings, and not in a good way. "What exactly is a Changeling? Is it a witch, a shifter, or a combination?"

Elana returned without the baby and sat next to him. For the next fifteen minutes, Ainsley spun an intricate tale of deceit and magic. Even if he'd read this stuff in a book, he would have labeled it as total fiction. She then explained about these mutated wolves, called Changelings, of which she'd been one until a goddess named Naliana, along with her immortal husband James had cleansed her. There actually came a point when he thought she was pulling his leg, but Kalan and Elana added their opinion and were quite serious.

Ainsley slapped her thighs. "I've taken up enough of your time, and I need to get back to Jackson, but I came to tell you something."

"I figured. What is it?" Kalan asked, his tone more serious.

"John Ernst came into the wellness center for another session with my magic needles." She looked over at Brian. "I'm an acupuncturist, and he's a Changeling—one who is high up in the Council ranks." She returned her gaze to Kalan. "In order to work on him, he undressed. It so happened, he placed his cell phone on the side table. In the middle of the procedure, a message scrolled across his screen."

"Which you just happened to read."

She smiled. "Why yes I did. I'm not sure what it meant, which is why I'm here. It was from someone named Daryl. It said something about putting an offer in on the old craft shop."

Elana's shoulders tightened. Clearly, this was someone she didn't like.

"What did Jackson say about that building?" Kalan asked. "Is that one built on top of the supposed sardonyx stash?"

"It is."

"Then our days of the Changelings being inactive might be coming to a close."

JILLIAN PUT IN another full day at the Blooms of Hope shop. Even though the hours were long and sometimes the work was menial, she enjoyed being there and meeting the customers. Everyone who stopped into the store was always in a good mood.

It was Anna who Jillian worried about. While she was sweet, Jillian wished she'd open up more. Being a lawyer, Jillian had grown good at sensing people's desires, their moods, and their level of honesty. She truly believed that deep inside, Anna was troubled, but since she was only twenty-five, hopefully she would find her happiness one day.

As closing time drew near, Jillian went into the back room to put away the ribbons, foam, and extra boxes and vases she'd set out in the morning.

Anna touched Jillian's arm. "Would you mind locking up? I have to take care of something and need to leave a few minutes early."

"Sure. No problem." Anna had just flipped over the Closed sign on the front door. As much as Jillian wanted to ask if anything bad had happened in her past to make her distant, she kept quiet. Anna would share when she felt it was the right time.

Once she left, Jillian closed out the cash register then wiped down the counters and the glass refrigerator doors. Alone for the first time in forever, she decided it was time to call Camille. Jillian felt guilty enough for running out of Los Angeles after Dalia's death and then turning off her phone, but it couldn't be helped. She didn't want that horrible man to find her by tracing her calls.

Jillian returned to the back room and hopped up onto the now clear table, ready to hear the worry in Camille's voice. Of all the people she knew in Los Angeles, Camille was the one she'd trusted the most.

About three years ago, Jillian had plans to meet with Camille at a bar on the edge of town. Camille had arrived first, and because it was a warm evening, she had decided to wait outside next to her car. Just as Jillian drove up, two thugs rushed out from some side alley and attacked her friend.

Jillian freaked. The deserted area lowered Jillian's shield about keeping all of her abilities secret. Instead of calling 911, she slammed on her brakes and stopped in the middle of the street. Two seconds after jumping out of the car, she was behind both men before they could even see her. She managed to wrap an arm around one man's neck while kneeing him in the back, and Camille used her police training to take down the other man.

Seconds later, the two thugs were on the ground in cuffs. Her friend said nothing until after the cops had been called and the men taken into custody. While Jillian hadn't shifted, she had to explain her super speed.

They had their drink that night, but it wasn't until they were back at Jillian's house that she revealed all the Wendayan stuff. The whole concept of shifters just happened to come out. Whether Camille totally bought into the idea that an alternate form existed, she didn't know, but Jillian suspected she did believe.

After that night, things between them changed. Camille starting asking questions about shifters and if they had any other super powers. All Jillian said was that shifters in general had a heightened sense of smell, sight, and hearing. That fact alone had Camille trying to convince Jillian to come to work for the LAPD. She said the criminals would leave town if they found out what she could do. That might be true, but Jillian wasn't interested.

Call her.

Jillian inhaled deeply and dialed Camille's cell.

"Hello?"

The tentative response threw her for a second until Jillian remembered she was on her burner phone. "Camille, it's me, Jillian."

"Jillian? Oh my God. I've been so worried about you. Where are you?"

"I'm staying with my brother."

"The brother in Tennessee?"

Camille had been listening. "Yes, though Dalton is my only sibling."

"Sorry. I forgot. Look, I know Dalia's death was tragic, but the detective running the case has been trying to find you."

I bet he is. "I need some time to myself. Don't worry. I'm doing fine."

"I'm sure that's true, but don't you want to find out who killed Dalia?"

She already knew who had murdered her friend. "Of course I do."

"Detective Whitlaw needs to ask you some questions. Can I have him call you?"

"No!" Damn, she hadn't meant for that to come out so strongly. At least she now had the name of the man who'd killed her father and good friend. At the moment though, she wasn't interested in pursuing him, but Dalton might.

"Jillian, what's wrong. This isn't like you."

"I'm sorry."

"When will you be coming home? I miss you."

If she told Camille the truth, it might put her in danger. However, this detective/killer knew they were friends. If she withheld information, Camille would see no reason not to tell him what she knew about Jillian's whereabouts. "If I tell you something, you can't mention it to anyone—especially Detective Whitlaw."

"My lips are sealed. You know you can trust me."

"I don't know if you ever believed that I could shift, but I'm telling you the truth when I say I can."

"I believed you. I think."

That was the best she could hope for. "Remember how I said that my ability to catalogue smells was heightened because of being a shifter?" Some shouts sounded in the background. Damn. "I thought you had the day off."

"I had to cover for someone. What does your ability to smell have to do with why you left?"

"I was in the kitchen the night my dad was killed." Just saying the words had her heart beating too fast.

"I remember you telling me."

Camille never forgot anything. "I might have only been six, but I smelled the killer and his scent has been with me ever since then." When Camille remained silent, Jillian continued. "I smelled him again the afternoon I came to your station, but I didn't say anything because I thought I was imagining things."

"What? Are you saying you think the person who killed your dad was at the precinct that day?"

Here came the hard part. "Not only that, when I rushed into my house the night of the murder, I smelled him again."

"Jillian, you were under stress. Seeing Dalia probably brought back the memory of your father's death."

She debated arguing with her, but if Camille didn't believe her and then said something to Detective Whitlaw, Jillian's life would be in danger—as might Camille's.

"I saw the man's scar at the precinct. It was the same crescent-shaped marking as the one my dad's killer had." More shouts sounded along with feet shuffling and phones ringing. "Cam, you still there?"

"Yeah. Listen I gotta go. Call me later okay?"

Something must have come up. Hopefully, Whitlaw wasn't nearby. Shit. If he had been, she hoped he hadn't overheard any part of the conversation. "Okay."

The conversation with Camille had shaken her. What Jillian needed now was a nice soak in the tub and a glass of wine. After she locked up, she ran to her car and fired it up. Fortunately, the heater knob was already on high. Before she took off, she called her boss in Los Angeles and told her she needed a leave of absence. To her relief, her boss said she'd already assigned her cases, figuring that when Jillian didn't report to work on Monday that her friend's death had hit her hard. When Jillian returned, she'd have to take Sandra out to dinner.

Needing to return home, she headed out, but not before checking the lot to make sure no one was watching her. Once she parked in Dalton's driveway, she rushed inside and tossed her purse on the sofa then slipped off her blue down jacket.

"Hey," she said to Dalton who had his feet up on the coffee table, drinking a beer and watching television. "You're home early."

He muted his program. "I started at six. How was your day?"

She chuckled. "About the only tragedy we experienced was cutting the stems off a few flowers. You?"

"Same ole, same ole. The troublemakers seem to be on vacation. Kalan and I were just talking about how calm things have been. With the red moon coming next week, I'm thinking something will go down soon, so don't get too used to my company every night."

"Oh, boo."

Dalton had kept her informed of the Changeling's movements, and these creatures weren't nice. If there were any of those mutant animals in Los Angeles, she was blissfully unaware. "Do you want me to make dinner?" she asked.

He looked up at her and smiled. "Will the sun rise tomorrow?"

Guess that was a yes. She'd gone shopping the other day and had bought ingredients for a tuna noodle casserole. When they were growing up, it was one of his favorite meals. Dalton was more of a carnivore now, but she bet he'd enjoy it nonetheless.

She pulled out the pan to boil water for the noodles and set out the ingredients.

"Did Brian contact you today?" Dalton asked.

She stilled at his question. "No. Do you know something to indicate he would?"

Dalton swung his legs to the ground, picked up his beer, and came over. "I'm thinking he'll have questions."

He should have, but she doubted he'd come to her for them. "Some men are in denial."

"You talking about me?"

She hadn't been, but her brother did have some issues he needed to resolve—mostly about how he didn't believe he fit in. How he could say that when he had Kalan as a partner, she didn't know. "No, but the things I told Brian would shock anyone."

"What happens if he doesn't call? If he's your mate, can you stay away from him?"

"Probably not, but I don't want to make things worse for him." It had taken all of her energy just to push his image out of her head today. She kept picturing them romping in the woods then rolling around. He'd laugh. She'd tease, and eventually, he'd let down his guard.

They were halfway through dinner when Dalton's phone rang. He checked the caller ID. "Hey, Kalan." His jaw tightened. "Sure."

He handed her his cell. "It's Brian."

Her pulse soared. "Hey, what's up?" She was pleased she'd kept an upbeat tone.

"I spoke with Elana and Kalan about shifters. My curiosity got the best of me."

At least he hadn't completely rejected what she'd told him. "What did they say?"

"She told me you spoke with her." Oh, crap. "Thank you. It made our conversation easier."

Jillian was thrilled he wasn't angry. "I'm happy for you and for Elana."

"I have more questions for you though."

That sounded hopeful. "Sure. Ask away."

"Can I come over?"

Jillian glanced at her brother who was chowing down on the casserole, trying not to listen, but no doubt heard not only her part of the conversation but Brian's too. She kicked him under the table. He looked up and nodded. "Sure."

Once she gave Brian directions, he said he'd be over shortly. Brian disconnected, and she handed Dalton back his phone.

"I guess Brian's coming over?" he asked as he pocketed his cell.

"Yes. Even though he talked with Elana and Kalan, he wants to speak with me, though I don't know what about."

"Do you want me to leave?"

He probably thought they'd be engaging in wild sex. As much as she would enjoy the dalliance, now wasn't the time. "I'd like you to stay. You might be able to help."

"If you think so."

She snapped her fingers. "I forgot to tell you. I spoke with Camille right before I came home."

"Your cop friend?"

"Yes. She told me the detective leading the case wants to ask me a few questions."

His eyes widened. "You mean the cop who killed Dad?"

"Yes. His name is Detective Whitlaw."

"Whitlaw, huh? I might just have to make some inquiries."

She smiled. "I was hoping you would."

Chapter Ten

F RANK WHITLAW LEANED back in his office chair and smiled. Jillian had finally contacted her good friend, Camille Williams. He'd put a trace on his fellow officer's phone, figuring Jillian would call to check in at some point. And she had.

Of course, he'd known where Jillian was, but it was nice to get confirmation. The fact she was staying with her brother who was a cop didn't really bother him. Frank was way smarter than any hick from Tennessee ever could be.

The hardest part in tying up loose ends was in covering his tracks. Given her location, it shouldn't be too difficult. He was working the murder case that he'd committed, and he was doing a fine job muddying the waters to throw all suspicions away from him. Since the investigation had stalled, his boss might grant him time off. Naturally, he would say it was personal reasons, like his mother had fallen ill again. That had worked in the past, so why not try again?

To make sure he succeeded in shutting Jillian up for the final time, he needed a good week to learn her habits and figure out a foolproof way to kill her. After all, she was a shifter. If she were a wolf like him, it would be easy, but he never liked to assume anything. She could be a bear, and that would make it more challenging, but still doable.

Sneaking into her brother's house and shooting her wouldn't work since he didn't want to do battle with two shifters at once. If they heard him enter, they'd both come out to investigate. He knew all too well that pulling off the perfect murder took planning and time. And time wasn't on his side yet again.

BRIAN CHECKED THE directions to Dalton's house once more before heading north on Robin's Ridge. His head was exploding with all this new information Elana, Kalan, and Ainsley had given him about Changelings, shifters, goddesses, and immortals.

Speaking of immortals, Kalan promised to speak with James to see if he'd grant an audience. The recluse usually only dealt with the Alpha and the Beta of the local Clan, but he might make an exception given the unusual circumstances. Kalan bet James had never met a man who was unaware he was a shifter.

When Brian had asked what advice a non-shifter could offer, Kalan said not to underestimate him. Apparently, the immortal had many talents, most of which were not understood. Rye and Kalan suspected that James's abilities came directly from his wife, the goddess Naliana. As much as Brian wanted to buy into this goddess thing, he was an atheist. He was, however, willing to alter his opinion should she prove him wrong.

Right now, Brian's biggest concern was whether a man his age could learn to shift—and if so, would it tear his body apart? Not only was he curious to experience something this fantastic, he wanted to do this for Jillian. She seemed intent on him giving this new opportunity a try.

Another thing he'd have to deal with was his volatile personality. What if he became angry and inadvertently turned into a clumsy bear? That scenario scared the shit out of him, as did the conversation he was about to have with Jillian.

Hell, he'd already tried to kick her out of his apartment more than once, had insulted her by telling her to put clothes on her beautifully naked body, and had practically called her a liar when she told him he was a shifter. Hopefully, she understood why he had been so hesitant to accept everything she'd told him.

A quick check of the instructions assured him he'd found her brother's place. Dalton's rental was one block off the main road, and the illuminated numbers by the door made it easy to locate.

Here goes. He marched up to the front door and knocked. Jillian answered, and as soon as her scent enveloped his body, his chest began to vibrate with an over-the-top sexual urge. If that wasn't a kick in the balls, he also had an insane need to protect her from danger, and the confusing combination threw him off his game once more.

"Hi," was all he managed to say, a little pissed he'd never developed any kind of slickness when around women.

As much as he wanted to tell her how hot she looked in her tight blue jeans and her bright green top, and how pretty she was with her hair falling gently around her face, he wouldn't. Experience had taught him he'd just mess it up.

"Come in." She clasped his arm, and her mere touch set his cock in motion. Not good at all. "This is Dalton, my brother," she said.

Brian peeled off his jacket and held it in front of him to cover his erection before offering one hand to shake. Damn. Compared to her brother, Brian felt average and even homely. Dalton stood six foot two, had thick brown hair and startling golden brown eyes, looking every bit like a celebrity. His shoulders were broad, and he didn't have an ounce of fat on him. "Nice to meet you."

From the outside, the cop appeared totally normal, but apparently he was just like Jillian—a white tiger. Brian was unconvinced he could ever get used to this whole shifter persona, despite having seen Jillian transform into a beautiful animal and then turn back to a human—albeit a gorgeous naked one.

"Come sit down," she said. "Can I get you something to drink?"

He'd had enough today and didn't need anything else messing with his already scrambled brain. "I'm good."

Brian waited to see where Jillian and Dalton sat before choosing his own seat. Dalton took the chair and Jillian the sofa, so he dropped down next to her. His pulse spiked and his gut tightened.

Jillian's nearness messed with his ability to think clearly, and he didn't like it one bit.

They both watched him, clearly waiting for him to begin. After all, he had called and asked to discuss something with her. *I can do this.* "When I stopped over at Elana's, Jackson's girlfriend Ainsley came by to see the baby and to tell Kalan something about some Changeling activity. If I recall, those are the bad shifters, right?"

Jillian grabbed his hand. "They told you about that? By the way, Ainsley is Jackson's mate, which is a lot more than a girlfriend. And, yes, the Changelings are very bad." She glanced over at Dalton who nodded.

"Mate, girlfriend, whatever. I'm still trying to process everything. I learned about James and Naliana, though their place in this world confounds me. Shifters are hard enough to comprehend, let alone immortals and goddesses."

Jillian squeezed his hand then let go. "Even I'm not so sure about those two, though Dalton has tried to clear up some of my confusion."

"Just so you know," Dalton said, "I've never met either of them. James deals mostly with Rye and Kalan, and Naliana supposedly returns to earth once a month on the white moon."

Brian nodded. "Kalan mentioned that too. Besides those two, I learned something important. Ainsley can tell one shifter from another, and apparently, I'm a bear shifter even though she said my signature was weak."

Jillian's smile nearly blinded him. "That's fantastic. I had no idea anyone could tell one shifter from another." She ran her gaze up and down his body. "Are you convinced that you are a shifter then?"

"I suppose, but until I shift, I can't be completely sure."

"Does this mean you want to try?" she asked.

His chest constricted, and his pulse soared. "Yes. Maybe. Not right now though. I'm overwhelmed." She ran a hand down his arm, and his thoughts changed from worry to excitement.

Jillian chuckled. "I wasn't thinking about doing it now. I'm thrilled you're willing to consider it though. It will open up a whole new world to you."

But would he like what he saw? "Kalan said he'd contact this James person to see if maybe he'll talk to me about it, and I wanted to see if you'd be willing to come with me."

Her perfect mouth opened. "You want me to go with you to meet James?"

"Yes. Would you?"

"If Kalan says it's okay, of course I will."

"What do you hope to accomplish by seeing him?" Dalton asked.

He'd given this a lot of thought. "I'd like to know my chances of succeeding. I'm no cub, you know."

A brief smile crossed Dalton's lips. "True, but I'm not sure that matters. Understand that James might not know the answer since he's not a shifter."

Brian lifted one shoulder. "Can't hurt to ask."

"Then I wish you luck," Dalton said.

JILLIAN COULDN'T BELIEVE she was on her way to meet a real immortal. It had been three days since Brian told her Kalan would ask James for an audience and she was more nervous now than at her first trial. Kalan had mentioned James looked like a youngish sixty-year-old, and she wondered if she'd be able to sense any other differences between him and a mortal. Thanks to her Wendayan mother, Jillian was more intuitive than most.

Dalton had told her stories he'd received second hand from Kalan about the strange hermit and his ability to understand things that a mere human couldn't possibly know. It would be an understatement to say that she couldn't wait to meet him.

They decided to take two vehicles. Since Kalan knew the way, Brian rode with Jillian as she followed closely behind. Kalan said he normally would have suggested they all ride together, but he wanted to play it by ear in case the two of them needed more time to speak with James alone. Elana was a lucky woman to have such a considerate mate.

"Are you nervous?" she asked Brian, who'd barely said a word since they'd left her brother's place.

"Yes, even though I took an anxiety pill. In retrospect, I probably didn't need to worry since I don't think James can tell me anything that will surprise me. Due to everything I've been hit with recently, I think I'm a few miles past total shock."

Jillian appreciated his attitude. "Well, I'm not so calm. Before we see him, I need to tell you something else."

"What's that?"

The bend in the road was rather severe, forcing Jillian to hold on to the wheel with both hands. This part wasn't paved, and the ruts in the road hadn't been attended to in a while.

She'd debated for a few hours today whether to bring this up. In the end, she decided it was best to have all issues out in the open. "According to your sister, James's mate, Naliana, is in charge of pairing people together."

"Pairing people? As in mating?"

She glanced over at him, surprised he was so well-versed in the concept. Then again, he had spent hours with Elana, Kalan, and Ainsley a few days ago. "Yes. What did Elana have to say about that?" Jillian glanced over at him, but Brian was looking out the window at the pure blackness that had painted the night sky.

"When you find your mate, you know it, because all you can think about is being with that person, and you want to protect her with your life."

"What a nice way to put it." She wanted to ask him if he had any of those feelings toward her, but it was too soon to throw that out. "I've been told that in order for the couple to be true mates, they must both agree to this bonding, and their consent is shown by biting each other on the neck." If that didn't toss him off the reality cliff, nothing would.

He twisted toward her. "That sounds barbaric."

Her shoulders sagged. How did she expect him to react? With joy? "I've never been bitten, but supposedly, it's not painful as long as it's done in the heat of the moment. When I'm excited, my animal teeth extend, but that's all I know about the mating process."

"Are they like your tiger teeth?" he asked. She quickly glanced over at him, and the whites of his eyes were showing even in the dark.

She felt herself sinking lower and lower. *Stupid, Jillian. I never should have brought up the concept of mating so soon.* Hell, they hadn't even kissed. "I can't really tell. They've sharpened a few times, but not by much. I think it's because I hadn't met my mate when it happened."

"Why are you telling me about this mate stuff?"

Why was she? *Because I need to know if you're feeling anything close to what I'm feeling.* "Because you're my mate," she blurted, immediately sensing a wave of hope coming from Brian.

Don't get too excited, her tiger warned. *Be cautious.*

So now her tiger decides to go the slow route? What was up with that? They'd have a heart-to-heart talk later.

"Back up a minute. You actually believe we're destined to be with each other? Like Kalan and Elana are?"

He didn't have to sound so surprised. "From the way I've been reacting to you, yes, but don't worry. I promise to control myself when I'm around you unless I know you feel the same way about me." Her heart jumped to her throat and remained lodged there. "The moment I walked into Teagan's party—before I even set eyes on you—my body went kind of crazy with lust. At first, I couldn't understand it, but the air smelled sweeter, and my heart practically fluttered. It was only after a day or so that I realized what that meant." She wouldn't go into any more detail.

"The way you described it, mating is purely physical without much emotional attachment." His tone came out bitter.

She was really messing this up. "That's not what I meant—or

rather what I've been told. Just ask Elana or Kalan. At first, maybe yes, it is lust filled. Think of this mating call as a fire starter. That's all. The emotional part is left up to the couple. At least, I think that's how it works. My dad was a shifter, but he died when I was six, so he wasn't around to explain it to me. My mom did the best she could."

He reached out and placed a hand on her thigh. "I'm sorry."

"Thanks." She pushed aside the rush of excitement at his touch.

"I have a confession to make too," he said.

Her body tensed. "What's that?"

"I experienced the same reaction to you. I felt you before I saw you, and the moment you walked around the corner, my brain froze. Other parts did not freeze, however, which was why I had to leave. I had this overwhelming urge to touch you, but I'd been taught to take things slow. I'm not always good at reading people. Besides, I didn't want to mess it up. It's not every day a beautiful woman walks up to me at a party."

Aw. That was so sweet. Kalan's brake lights lit up, and she took her foot off the accelerator. Damn. They'd arrived. "I had no idea you felt anything. When I asked you a simple question and you ran, I thought you didn't like me."

"Quite the opposite. You were so out of my league that I kind of freaked. My intense and sudden feelings scared me."

She swallowed a smile. "I'm glad you told me. Bottom line is that we need to get to know each other and see how we feel before we even consider mating. First comes the physical, or rather, the intense animal attraction, and then the caring and eventually the loving. Are you willing to give it a try?"

"I'm willing." He huffed out a laugh. "I gotta tell you, Jillian, I didn't think my head could be any more twisted, but you've managed it."

At least he didn't sound upset. "Life can be a wild ride some-times."

"You got that right."

She stopped, cut the engine, and twisted toward him, every nerve electrifying her senses. Before she could ask him anything else, Brian grabbed the door handle, pushed it open, and jumped out. A second later, her door opened. "Ready?"

"I hope so."

"Then let's see if it is possible for me to shift." He held out his hand, and she placed hers in his, loving his calloused palms and strong fingers.

Kalan was waiting for them at his car. "Don't be surprised when James seems to read your mind," he said. "I sure as hell have never figured him out. If he doesn't answer your question directly, don't push back. Remember, he's doing us a favor by seeing us."

"I appreciate the warning. Whatever pearls of wisdom James offers will be welcome," she said.

Kalan knocked, and the mystery man answered seconds later. He looked exactly as Kalan had described—about six feet tall with close cropped white hair and a handsome face. Immortality had served him well.

"Come in."

Chapter Eleven

THE THREE OF them entered James's rustic home, and the pleasing scent of fire mixed with some kind of incense flavored the air. The living room looked ancient with its handmade furniture, stone walls, and dim lights, but the fire made it super cozy—and warm. James motioned for them to sit on the benches that flanked the fireplace, while he took the chair facing the blaze.

Kalan introduced them, though Jillian suspected he'd already given James a briefing on who they were and their situation.

"Brian, Kalan tells me that you want to learn how to shift." *Yep! She had guessed right.*

"Yes. I figure if I'm a shifter, I should try."

James smiled. "I would want to try too, if I had the ability."

"Can I ask you something then?"

"That's why you came, right?"

James would make a great attorney.

"It was. My first question is whether there will be any side effects if I do shift? I am thirty-eight, and my body isn't used to being taken apart and put back together again in the blink of an eye."

Jillian had never considered shifting as being rough, but then she'd learned by the age of two.

"I don't have experience on that topic, but one thing I believe to be true is that shifting should help stabilize your hormones since shifter hormones are more powerful than human ones. I know you've suffered your whole life with bipolar disorder."

His leg bounced up and down. "How do you know?"

Jillian wondered the same thing. She glanced at Kalan to see if he thought James was making that up in order to encourage Brian to try shifting, but all she could detect was a glint in his eye. Perhaps Kalan was thrilled his mate's brother might have some of his demons vanquished.

James smiled. "Any other questions for me?"

Why hadn't James answered Brian's first question? Was if because he didn't want to divulge where he received his information? Or did he like to be mysterious?

Brian grabbed Jillian's hand, and her heart nearly burst with joy at this sign of affection—if that's what it was. Possibly, he was overwhelmed again and needed some support. That worked too.

"Yes. How do I shift? Besides thinking about being a bear shifter." He looked over at her. "After Jillian told me that I was more than a mere human, I closed my eyes and tried to imagine being an animal, but nothing happened."

"Hmm. Well, I'd try again on the white moon. When a shifter bites his human mate, her first shift can only happen then. I'm not sure if it applies to you, as you are already a shifter. Mind you, it's possible given your advanced age, you won't be able to shift, so don't get your hopes up too high."

"What?" Jillian blurted before Brian could respond. "Why? If his animal is inside him, there has to be something to coax it out." Please say that a lot of good loving might give his animal a boost.

Now that she'd spent time getting to know Brian, her animal was demanding some satisfaction—when she wasn't telling her to be cautious, that is. Fickle beast. James could help her cause with a few choice words.

Sure, Brian was challenging, but deep inside, he was a sweet man, waiting for love. To accept that love however would take trust—something that had been in short supply in his life. Thankfully, Elana had been there for him when he'd reached out.

James held up a hand. "It's like learning a second language. The younger a child is, the quicker he picks it up. If the child is exposed to another language at a later age, it's more difficult, but still possible with hard work and perseverance."

Brian sat up straighter. "I'm willing to try. If I can't, then I won't be any worse off than before."

James smiled. "I like your attitude." He turned to Kalan. "If you'll excuse us, I'd like to discuss the concept of mating with these two."

Was he kidding? Thank goodness she'd brought up the topic in the car. Otherwise, Brian might have freaked.

Kalan couldn't jump up fast enough. "Call if you need me for anything," he told them. With that he left.

Sex education wasn't something she enjoyed, but there were some holes in her knowledge, especially regarding her blue glow and the best location to bite her future mate.

"Let's begin with your blue glow, Jillian."

EVEN A FEW days after the meeting with James, Brian was still processing what the immortal had told him about shifters and mating. The most disappointing part was that until he shifted, he wouldn't be able to mate with Jillian. It wasn't like what happened with his sister and Kalan. James said Brian was not considered merely a human anymore. In the eyes of the goddesses, he was a shifter. Just as Jillian had explained, for two shifters to mate, they each had to bite each other. Well, he had teeth, but unfortunately they weren't sharp enough and would hurt her. Depression nipped at him. Until he shifted, no mating could occur, which was why he was on his way to try his first shift.

As Brian focused on the road, he thought about something more pleasant to help push his negative thoughts away. The night after their meeting with James, Jillian had stopped by his apartment bearing pizza and drinks. Once they ate and chatted a bit, they huddled next to each other and watched an Avengers' movie that she was able to stream on her iPad. It made him realize how much he'd missed out on in life. If only his therapist could see him now, he'd have been proud.

Brian wasn't as bitter as he thought he'd be about having been kept in the dark all these years about his true identity. Jillian kept talking about living in the moment, and that was what he planned to do.

The following night she stopped by again, but this time it was just to say hi, since she had promised Dalton she'd cook for him. Thankfully, she didn't drop any more bombshells on him or pressure him into trying to shift. She seemed to understand what he was going through and that meant the world to him.

Then, last night, she came over and dragged him out to the Lake Steakhouse, which was a real treat. The food was amazing and the company exceptional. The more time he spent with Jillian, the easier it was to relax and just be himself with her. She listened to his stories about growing up but never judged him like so many had.

"Are you nervous?" Jillian asked, jerking him back to the present.

The white moon was full, the sky was clear, and the night unusually cold.

"Yes and no. What you said to me at dinner last night really resonated with me."

"What was that?"

"I can see now how much I missed out on when I was growing up. Not only did I live in an institution for much of it, I didn't live up to my potential."

"You can't blame yourself. You didn't know you were a shifter," she said.

"True. My whole life, I had this feeling that something was missing. I think if I can learn to shift, I'd have a chance at being whole."

Jillian reached over and rubbed his arm. "You can do it. I know you can."

He hoped so. Regardless of what happened tonight, it was time to move on and take responsibility for who he'd become. No longer would he allow his deceased parents' previous actions to control his thinking.

Even though he was nervous about attempting this mind-blowing and physically challenging feat of changing from a human into a wild animal, he was excited. If he succeeded, his whole life would change. If he failed...

Don't go there. Just concentrate.

He planned to, which was why he'd refrained from taking any anxiety medication. Not having that crutch however, added to his unease.

While this white moon was full and high, Jillian's expectations seemed to be even higher. No one liked to fail, and Brian trying to do this in front of the woman he cared for—or rather the woman who'd already wormed her way into his heart—would most likely cause a lot of damage to his male psyche if he didn't succeed.

"Pull up here," Jillian said, pointing to a dirt patch on the side of the road. They were in the same neighborhood where Elana and Kalan lived and then had driven another mile past Elana's house down a dirt road.

"I'm surprised your brother doesn't rent a house around here if most shifters live in this area."

"I asked him that," she said. "He said he didn't want anyone to know he was a tiger."

"What difference should that make? The few shifters I've met seem eager to share their stories about who they are and what they are capable of. Like you. Besides, didn't you say a shifter can detect another shifter?"

"Yes, but not what kind—other than that one woman you met."

"Ainsley. I forgot that Elana mentioned that."

"Dalton's different from everyone around here and that bothers him. It's why he's kept to himself."

"You aren't."

She smiled and dragged a hand down his arm. "Thank you, but

that's not quite true. In Los Angeles, I've always buried my shifter persona. Only one person in California even knows what I am."

Brian twisted toward her, telling himself he wasn't procrastinating, that the moon would be full for another few hours. "Didn't it bother you to have to ignore who you were?" The light from the moon shone on her face, enough to see her slightly lowered chin and pinched brows. He wanted her to open up to him as much as he had to her.

"At times, but I try not to think about it. I will admit that when I shifted for you, something inside me kind of opened up. All the memories of Dalton and me running around as kids and chasing each other came rushing back. It was an idyllic time." She sat up straighter. "Then dad died and things changed. I grew up, went to school, and put all of that behind me."

"So you miss shifting?"

"Yes, but Los Angeles isn't conducive to running around in my tiger form."

All the more reason for her to stay here. Brian feared the day Jillian returned home. He wished there was something he could say or do that would make her want to remain in Silver Lake, regardless of him. "Then why live there?"

"The job's great, and I have my friends—not to mention the weather is a lot warmer." She twisted around and grabbed some clothes off the back seat. "Enough about me. Let's do this," she said, her voice sounding far off.

"You sure you won't get cold being naked?" After she shifted, she would return to her unclothed human form, surrounded by patches of snow.

"Hell, yeah I will. It's freezing out. It's why I suggested we wear our crappy clothes until we shift. We'll stay warmer longer. If I remember correctly, being in my animal form keeps me warm for a while after I shift back. At least we'll have our winter clothes to put on afterwards. Come on."

"Maybe we should wait until the weather turns warmer."

She lowered her pile of clothes. "Brian Stanley, we are not waiting one more month."

She was one determined woman. "Okay." They both slipped out of his truck. "Where do you want to do this?" he asked, inhaling the cold that made his nose twitch.

"Dalton and I came here yesterday on his day off and scoped out the place. We figured it would be better to have an open field to run around in since our human bodies aren't as sure footed as our animal counterparts."

He stuffed both sets of clothes in his small backpack. "Lead the way."

Jillian took him through a forest that opened onto Silver Lake. The bright moonbeams bounced off the flat surface and created a magical scene.

She stopped and grabbed his hand. "It's really beautiful here isn't it?"

"Not half as beautiful as you." How that had slipped out he didn't know since Brian normally wasn't that bold.

You've changed since meeting her that little voice in his head said.

She spun around and then lifted her arms around his neck. "Why Brian, I think you're becoming romantic."

He grinned. "It's easy when I'm around you."

Kiss her that pesky voice urged. *You want to.*

When Jillian looked up at him, he shoved his past aside. This was where he wanted to be—needed to be—with her. As if an invisible magical hand pushed down on the back of his head, their lips finally met. Despite the winter air, warmth spread throughout him, and his body swam with endorphins. That, or the blood had rushed straight to his cock and left him breathless.

Jillian tightened her hold around his neck and when she drew him closer, he deepened the kiss and savored her taste. Inhaling her sweet scent, his body seemed to change from the inside out. He let his hands roam up and down her soft, yet firm body. Man, did she fit perfectly in his arms or what?

Brian wanted to drag her back to his truck and explore her thoroughly, but she deserved more. They deserved more. Before he lost control, he broke off the kiss.

A smile lifted his lips as pure passion continued to envelope him. "That was nice," he said.

"It was more than nice," Jillian said.

He cleared his throat. Her touch and taste had pushed away his nerves. "You ready to show me how it's done?"

"Absolutely. The field is a little beyond those rocks and then behind a small copse of trees."

Probably because it was cold, Jillian jogged and Brian loped right beside her. The stars winked brightly in the sky as the clouds gave the moon a wide birth. His body warmed as he inhaled the fresh scent of pine and the loose loam on their path.

Jillian had told him to clear his head of all bad thoughts, and to his surprise, he was able to picture bright colors instead of the dull browns of depression.

She eased to a stop at the edge of the forest. "Let's leave our change of clothes here." He slipped off the backpack and set it next to a large pine tree. "You know what to do?" she asked as she peeled off her jacket and set it on top of the pack.

"Yes, think furry thoughts."

He removed his coat and tried not to worry about the cold. Because Jillian was rubbing her hands up and down her body, all he could think of was holding her tight and warming her up, but if he started, who knew whether he'd be able to stop.

She laughed. "Yes, but it's more than furry thoughts. Your bear is inside of you, so all you have to do is give him permission to let loose. Think free. Think wild. Think powerful."

If he ever met this Naliana woman, he'd give her a big hug for bringing Jillian into his life. "I'm ready." *I think.* When the familiar tingling in his gut began, signifying his anxiety was building, he growled to keep it at bay.

"That's it. Stay fierce. I won't shift until you do, okay?"

He gave a thumbs-up sign, "Gotcha." He studied the terrain, needing to be sure he didn't trip and fall. Despite not participating in any team sports, he was unusually strong and rather coordinated. Only now did he understand why. *I can do this.*

"Catch me if you can," Jillian said with a laugh.

A split second later she was out in front.

Move. Wanting to catch her, Brian's chase mechanism clicked in. For a moment, his only thought was to grab her and kiss her again. Then he remembered why he was there. He was a bear—an animal who needed to be freed.

Focus on being one with the earth.

As his feet pounded the ground, his heart rate increased. *Think bear.* He curled his fingers like his inner beast would and hunched over a little, hoping to coax him out. A second later, his foot tripped on a root and he stutter-stepped but managed to stay upright. With her back to him, she hopefully hadn't noticed the change in his gate.

He'd run a good half-mile yet nothing had happened. Hadn't James and Jillian said he should shift within seconds? She looked back over her shoulder as if to check on his progress, but when he looked down, his hands were all human.

Brian had to be realistic. He wasn't going to shift, so he slowed and then stopped, angry that he'd failed. It was the story of his life.

Stop it. As Jillian would say, *Pity has no role in anyone's life.*

Be a man, that voice chided. He huffed out a throaty growl and planted his hands on his thighs. It was about time he listened to that little voice.

Chapter Twelve

WHEN BRIAN'S FOOTSTEPS stopped, Jillian spun around. He was bent over, causing her heart to crack. She rushed over to him. "Are you okay?"

Jillian worked hard not to sound disappointed because Brian really wanted to shift.

He stood and held up a hand. "I'm fine. I don't know what happened. Maybe my bear is too deep inside me."

The angst in his voice tore at her, and she rubbed his back. "It's okay. James warned us that you might not succeed on the first try. Let's grab our jackets and get out of here."

"I'm sorry."

"You don't need to be sorry for anything. For thirty-eight years, you've denied your bear access to your mind. You can't expect him to suddenly jump out and go for a romp."

"Yes, I can."

She grabbed his hand, and together they walked across the field to where they'd stashed their clothes. Neither of them said anything more. Clearly, he needed time to process what might have gone wrong.

Once they donned their jackets, they returned to the truck. "What do you think happened? Were you distracted?" she asked. As much as Brian would want to forget he'd even tried, it wouldn't solve anything. Facing the problem head on was the only solution.

"Don't know."

O-kay. "You pictured yourself as a bear and—"

He jammed the key into the ignition and then faced her. "Yes. Yes. Yes. I did everything right. I really believed it would happen, and I did keep trying and then—nothing. I guess it's not meant to be."

His frustration cut through her. "Don't say that. We can try again."

Brian put the truck in gear and took off, his focus straight ahead and his jaw clenched. He was headed toward Dalton's, but she had another idea. "I think I know what happened."

"What's that?" he said with too much bitterness.

"Your muscles were too tight. Do you stretch a lot?"

He glanced over at her. "Stretch? Fuck no. I lift wood all day. That's all."

"Then that's the problem. Let's go back to your place. I'll give you a good massage to loosen up your muscles."

Yes, she'd made that up, but Brian was hurting. Besides, once she had her hands on him, she bet she could get him to relax by using a more loving way.

"You think that's the problem. I was too tense?" She swallowed a smile from the hope in his tone.

"I had a law case once that I really wanted to win, mostly because I yearned for a promotion. I'd won four straight cases in a row and the case that mattered the most? Yup, I lost it. I had all of my questions prepared, but I didn't listen to the defendant's answers closely enough. I was not paying attention to the most important part of the case."

"So you're saying that wanting something too much could botch it up?"

"Yes, if you focus on the wanting part more than the feeling, it can. Maybe you haven't learned how to listen to your body. Remember the first time I came to your apartment?"

"I'll never forget it."

She bet. "I wanted to convince you so badly that you were a

shifter that I ignored what you were telling me. I didn't listen to you."

"What was I saying besides asking if you were crazy?"

He had accused her of that. "That *you* weren't ready to accept that much change. It was stupid, or rather egotistical, of me to shift on you. I just wasn't thinking."

He turned onto the main road and headed toward town. When he pulled behind the Blooms of Hope shop, Jillian's tiger went wild.

It's just a back rub, she told her anxious animal.

You aren't a very good liar.

Why couldn't Jillian hide anything from her suddenly overly active tiger? This time she would take it slow. Brian was tense. If relaxing his muscles would help him shift, she was all for it. However, if he became a little more amorous, she certainly wouldn't turn him down.

He parked, and when he led her upstairs to his apartment, one of the steps near the top creaked.

"That's my alarm system," Brian said with suddenly more humor in his voice.

Jillian smiled, happy he was able to joke at a time like this. He let them in, flicked on the living room lamp, and tossed off his jacket. "You want something to drink?"

"Have any wine?" She wasn't in the mood for a beer.

"Just so happens, I picked up a bottle of Chardonnay today."

Her favorite. She wondered who he'd asked. "Fantastic."

Oh, crap. Maybe he'd bought it to celebrate his shift. Well, darn. While Brian poured them a drink, Jillian removed her jacket and then kicked off her shoes. She was wearing a baggy shirt, one that she'd painted her living room in, and a splotch of khaki still resided on the lapel, despite its many washings. It was the only junky top she'd brought, in case she needed to shift.

Carrying two glasses of wine, he met her in the living room and handed her one. "Here's to the fickle world of shifters," Brian said.

While he wasn't smiling, Jillian was pleased he wasn't throwing things across the room. "To shifters. Even though your first attempt did not go as planned, don't give up. After a Jillian Garner rubdown, you'll be so relaxed you might wake up your bear."

He widened his eyes. "Let's hope not. I want to be able to control the beast."

She laughed then drank half the glass. It was smooth and rich. "Ah, the perfect drink on a cold night."

After tossing back some of the golden liquid, he set down his glass and then slipped hers away from her fingers, placing it next to his. His eyelids lowered and his mouth parted. "If you need warming up, I have just the thing."

Jillian wrapped her arms around his neck and looked up at him, her heart pounding hard. "What do you have in mind?"

"This."

Brian dipped his head and sucked on her bottom lip. The slow, sensual pull ignited her from head to toe, and his earthy scent stimulated every one of her human and shifter senses. Jillian had to work hard not to rip off both of their clothes, wanting more than anything to press against him naked. Rushing him would be a mistake though, which was why she cursed the groan that had just escaped.

As he hovered his lips over hers, their breaths mingled. What was he waiting for? Did he want her to make the first move? If so, she was more than willing to oblige. Jillian latched onto his lips with hers and kissed him fully with all of her being, but it wasn't enough to satisfy her inner animal. She needed to taste and touch him, too. Running her tongue along the seam of his lips, she begged for entrance. When he opened up, the room's lights seemed to dim, encasing them in their own world, and their first touch had blue sparks shooting off her forearms. Holy hell.

He wrapped his arms around her waist then dragged his hands up her back, pressing strong fingers against her body. Brian must have been in his own world because he didn't freak at how her body was reacting, and his oblivion encouraged her. She wanted more.

Tongues entwining, they probed and explored, and soon his taste became one with hers. She could almost feel the bear inside him vibrate with desire and passion, and she couldn't wait to explore all of him.

Breaking the kiss, Brian lowered his arms. "It might be faster if you shift and then return to your human form right away."

It took her a moment to understand his intent. "Are you asking me to get naked?" *Please say yes.*

Brian dragged a finger down the middle of her chest. "Would that be such a bad thing?" His voice came out so low and gravelly that she wanted to purr at the delicious sound.

"Not unless I'm the only one." Her fingers found his pants, and she undid the top button. One metal tooth at a time, she lowered his zipper. *Click, clack, click, clack...*

Keeping his gaze on her, Brian undid the top two buttons of her shirt. His slow movements turned her on more than if he'd been in a hurry. Foreplay was a powerful aphrodisiac. Still working on her buttons, he toed off his shoes. Once he finished with her shirt, she stepped back.

"My turn." She eased off her paint-splattered shirt and let it drop to the floor.

"What happened to your br...bra?"

She looked down and pretended to be surprised she didn't have one on, but then relaxed. "I didn't want to ruin another one."

He smiled. "I really like how forward thinking you are."

"Were you as forward thinking?" she asked, nodding to what he wore under his pants.

"Did I go commando, you mean?" She nodded. "Why don't you look?"

Brian had been shy when she'd first met him, but he was becoming more confident—at least with her—and she loved it. Whatever it took, she would try to keep him that way. For her, it didn't matter what happened in the field. The fact he seemed willing to accept his failure made him more of a man in her eyes.

Jillian moved closer, hooked her thumbs in his waistband, and eased his khaki pants over his hips, revealing black boxers. "You tease!"

He grinned. "If you were a man, you'd understand that running without support would be painful."

She cupped her tits and gave him her best pout. "These babies bounced around like crazy. Don't think for a moment that was fun for me."

Brian finished taking off his pants then eased her hands away. "It's my fault that you had to run for so long. Let me make it up to you."

Yes! Her ploy worked. When he rubbed his thumbs over her distended nipples, his rough fingers created the right amount of friction, and sparks of need shot through her. Goddess, that felt divine.

Wanting to watch, or rather needing to watch, she glanced down just as he twirled both nipples then pulled them taut. "Oh, yes. I like that," she cooed.

When he released the hard peaks, her chest glowed blue, something she'd never seen before.

He flashed a quick smile. "So I see. It's cool that you can't hide your feelings."

She dragged a finger down his covered cock. "Neither can you."

Brian laughed, and she arched her back to give him better access. He stroked the tips until each nipple puckered fully. His gentle touch was sure, and he seemed to know the perfect pressure and speed. Wanting to give him some satisfaction, she reached out and cupped his balls.

He stiffened. "Jillian, you're playing with fire."

"I like fire."

"You might get burned. If I can't shift, we can never mate." His voice nearly cracked.

She had something more pleasurable in mind. "Let's worry about that later. My tiger is about to claw out my insides if I don't get a taste."

"I wouldn't want to piss *her* off. I could never defend myself against your tiger. I've seen those claws."

"I admit she has really long nails." Jillian scraped her human nails down his chest, and when she tugged off his briefs, her eyes widened at his size and girth. "Holy shit. You are a bear of a man."

His eyes shone. "After you test drive him, you can tell me if he's too big, too small, or just the right size."

"I like a good Goldilocks challenge. I think a long taste would help me decide."

"Be my guest." He slipped his forest green T-shirt over his head. Nice. His shoulders were wide and ripped with muscles from all the lifting he did on the job.

Feeling dowdy in her sloppy pants, she slipped them down her hips then stepped out of them. Thankfully, her undies were pink cotton—not fancy, but not shabby either.

Brian whistled, and as he reached out, she stopped him. "Uh-uh. Me first," she said in her most sultry tone.

Before he could change her mind, she dropped to her knees. Reaching around him with her left hand, she drew him near. Taking a long inhale, she let his earthy scent travel down the length of her body, familiarizing her with his essence. As much as she wanted to draw him deep down her throat, she had to make sure he was comfortable with her loving ways—assuming she could keep her tiger in check.

With her finger, she traced the puckered rim of his cock. It jerked. She then cupped his balls and rolled them slowly in her palm, hoping he wouldn't stop her.

Brian threaded his fingers through her hair and tugged. "If you keep that up, it won't be long before I explode," he said, slightly panting out his words.

Suck him now, her tiger said, clearly worried that he might go off prematurely.

This is about Brian's pleasure, not mine, she chided. *At least not yet.*

Jillian wanted to show him how good it could be between them. She leaned closer, dragging her tits up his thighs right before encompassing his cock with her mouth. His quads bulged as he pressed into her mouth.

He likes it!

"That's so fucking good," he groaned.

Just wait until I'm done with you. She wanted this to be one of the best nights of his life.

Brian's groans increased with each pump of her fist. Soon, she let her tiger set the pace, stroking him and sucking him deeper and deeper. The sparks of desire increased, tripping up her arms and chest, setting her skin on fire. She was so intent on taking in as much of him as she could that when his hot spray coated the back of her throat, she jerked. Swallowing quickly, she lifted off him.

Brian stepped back. "Fuck. I'm sorry. I've never had anything that amazing in my life."

She couldn't be upset after that compliment. "I'm glad you enjoyed it."

"Enjoyed it? It was so much more than that. I don't know what you did, but something inside me is rumbling around. If you think your tiger has claws, you should feel my bear's claws."

She smiled. He leaned over and drew her to her feet. Brian tilted his head down and Jillian thought he'd kiss her, possibly to give him time to recover, but a quick glance at his glistening cock convinced her he was raring to go. To make sure, she grabbed his thick shaft and squeezed. Yup, hard as a rock. *That's my bear man.*

Brian clasped her hand. "Come with me. My bear would like to invite your tiger to frolic in a more comfortable surrounding."

She leaned her head against his shoulder. "My tiger accepts."

He led her into his bedroom. With no lights lit, all she could make out was a made bed and a small dresser across from it. A nightstand abutted the bed on the side closest to the closet. She expected him to place her on the spread, but instead he turned her around so her back was to the bed.

"Don't move unless I tell you to," he commanded.

Ooh, she couldn't wait to see what he had planned.

Chapter Thirteen

S HIVERS OF ANTICIPATION coursed through Jillian, and she wanted to know where this dominant man had come from all of a sudden.

His bear is slowly emerging, her tiger said. *I can feel him growing stronger with our every touch.*

Then we need to do a lot more touching.

Brian stepped behind her, and when he pressed his chest to her back, every hair tickled her skin. As much as she wanted to reach around her and stroke his thighs, she obeyed and remained still.

"Lift your arms," he commanded.

Jillian had no idea what he planned, but whatever it was, her tiger sure seemed happy, as evidenced by the pulsing blue glow. Brian brushed his callused palms across her nipples, and a wave of desire nearly buckled her knees.

Touch me lower. While they didn't have a telepathic link yet, she hoped he could sense her desire. Ever so slightly, she arched her back for more, pressing her rear against his groin.

"No moving. That's cheating."

Cheating? Was he kidding? "I need you."

"In due time." Brian lowered her arms and stepped around in front of her.

"Can I touch you now? I really need to." Her teeth had already sharpened, and having Brian in front of her, naked, and not being able to indulge in him was testing her resolve.

"No."

To her relief, he cupped a hand between her legs then pressed a finger into her wet opening. When he wiggled his digit and then pushed on her most sensitive spot, bolts of pleasure rocketed through her, forcing her to squeeze her inner walls together. "Got anything bigger?" she panted.

"I'll let you be the judge."

In a flash, she was in his arms and then on the bed. Jillian expected him to crawl on top and impale her with one long thrust, but instead, he knelt between her thighs and lifted her legs over his shoulders, his mouth an inch from her apex. As he hovered over her opening, she grabbed onto the knobby bedspread.

Eat me. She tried sending the message to him mentally, but either he didn't receive it or else he chose to ignore her. Never would she have expected Brian to be so seductive. It thrilled her to think he wanted their first experience to be so special.

When he leaned over and flicked her clit, she nearly flew apart at the seams. Holy goddess almighty. Slipping a hand between her legs, he pressed his thumb into her weeping opening while he sucked on her clit. Jillian firmed her butt to help lift her hips and nearly ripped the bedspread with her now-sharpened nails. The intensity was too much, and she couldn't control her glow that was pulsing brighter and brighter with each stroke.

"I swear I'll shift if you don't take me now." Jillian rarely demanded anything from a lover, but she was desperate.

"That so?" Brian lowered her legs and crawled up her body, his gaze focused on her tits.

He swooped down and plucked the left breast while he palmed the right one. Drawing the nipple taut, he sucked hard, sending spikes of need straight to her core. Jillian grabbed his shoulders and dug her sharp nails into his skin. She couldn't last much longer.

"What are you waiting for? I'm on the pill. Please."

Brian moved his attention to the other tit and drew a lazy circle around the delicate peak before dragging his mouth down her belly.

With each inch, her need grew. If he didn't plunge into her in the next two seconds, she'd have to take control. Her breaths shortened and her teeth sharpened.

Ride him, her tiger urged.

Jillian was tempted.

Brian reached the apex of her thighs and pressed his mouth over her mound. His tongue went to work, ratcheting her desire off the charts while his hands roamed up to her breasts and captured them. Twisting her nipples slowly while he licked her up and down was driving her crazy. It was too much. Her bones cracked and white hair sprouted.

"Brian!" In one quick move, she rolled out from under him, her body pulsing. Jillian pushed on his shoulder. "Get on your back, please."

He winked at her. "Feel like taking a ride, do ya?"

A second later, she was straddling him, her hand holding his thick, hard shaft. For good measure, she leaned over and drew him deep into her mouth, and dragged her tongue around the rough edge of the head of his cock. Brian groaned and mumbled something she couldn't make out.

When he reached up and pinched her nipple, her body convulsed with need, and her tiger screamed for release. Jillian lifted up then guided his shaft straight into her. As she plunged down, overwhelming desire consumed her. His cock stretched her wide and stars burst on the back of her lids as bolts of pleasure tripped up her spine.

Jillian gulped in oxygen as she waited for the slight pain to subside. It had been too long since she'd let herself be with a man.

You were waiting for your mate, her tiger reminded her.

I never thought I'd find him.

You have now.

Brian clasped her waist and lifted her up. "Stay there."

It would be impossible not to move, but she'd try. Brian eased out, waited a long second, and then plunged back in, sending her closer to her climax. Wanting it all, Jillian leaned forward and kissed him. His beard had turned rougher and his nails had extended, but he probably had no idea that his bear was clamoring for freedom.

She cupped his face and kissed him hard, needing him, wanting him, desiring him. Sparks flew as he pounded up into her. When his hard cock banged against her back wall, she lowered her mouth to his neck.

Bite him, her tiger urged.

No, it's too soon. I don't want to pressure him.

Just break the surface, enough to coax out his bear.

"Jillian," Brian shouted. "I'm so close."

So was she. As if the floodgates were about to open, she met each of his thrusts with equal power. He clamped his mouth on her shoulder and her breath hitched. He dug his fingers into her butt and squeezed tight. She pressed her teeth to his neck, hoping to coax out his bear.

On the next thrust, she lost all control. Her orgasm swept down so hard she had to gulp in air to keep from passing out. As Brian let loose his seed, she slid her hands under his body and hugged him tight.

His cock pulsed, and she soared. Exhausted, she collapsed on top of him. A minute later, he lifted his hands and gently rubbed her back. "Did I feel you bite me?"

"No, I was merely tasting you. I was hoping your bear would rear up and roar."

"Well, something just reared up." They both laughed. "How's this? Ro-ar."

She laughed again. "Close, but no cigar."

"I guess you'll have to keep coaxing him then."

"It would be my pleasure."

BRIAN WAS SURE he'd succeed at shifting tonight. Making love with Jillian last night had altered something inside him, and he wasn't just talking about the self confidence and joy she'd brought. She'd woken up his bear; he could feel it. While it might not have been noticeable to Jillian, his incisors had definitely been sharper, his hearing more acute, and his body stronger. Jillian had made a difference—or else her little taste of him had been more than she'd let on.

He returned to the same field where she'd brought him yesterday. The moon looked about the same, only this time, dark clouds were scudding across the sky, and the air had more of a bite to it. He reminded himself that bears liked it cold. So what if his human did not?

Stop being a wuss, that voice said.

Without Jillian to watch his attempt to shift, he was more relaxed. If he didn't shift, at least he'd get some much-needed aerobic exercise.

In case he succeeded, he'd brought a change of clothing and stashed them at the edge of the field. He then did what Jillian suggested and performed a series of warm-up exercises including an attempt to touch his toes. Yeah, that wasn't going to happen anytime soon, but he still tried. If nothing else, he needed to add stretching to his daily routine.

Stop procrastinating.

He slipped off his jacket and mentally blocked out the cold. Brian started out with a jog then slowly increased his speed, focusing on his inner bear. The image of Jillian popped into his head, and his cock stirred at the thought of her naked, tempting, delicious form. His foot slipped on a patch of snow and broke his train of thought. Damn. When he was making love with her, his bear had urged him to be more aggressive. So where was his randy bear now?

Pay attention!

As his body warmed and his muscles loosened, he was sure he'd suddenly find himself on all fours lumbering across the field. But so far, it hadn't happened. He changed his stride length thinking that perhaps one speed was better than another.

As much as he tried to bring his bear out, it was Jillian who sat at the forefront of his mind. He thought it might have been the calm he experienced around her that was blocking his excited bear from escaping. If he had to choose between being with Jillian and shifting, his bear would have to stay hidden.

The clouds passed over the moon, hindering his sight and forcing Brian to slow down. He'd encountered the uneven terrain last night, along with some rocks in the field, and he didn't need to show up with bruises if he fell.

Learning to shift was more than just about him connecting with his bear. He wanted to shift so that Jillian and he could run free together. She claimed she wasn't in her tiger form often, but hopefully he could change that.

After one more lap, Brian admitted to himself that it wasn't going to happen tonight. He lacked the concentration mostly because his thoughts kept jumping to the two of them in bed the night before. Everything about that woman was perfection, which made him want to keep trying—night after cold night.

AS JILLIAN TRIMMED some greenery for Anna, her thoughts jumped to Brian's green T-shirt he'd worn the night they'd made love. She could tell he had a nice body under all his clothes, but she hadn't expected such thick shoulder muscles. And he certainly hadn't been shy or fumbling in any way when it came to using that body. In fact, no man had ever excited her the way Brian had.

Anna came into the back room with some wild flowers and smiled. "Thanks for cutting the greens for me."

Jillian liked watching Anna create bouquets. She said she wasn't as good as Elana, but Anna could have fooled her. "No problem. You want me to flip the door sign to Open?"

"Sure."

Just as Jillian stepped into the main room, Brian's voice sounded from the back and her pulse sped up, causing her body to throb. Really? It was as if their lovemaking hadn't satisfied her.

You want more, her tiger snickered. *Or rather you need more.*

It was true. One little taste of Brian seemed to make her cravings worse.

Brian entered the main part of the store. "Hey, I was on my way to work and wanted to say good morning."

Brian looked not only professional wearing jeans with his orange work shirt, but he was sexy too. "Good morning to you. How was your *field* work last night?"

Most likely he hadn't shifted. If he had, he would have called her. She just wished there was something she could do to help his bear emerge.

"Nothing's changed."

She tried to hide her disappointment. "Did you get any sleep afterward?"

He looked over his shoulder and moved closer to her. "Not really. It was lonely in my bed."

Heat raced up her face. Brian wanted her to stay with him, but she thought it was too soon. He'd asked her what too soon meant, but she wasn't able to articulate her thoughts. All she knew was, for this mate stuff to have any chance of working, they needed to take it slow. Brian seemed to understand, but she feared if he became frustrated over one of her quirky habits, it might cause more tension. It was hard enough keeping him upbeat since he hadn't been able to shift.

Besides, with that crazy killer-cop on the loose, she was safer with Dalton. Probably because she didn't know how Brian would react, she hadn't divulged why she was even in Silver Lake—other than to visit her brother.

A customer appeared outside the store's front door and then entered. Brian moved closer. "I have the late shift tonight, but do you want to have dinner tomorrow night?"

Her muscles relaxed. "I'd love to."

"Great. I'll call you later."

When Brian leaned forward, she smiled and pressed her finger to his lips, not wanting to kiss him in front of the customer. In part, she feared one kiss would lead to something else. When she was around Brian, her control wavered.

Brian left just as Anna emerged from the back with the vase of wild flowers. She placed them in the cooler first then helped the woman pick out a nice bouquet for her boss who was retiring. All throughout the interaction, Anna kept shooting Jillian sly glances.

Once the women chose the bouquet, Anna wrapped a pink ribbon around the vase while Jillian rang her up. The woman thanked them both and left.

"Jillian Garner, is there something you want to share?" Anna placed a hand on her arm, but quickly removed it. Her mouth opened and then shut as the sparkle that had been in her eyes turned painful.

"Anna, are you okay?"

"Yes. I'm fine." She looked off to the side and then smiled. "So you and Brian are a couple?"

Her comment was a cover up, but Jillian had learned when to pry and when to go with the flow. "Yes, we are, but you looked like you remembered something. Are you sure you're okay?"

"Yes, I just remembered that the winter carnival is this weekend."

"Really? I wonder why Dalton never mentioned anything. Have you been?" Elana told her that Anna hadn't been in town that long.

"Yes. Once. I met a guy last year when I'd first arrived in town. We hit it off really well, and he asked me to go with him."

Because Anna didn't seem to be dating anyone now, the relationship must not have worked out. "You didn't have a good time?"

"Yes, it was awesome, but about a month later a freak storm descended on the town. Chris was a first responder and was called out in the middle of the night to help a stranded motorist. We're not sure what happened, but his car was found at the bottom of a ravine the next day."

Jillian grabbed Anna's hand. "I'm so sorry."

"Thanks. It's particularly bad when the carnival returns to town."

Jillian understood. She had issues on June 15th, the day her dad was murdered. While she believed Anna's story, something else was going on with her. To demand answers right now though wouldn't be wise. "What's the carnival like?"

"It's wonderful. They have rides, fun houses, and a ton of vendors selling everything from fudge to elephant ears to delicious stuffed meat pies. No one goes home hungry. Last year, they had a skating rink and a concert."

She bet that she and Brian would have a good time. "I might check it out."

"Do. You'll like it."

For the rest of the day, Anna didn't act like herself. Whether she was thinking about the man she lost or something else, Jillian didn't know.

They'd just closed up, when an idea struck Jillian. Brian would be working late, and Dalton said he was on a big case and didn't know when he'd make it home. "Do you want to go get a drink?"

Anna hesitated but then studied Jillian. "Yeah, I'd like that."

"What do you think of McKinnon's Pub and Pool?" The place would be filled with shifters, but that shouldn't be a problem.

"I've never been, but I'm game to try a new spot."

Chapter Fourteen

J
ILLIAN SUSPECTED ANNA had agreed to have a drink with her because she wanted to get the inside scoop on her relationship with Brian. While Jillian didn't have a problem sharing a few tidbits, it wasn't as if she could tell her coworker they were mates, or that Brian was trying to learn to shift. Wouldn't that blow her mind?

They were on their second glass of wine when Jillian decided it was time to ask Anna again why she'd had such a haunted look on her face back at the store. It was the second time since Jillian started working there that Anna had a strange reaction after she'd touched her arm.

"Can I ask you a personal question?" Jillian asked.

Anna smiled. "You can always ask."

That translated to mean she might not answer. "Why did you move to Silver Lake?"

Tackling the real question from a different starting point often worked. She needed Anna to let down her guard, and the wine was definitely helping.

Her brows rose, clearly not expecting such a benign question. "I love the mountains here, even if they are just rolling hills."

Jillian could relate. "Where are you from?"

"Montana."

"Ah." Jillian had driven through the area just last year. "It's lovely there. The ragged mountain peaks are breathtaking."

"They are, but my town held bad memories."

"Were you thinking of them when you touched my arm?"

Anna gulped most of what was left in her glass. "No." She let out a breath then watched as she twirled her glass on the tabletop. Finally, Anna looked up. "Since you seem determined to find out, I'll tell you, but please don't judge me."

How sad that she believed Jillian would. "At the risk of sounding egotistical, not judging a person is one of my better traits. Over the years, I've learned it's better to understand a person first before drawing any conclusions."

Anna's chin trembled. "Okay, here goes. When I touched your arm, I saw one of *your* memories—a bad one." Anna leaned forward slightly, and her hand tightened around the stem of the glass.

That comment took Jillian by surprise. "I don't understand."

She finished her wine. "Let me begin by saying I'm a very observant person. I knew Elana before she met Kalan, and I watched how she changed after they were together for a while."

Jillian tensed, wondering if after Elana and Kalan mated, her friend exhibited any shifter traits. "How? What exactly was different?" Had her teeth sharpened? Had her hair suddenly sprouted on her arms and face? Or worse, had her bones cracked?

"Her hearing was better, her smell more acute, and her eyesight was sharper."

All were shifter qualities, but nothing that would give away her new status. "Fascinating. What do you think caused it?"

Anna leaned back in her seat. "You should know. You have the same traits."

Oh, shit. Did she know about shifters? Anna wasn't one. "I'm glad you think so. So tell me about this memory of mine that you saw."

Anna looked around the room then back at Jillian, as if debating how far to push this line of questioning. "I get it. You don't want to divulge your secret, but how about I tell you mine and you tell me yours?"

Jillian wasn't a lawyer for nothing. She didn't like being evasive, but she wasn't about to be the one to leak the concept of shifters to a human. "I'm listening."

Anna twirled her glass. "Let me start by saying I'm cursed." Jillian raised her brows and downed the rest of her wine. "Ever since I can remember, if I touched someone, I often would see a bad memory they'd had."

Now she was intrigued. "Which one of mine did you see?"

She had two horrific ones, but she didn't believe Anna really had that talent. Jillian hadn't told Anna anything about her circumstances for being in Silver Lake, and she doubted Elana had spilled the beans either.

"I saw you standing in a bedroom with beige and white striped wallpaper looking at a blonde woman lying on a bed. She'd been shot in the head."

Jillian's blood nearly drained from her face. "How did you know? Did Elana tell you?" She waved a hand. Jillian hadn't mentioned the wallpaper. "Never mind."

"You see? It's a curse," she whispered.

That kind of talent would be. Then it dawned on her. "You're a Wendayan!"

Anna's brows scrunched. "A what?"

What was it about people in this town not knowing who or what they were? "A Wendayan is a kind of witch—a good one, mind you. In fact, I have a touch of Wendayan in me." She didn't mind sharing that aspect of her life.

Seeing their empty glasses, the waitress came over. "Another round ladies?"

They both nodded. Given their waitress was a shifter, Jillian didn't care if she overheard.

"Does that mean you can touch someone and see into their past too?" Anna asked, her voice laced with excitement.

"No. Each Wendayan is different." She tried to remember what Elana told her about some of the Wendayans in town. "Some have premonitions, others can put thoughts into people's minds without them knowing, and still others can control fire, wind, and earth. As for me, I move fast. Really fast."

"Shut up! Really?"

"Yes, really."

Anna's smile lit up her face. "I thought I was the only one who was weird like that, though controlling fire and wind is way beyond what I can do."

The poor girl. Here she had thought she was alone all her life. "There is a fairly large group in Silver Lake who possess talents similar to yours and mine, but I'm surprised your parents didn't tell you about them. Your mom or dad, or both, must have been Wendayans."

Anna glanced away. "I was adopted."

Her heart squeezed. That explained a lot about her. Anna was similar to Brian in a way, except she was able to discover her true self without help. While it was probably wrong to ask Anna to break confidence, Jillian had to ask. "Did you ever get a vision off Brian?"

Anna cast her gaze downward. "Yes."

"Does he know that you did?"

She shook her head. "I see no reason to tell anyone what I've seen. It's not like they aren't aware of their own memories."

True. "Was Brian's bad?"

"More like sad, but still traumatic."

"Care to share?" Since Anna was a Wendayan, it wouldn't matter if she learned about shifters since the two groups co-existed. Dalton had said the Silver Lake shifters protected the Wendayans. Explaining all that right now might blow Anna's mind. In due time, Jillian would tell her.

"I saw Brian as a young boy sitting at his kitchen table. He was maybe six, and his mom was fixing him a glass of milk. He watched her put an eyedropper full of something in his drink then hand it to him."

The implication crushed her heart. "What did Brian do?"

"He refused to drink it at first, but his mother forced him. I wasn't touching him long enough to see more."

Brian must have believed his mother couldn't be trusted. Hopefully, the eyedropper contained some kind of medicine and not some drug to help calm him.

If Jillian had Anna's ability, she might not want to touch anyone—ever. "Do you see good things?"

"Not really. Most of the time though, I can't get any reading off a person. Only those who have had something tragic happen in their lives that is still unresolved seem able to send any images, if that's the right phrase."

"Who else knows about your special talent? Sharing can often lighten one's load."

"Only Elana, so please don't tell anyone else. I just thought you might be like me."

"I can't read people's minds or thoughts."

"Maybe not, but you are intuitive. You're more open-minded than most."

Then why did Anna think she'd judge her? "Thank you."

"You don't treat Brian like anyone I've known. I've watched people around him. He can be a little standoffish at times, yet, you can see right through him. You could tell he is a good person."

"I could." But that might have been because he was her mate.

"As long as we're sharing, why did you come to Silver Lake? Elana said you were a lawyer in California."

Anna deserved to know the truth, especially if that cop ever showed up. "I saw the man who murdered my friend—the blonde you saw—and I think he knows I know."

Anna sucked in a breath. "You're on the run?"

"Yes. I'm staying with my brother for protection until I figure out what to do."

"Do you think he'll come after you?"

"I hope not, but since the killer is a cop, he has the resources to find me."

"I have a gun. Maybe I should bring it to the store."

Jillian smiled. "I don't think that would be wise." To be safe, Jillian briefly described the fifty-year old, including the scar on his jaw. "If you do see him, don't react. Pretend you have no idea who he is."

If he thought she knew, Frank Whitlaw would shift and attack before Anna had the chance to move.

Their next round of drinks arrived, and Jillian held up her glass. "To those who are different."

Anna lifted her glass. "To being different."

"I'VE NEVER BEEN to a carnival," Brian said, holding Jillian's hand and glancing around wide eyed.

Country music was being piped through tall speakers located around the large venue. She estimated the carnival was spread out on about eight acres and parking took up several more. Everywhere she looked, vendors were hawking their goods or trying to draw in the crowd to look at what they were selling. She didn't know the population of Silver Lake, but she bet half of them were there.

"I don't think I've been to anything like this since I was six," she said. "Los Angeles has festivals, but nothing like this." Jillian pointed to a stand fifteen feet from them. "Oh, look, cotton candy!"

"Let's get you some." They hightailed it over there. Brian then reached into his pocket, withdrew his wallet, and paid the man who handed her the foot tall sugary confection.

"You aren't getting any?" she asked.

"I'll try a bite of yours first, if that's okay?"

"Absolutely." He leaned over and together they chomped on opposite sides of the sweet. Brian must have never eaten something like this before, because the sticky wisps of sugar coated his cheeks and lips. Jillian laughed. "You're a mess."

"What's this stuff made out of?" he asked peeling what he could off of his face. For a moment Jillian feared he'd become angry, but soon he laughed. "I think I'll stick to fudge."

"Good plan."

She'd never seen him so relaxed. Hopefully, their new relationship had a hand in that.

"Come on, let's explore," he said as she scarfed down her new treat.

The bright sun had warmed the air to temperatures in the high fifties or low sixties, and she couldn't ask for a nicer day. Brian led her over to the ring toss station where a large rack of stuffed animals sat off to the side. Two teenage boys were each trying to win an animal for the two girls with them, and Jillian smiled at their enthusiasm.

"Which one do you want?" Brian asked.

"I don't need a stuffed animal."

"How about if I want to win one for you?"

She smiled. "Then I'll treasure it for life."

After the teens finished showing off, they left. While only one of the girls won a stuffed unicorn, both girls seemed impressed with the boys' efforts.

"Four tosses for a buck!" the gamer told Brian.

He fished out a dollar and handed it to the bearded man. For Brian's sake, Jillian hoped he won. The first toss bounced off the glass, but Brian didn't appear worried.

"That was practice," he told her.

The second toss hit the mouth of the bottle, rattled, teetered, and then landed around the neck. Brian held up his hands in victory and Jillian clapped.

"That was awesome! And you said you didn't play sports."

"This is hardly a sport."

To her it was. She was so excited for Brian. In the last few days they'd talked a lot about what it was like growing up without his parents around, and he seemed to have come to grips with everything. He'd told her about some tales of fun things he did at the institution, but for the most part there wasn't much joy in his life. It had made Jillian want to hold him forever.

"You get two more tosses," the gamer said.

Brian glanced over at her and grinned. "Pick out something big."

She was about to say she'd wait and see if he landed either of those two, but Jillian kept quiet. "Good luck."

The next toss ringed another bottle, but the last one missed. He puffed out his chest. "Hey, I got two!"

"You were awesome." Jillian picked a rather large stuffed bear, surprised at how excited she was at the gift. "Growing up, we didn't have many toys."

"I'm glad I could win it for you."

"Me too." For the next half hour, they sampled way too much fair food, and then Jillian announced she'd reached her limit.

"I can't eat another bite either."

For the next hour, they wandered about the carnival, checking out the booths, and watching exhibitions. Brian's favorite was the man using a chain saw to carve totems while hers was the woman painting portraits in about five minutes. No matter where they were or what they saw, Brian seemed so happy, and she couldn't have been more thrilled.

"Hey, Brian," a pretty woman said coming toward them. If she hadn't had a handsome man on her arm, Jillian would have been jealous. The cute woman had short blonde hair streaked with purple and black highlights. "I don't think you've met Jackson yet."

"No, I haven't." They shook hands.

Jillian introduced herself, wondering where Brian had met them. Both were shifters, that much she could tell.

"Jackson is Kalan's brother," Brian told her.

Ah, yes. Ainsley was the shifter who'd stopped by Elana's house the night Jillian had dropped the You're-A-Shifter bombshell. And she was the one who'd recognized Brian was a bear.

"Nice to meet you. Thank you for helping Brian out the other night. I wasn't very subtle with my revelation, but you confirmed what I was trying to tell him."

Ainsley smiled. "You must be Dalton's sister."

"Yes." The woman was good, if she could tell the two of them were the same breed.

Jackson tightened his hold around Ainsley's waist. "We're having a big birthday bash in about a month and hope you two can join us. Ainsley never celebrated her own birthday growing up, and since our birthdays are only a week apart, we're having a joint celebration."

That was so sweet of them to ask. Brian squeezed Jillian's hand as if he wasn't sure he wanted to be around so many people.

"We'd love to, thanks," Jillian said without conferring with Brian. He'd been making steady progress in dealing with people and she was confident he'd be fine.

"We're headed off to grab something to eat. Nice meeting you," Jackson said. "We'll be in touch about the date."

"Great," she said. Once they disappeared, she moved in front of Brian. "Are you okay with going?"

"As long as you're by my side, I'll be fine."

"Always." As soon as she said that word, Jillian realized she'd have to leave at some point, and hoped it wasn't during their birthday bash. "Just so you know, I'll have to take a trip back to Los Angeles at some point. I need to turn over my practice there to one of the associates and sell my house."

"So you've decided to stay?"

"Yes. We're a team now." Brian grinned and her heart soared.

With his arm around her waist, they continued to check out what the carnival had to offer. "Hey, there's a skating rink." Brian pointed to a large white tent.

"You skate?" she asked.

"We had an ice skating rink near the institution. The caregivers took us over on weekends."

"Lucky you. I've never skated," she said.

"What? Are you kidding? Come on, you'll do great."

No, she wouldn't. Jillian was comfortable in the ocean, assuming she wore a wet suit, and while she'd never surfed, she suspected she'd be rather good given her excellent balance.

Brian seemed so excited to show her the rink that she couldn't turn him down. As he led her over to the large tented arena, he carried the bear he'd won for her. The generators used to keep the ice solid, rattled loudly off to the side. She was glad to step inside where about fifteen kids and their parents were skating to an up-tempo song. Most were good skaters, but a few looked like this was their first time. She'd probably look like them soon—wobbly and unsure—unless her tiger offered up some of her agility. In truth, Jillian didn't really care what she looked like as long as she didn't fall.

After finding out her shoe size, he rented them skates and then laced hers up.

"If I fall on my butt," she said, "I won't be a happy camper."

"If you fall on your butt, I'll be sure to kiss the bruise away."

She laughed, always surprised at what came out of Brian's mouth. That first afternoon when she'd met Elana for lunch, his sister had told Jillian how hard it had been for Brian to interact with people. Add in his anger issues and most people avoided him. When Brian came to Silver Lake though, he'd changed. Jillian suspected that his bear liked being around other shifters, and while she'd never felt the pull of Silver Lake, Dalton had told her the pink quartz lining the bottom provided strength to bears and wolves.

When Jillian asked Brian about his change of attitude, he'd attributed a lot to his sister's love. For the first time in his life, he felt wanted.

Don't cry. Just enjoy him! her tiger said.

He held out his hand. "Let's give this skating a try."

When she stood, her ankles nearly buckled, and Brian steadied her. "Don't let go," she said.

"I won't."

Tentatively, she walked onto the ice and stood for a minute to watch the other skater's techniques and to get her balance. The general movement of skating involved pushing off with one foot then gliding on the other, alternating as needed. "Why don't you go around once and I'll study how you do it."

"You sure?"

"Yes." Mostly, she just wanted to watch him.

He toed the ice and sped away from her. With sure, smooth strokes, he wove around some of the slower skaters, and even flipped around in mid stride to skate backward. She had no idea if bears were usually light on their human feet, but Brian sure was. When he came around full circle, she clapped. "You were awesome."

Red tinged his face. "Thanks. I didn't participate in any group sports, so this was my exercise. My therapist encouraged me to let out my aggression on the ice, as well as to build things with my hands in order to get in touch with my inner being." He chuckled.

"I think your therapist was wise."

"Maybe he was. After all, he suggested I come to Silver Lake and reconnect with Elana."

"Definitely a smart man." Jillian inhaled the cold. "Okay, let's try this, but don't laugh."

"Never."

With Brian holding her hand, he let her skate close to the railing in case she needed to grab onto something else. To her delight, after two times around the rink, Jillian let go of Brian's hand and managed to keep upright. "I'm doing it!" she exclaimed.

"You sure are." Brian flipped around and grabbed both of her hands then skated backward, pulling her along.

Jillian laughed at how much fun this was. As he wove them between the groups of people, her coordination grew. The best part about being here was seeing Brian have a great time. Jillian delighted in Brian being in charge of an activity for a change. Ever since she'd met him, she'd been the one forcing him to change and trying to shift. On the ice, Brian was the leader.

They'd almost returned to the starting point, when a unique shifter signature floated by her. At first, she ignored it, as many of the people at the rink were shifters, but for a split second, she caught *his* scent.

Brian slowed. "Are you okay?"

As much as she wanted to blow it off, she couldn't. "Yeah, I'm good. Just a little tired that's all. Do you think we could go?"

"Sure." His shoulders sagged.

Brian led her over to the benches where they took off their skates. While he returned them, she glanced around for the scar-faced killer, but didn't spot him anywhere. She hoped she hadn't been imagining things. If Frank Whitlaw had found her, she needed to warn Brian. It was time to tell him everything.

Chapter Fifteen

F RANK WHITLAW WAS pissed. He'd blocked out four days to tie up loose ends, and now it seemed it might take longer. Figuring out a way to kill Jillian Garner should have been easy, but the woman was never alone. She worked at a local flower shop where some brown haired, tattooed woman worked right along side her. When Jillian left for the evening, she either went straight home to her cop brother's house or hung out with that human friend of hers. From the way those two were holding hands at the skating rink, the man seemed to believe they were an item.

Frank knew better. Jillian was in Silver Lake merely to hide, probably believing once he was in jail, she could return home. *Guess what, Jillian Garner? You're never seeing Los Angeles again!* He was leading the Dalia Swanson case and had done a masterful job of tainting the evidence, enough to throw off the best forensic team.

After watching Jillian's movements these past two days, he needed to figure out a way to get her alone—and that meant dangling some bait in front of her so that she'd come running. Right before he killed her, he'd tell her what a snitch her dad had been. Frank would enjoy seeing her try to defend her righteous son of a bitch dad, but then she'd get what she deserved. It was just a matter of setting up a few things and then he'd be ready.

RELIEVED TO BE away from the carnival, Jillian tossed her coat on the back of Brian's sofa. "I needed to leave because there are a few things I have to tell you."

He spun around, his eyes haunted. "Don't tell me James confided in you that I can never shift and that we can't be together."

She rushed up to him and placed her hands on his chest. "No. This isn't about us. It's about why I'm here in Silver Lake. Why I'm *really* here."

"I thought you came to Silver Lake to visit Dalton."

She didn't want him to think she'd hid everything from him. "That's partially true. Come sit next to me, and I'll tell you the rest."

"Why now?" His voice had turned gruff and his movements stiff.

"I didn't tell you before because I'd already dumped enough crap on you. How much could you have handled after I told you shifters existed? And guess what, sport, you're one too."

"Fine, so you had your reasons. Go on."

Jillian ran a hand down his arm, as much to calm him as herself. "The night before I came out here, I witnessed a murder—more or less."

"Oh, shit. I'm sorry, but what does kind of witnessed a murder mean?"

She began with how she'd seen her father's killer when she was six, and how she'd spotted the same man in the police station before noon the same day as the second murder. "Mind you, it was twenty-five years later."

"Are you sure it was the same man? Memories can blur in that time."

"Trust me. I know. I smelled him, and scent is ingrained in my brain," she said.

He shook his head and glanced off to the side. "I can't imagine waiting all that time to find him. What did you do when you realized who he was?" His concern warmed her heart. Brian was such a protector.

"I acted as if I'd never seen him before, but I don't think he believed me. You probably wonder why I think that. It's because that same night was when he came to my house and murdered my friend Dalia who was asleep in my guest room. The two of us look similar—same length blonde hair and same height—so I'm thinking he must have thought it was me that he had shot and killed."

Brian reached out and drew her close. "I'm so sorry. What did the cops say?"

He must not have connected the dots. "I didn't tell them. The killer is a cop, and he was assigned to lead the case."

His jaw slowly lowered. "That's horrible. Can't you complain and ask for a new detective?"

She actually chuckled. "What would I say? I recognized Detective Whitlaw as my dad's murderer, but since I was six at the time, I have no proof—other than his scent."

"Ah, I see. And you can't say you recognized his scent without telling the world you're a shifter."

"Exactly. Even worse, Whitlaw is a shifter too."

While holding her in his arms, he leaned back. "What are you going to do?"

She twisted toward him. "What I'm already doing. Hiding out in Silver Lake. Just so you know, when we were at the skating rink, I smelled him again."

Brian jerked up. "He's here? In Silver Lake?"

She wanted to be completely honest. "I think so, but there were a lot of people in that rink and the smells might have mingled together. I looked around but didn't see him. I'm hoping I'm wrong."

He shook his head. "I don't like it. You need to tell Dalton right now."

"I will. I just needed a moment to think this through."

"Dalton is a cop. Maybe he or one of his friends can track Whitlaw down. You know what he looks like, right? Can't they put out flyers or something?"

That almost made her smile. "I don't think wanted posters in the post office work for men like Frank Whitlaw. Besides, what would anyone do if they found him? They can't arrest him. He's covered his tracks."

"If a Los Angeles cop suddenly shows up in Tennessee, doesn't that implicate him?"

"No. He'll say he's here on vacation in the beautiful Great Smokies. I'll ask Dalton to look for him, but if Whitlaw's not here, it'll cause a lot of work for people."

Brian dragged a hand down his face. "But if he is here and you say nothing, the consequences could be lethal."

"True." She snapped her fingers. "Duh. I'll ask Camille."

"Who's Camille?"

Jillian felt bad that she hadn't let Brian in on anything about her life. "She's a good friend of mine who I was visiting at the police station in Los Angeles that day when I saw Whitlaw."

"She's a cop?"

"Yes." Jillian swiped her finger across the burner phone and dialed Camille's cell. Her friend would either be out with their usual gang, or curled up on her sofa reading a good book.

"Jillian! How are you?"

"I'm good. Say listen, was Frank Whitlaw at the precinct today? Or didn't you go in."

"It was my day off."

Shit. "Was he there yesterday?" Jillian held her breath.

"I don't think so, but then I don't always see him. It's not like we work together."

"Do you think you can find out for me?"

Jillian was met with silence for a few seconds. "What's going on?"

"I think Whitlaw followed me to Tennessee. I swear I caught a whiff of him."

Brian was leaning close, the lines around his eyes pronounced.

"Oh, my God, Jillian. Sure, I'll discreetly ask Maria Rodriguez. She's Frank's partner."

Poor woman. "Be careful."

"Always."

They chatted a few more minutes. "Look, I gotta go."

"Stay safe." Camille disconnected.

Jillian stuffed the phone back in her purse and faced Brian. "My friend isn't—"

"I heard," Brian said. "It's inconclusive."

"Yes. I hope you don't mind, but I should call Dalton."

"Absolutely."

From the noise in the background, her brother was still at work. She explained she thought she'd smelled their father's killer.

"If you're right, you'll have to be extra careful. I'll do some checking to see if he flew in, and then I'll check the rental car companies too. I'm thinking he won't bother with a fake ID either since he won't have any clue that we're on to him."

"Can you get that information without a warrant?"

"I can't, but I bet Jackson Murdoch can. The man can hack into anything."

As a lawyer, Jillian frowned on illegal activity, but for this she'd make an exception. "That's good to know."

"Jilly, if Frank Whitlaw is in town, we'll find him."

"Even if you do, you can't touch him. Technically, he's done nothing wrong." She didn't need to be lecturing her brother on the law.

"Even so," Dalton said, "we can watch his every move to make sure he doesn't harm you."

Knowing Dalton, he'd ask someone to keep an eye on her. Finding out if Whitlaw was in town would require calling in quite a few favors or hiring people for the job. "Do whatever you need to do, but if you hire McKinnon and Associates, I can't pay until I get home."

"Don't worry about it. Connor McKinnon will do right by you. Where are you now?"

"I'm with Brian."

"Have him follow you home. I don't want anything to happen to you."

"I will."

After they both disconnected, she faced Brian. "Dalton said he'll speak with McKinnon and Associates about finding Whitlaw."

"Who are they? The name sounds familiar."

"You've met one of them—Jackson Murdoch. Apparently, Jackson and the team he works with are Jack-of-all-trades security specialists. They do everything from finding people to doing what needs to be done for the greater good so to speak—especially if Changelings are involved."

Brian smiled. "So, basically they tread anywhere the cops can't legally go."

"That's what I've gathered from Dalton. By the way, because my madman might be in town, Dalton asked if you'd follow me home tonight."

"Of course." He scooted closer. "You've done all you can for now. You're safe here."

"At least he can't enter this building without a key code." Then she remembered the man had broken into her place with ease. "Just in case, do you think you could put the deadbolt on the door?"

He smiled. "You got it." Brian secured the door then dragged a chair over and jammed it under the doorknob. "Not sure if this will stop anyone, but they always do this in the movies."

She laughed. "That they do."

"I know what will cheer you up."

"What's that?" *Making mad passionate love with me?*

"Wait and see." He disappeared into the bedroom. A door slid open then closed. Seconds later, he came out with a beautiful box. "I made you a jewelry box."

Jillian was stunned. The box was slightly bigger than a loaf of bread. What was so amazing was that the lid had wood inlays in different colors that were cut and placed together to form flowers. "You didn't have to get me anything or make me this. It's too beautiful."

"Like you."

"Aw, thank you. How did you do this?" She lightly ran her fingers across the top.

"I just made a pattern, cut out each piece, and then glued them together. Open it."

He made it sound so simple. Inside was a drawer that lifted out. "It's like a secret hiding place," she said, her voice full of awe. Jillian closed the lid and once more smoothed her hand along the surface. "What are you doing working at a hardware store if you can do this? You should sell your work."

He looked away, clearly not comfortable with compliments. "If I ever get enough money, I'd like to open my own woodworking shop and make custom furniture and stuff."

"That sounds wonderful."

"What sounds even more wonderful is a kiss. I've been staring at those lips all day and have been dying to taste you," he said with eyes so dreamy that Jillian wanted to dive right into them and search his soul.

"What's stopping you?" she asked, placing a hand on his thigh. It was fun to tease Brian. Every experience they shared was fresh and novel.

"Absolutely nothing." Brian slipped his present from her fingers and set it on the coffee table. A second later, he was sprawled on top of her on the sofa. Brian then brushed her lips with his, and the soft kiss sent spikes of pleasure across her body. As much as she enjoyed it, she wanted to be taken—hard and fast.

"Thank... you... for... a... wonderful... day," she said, kissing him with tiny pecks in between each word, hoping he'd be equally frustrated with the brief contact.

Brian lifted his head and looked deep into her eyes. "No. Thank *you*. I've never met anyone like you, Jillian. Not only are you beautiful, you're smart, kind, and thoughtful. I'd need at least another thousand more words to describe you."

Brian was so sweet. "Have I told you how much I love your eyes? They're soulful."

"Soulful, huh?" He quirked his lips to the side, seemingly unable to decide if that was a good thing or not.

"Yes. They show a depth of character few men possess. They intrigue me. You intrigue me. I know that big heart of yours is hiding inside you, and it's your eyes that reveal your fear of showing your true self to people."

His confusion changed to delight. "That so?" He tapped her nose. "I was waiting for the right person to come along. Then I will give my heart to her freely."

"You mean me?"

"Of course."

Her heart nearly burst. Jillian didn't believe she'd earned his trust, but if she had, she needed to do everything in her power not to break it. "I accept."

"Right now, my brain is only thinking of one thing I can give you," he said as he pressed against her a bit harder.

She wiggled her hips, loving how hard his cock was even through their clothes. Excitement coursed through her knowing he wanted her just as much as she wanted him. "I can tell."

Kiss him.

And she did—fully, totally, and with complete abandon. Wanting more, Jillian tugged his shirt from his jeans and ran her hands up his corded back. The skin-to-skin contact ignited her. Who knew lifting wood all day would make him so ripped?

Brian dipped his tongue into her mouth and immediately possessed her, his scent making her tiger beg for release.

After a long, intense exploration, she broke the contact. Breathless, she ran her gaze downward, as if inspecting both of them. "I think we're both overdressed."

"Totally." He sat up and unbuttoned his jeans.

While it was more efficient if they each took off their own clothes, it definitely wasn't as rewarding. "How about if I do that for you?" she asked. "Can you stand up? I want to take off your clothes this time—slowly."

His eyes widened, and a second later Brian climbed off her. The last time, he'd made her stand still. Now it was his turn to be tormented by need. "Where do you want me?" he asked.

She glanced over at the window and found the curtains drawn. Perfect. "Right where you are is good, but first take off your shoes."

As he shucked off his boots, she kicked off hers. Her tiger took over and Jillian stalked toward him with one thing on her mind—having Brian. Even with all the injustice this man had gone through, he'd managed to fight his own inner demons and found a place in his heart for her.

Mate, mate, her tiger huffed out.

You know it can't be completed until Brian shifts one time and returns my bite.

Brian stood in front of her and held out his arms. "I'm all yours."

Chapter Sixteen

J ILLIAN LOVED BRIAN'S attitude and hoped he meant it when he
said he was hers. She tapped her lips and hummed as she perused
his body. "Where to start? Where to start?"

He tossed her a fake scowl. "If you don't decide quickly, I'll go
first. If I do, you better watch out, because I plan to strip you naked
slower than paint can dry."

She laughed, amazed at his sense of humor and his newfound
confidence. Knowing Brian, he would be true to his word. From the
way he made incredibly tender love with her, he understood what a
woman wanted. "I'll start with your shirt. I do adore a good chest."

Jillian slipped her hands under his black T-shirt. Running her
palms up over his abs, she halted when she captured his pecs. She
squeezed his hard flesh, loving the size of his muscles. He growled,
and she swore he sprouted hair right under her palms.

His eyelids lowered, and Brian looked like he was ready for a
feast—with her as the main course. Jillian slowly eased his shirt
upward until it cleared his body. Dropping the material on the floor,
she rubbed up against him. "You're fun to undress."

"Oh, yeah. Remember, it's my turn next. As they say, do unto
others as you would have them do unto you."

"I can't wait." As Jillian nibbled on his lips, she eased his pants
over his hips.

Brian stepped back. "Did you forget what happened the last time
you teased me too much?"

"No." She'd never forget anything about their first lovemaking session, which was why she'd be cautious. This time she wanted them to come together.

Before she could stop him, Brian stepped back and slipped off his pants and briefs. What he revealed had her licking her lips once more.

Brian groaned. "You are so tempting."

"Thank you." She nodded to his cock. "Someone's excited I see."

"That shouldn't come as a surprise. I can't keep my mind off you."

She smiled. "Spoken like a true bear."

"I wish."

If Jillian could snap her fingers and make him shift, she would.

No, you wouldn't, her animal shot back.

Her tiger was right. Brian needed the satisfaction of transforming into a bear himself. Perhaps that was what was blocking him—his fear that his life as he knew it would change. Jillian wanted to show him that it would be different for sure, but in a much better way. The best way to accomplish that would be to love him completely.

A very naked Brian closed the gap between them. "My turn," he said as he slid his hands under her shirt until he cupped her covered breasts. "I do love these."

She laughed. "If you take off my shirt and bra, I bet you'll get a better visual and feel for them."

"That so? Then I guess I'll have to see for myself."

You're stalling. Get going. Her tiger clawed at her to get on with the lovemaking.

I like foreplay, so shut up.

Jillian felt the kick in her gut. Jerk.

Just as she'd done to him, Brian lifted her shirt over her head and tossed it to the floor. After undoing her bra, he dropped it where her shirt had landed. "Nice."

He leaned over, and when he kissed her neck, thoughts of mating whipped through her, sending heat straight between her legs. She wrapped her arms around him, yearning to explore every inch of his body.

Starting with his back, she slid her hands downward, enjoying his strength. Passing his waist, she reached his bare butt, and when she squeezed his delicious rear, something inside her snapped, and every hormone in her body exploded. The kiss that followed more than curled her toes, and with each dip of her tongue, Brian walked her backward. She thought he was taking her into the bedroom, but apparently the wall next to the door was far enough.

"I have to taste you," he whispered. Brian dropped to his knees and spread her legs wide.

Anticipation had her pulse shooting skyward, and the first lick took it from there. She threaded her fingers through his thick hair and noticed how the strands seemed to have grown coarser. It was as if his bear was slowly emerging from a long hibernation. For Brian's sake, she hoped that was true.

As soon as he slipped a finger into her opening, Jillian nearly came on the spot. She'd hoped that after having made love with him the first time, her tiger would have calmed down. Wrong! Her animal was more determined than ever to climb the highest peak of ecstasy again. And again.

"More," she begged Brian.

He winked, leaned over, and swiped his tongue across her clit, all the while wiggling his finger inside her. Her nub exploded with need and set off a chain reaction that started at her core and worked its way up her spine. She tugged on his hair and grunted. "Please, Brian."

As if her plea was what he'd been waiting to hear, Brian eased up to his feet and then pressed his body against hers. Every inch of her, yearned to become one with him. When their lips met, he tasted like her, and the heady aroma of sex had her delving deeper into him.

After a long, amazing, taste, she broke the kiss and cupped his face. "Fuck. Me. Now." Jillian hadn't meant to sound so demanding, but between her tiger and her human, she had to have him.

"I can't wait any longer either." He grabbed her butt. "Wrap your legs around my waist. I don't know what's happening to me. It's like I'm combusting inside."

If Jillian had the strength, she would have smiled. She bet his bear was ready to roar, and when he did, she'd be right there alongside him. With her back to the wall for support, she hung on tight as Brian placed his thick cock at her entrance. He hesitated.

Take him, her tiger demanded.

Hell yeah she would. Jillian sunk down on him but had to stop halfway when the stretching became too intense.

"God, you feel good." Brian trailed kisses up her neck before nabbing the shell of her ear with his teeth.

Her body caught fire as he traced the edge with his tongue. Why was he taking his time? He'd lick then inhale as if savoring the moment. Wait until his bear emerged fully. They might never see slow again.

Withdrawing part way, he waited a second before easing back in. This time she was able to handle all of him. She sat up straighter and arched her back, begging him to suck on her tits.

Taking the hint, he stepped away from the wall and dipped his head. The first tug on her nipple left her breathless. He licked, sucked, and twirled until she was so hot that her nails sharpened into points.

"Hurry, Brian. You don't want me to shift on you." And she would too. Soon.

"No." Slipping his hands up to her waist, he lifted her up at the same time he eased out.

Capturing her lips, he thrust into her, and all hell broke loose. Jillian dug her heels into the sides of his thighs for better purchase and rode right along with him. He'd plunge in just as she'd drop down. They kissed, moaned, dipped, and fucked hard. Time seemed to stand still, and no matter how fast he drove into her, she wanted more. With each foray, he took her closer to that point where she'd reach wonderful oblivion.

Tongues entwined, and on the next surge, Brian plunged into her so deeply that Jillian cried out his name as her release shoved her over the edge. His cock exploded a second later and he dipped his head to her neck. For a second, she allowed herself the luxury of imagining his sharp bear teeth sinking into her skin and mating with her.

What if it never happens? her tiger asked.

It will.

NOT WANTING TO let go, Brian kept his arms around Jillian, long after both of their hearts had slowed. His whole life he'd wanted to be with someone who understood what he'd gone through. Then Jillian had walked into his life with a fury and embraced him. Her tiger and his bear were so close to becoming one that he could taste it, but his head just couldn't figure out how to draw out the creature inside him.

If I fail, will she leave me? that stupid voice asked.

Brian refused to worry about something that far in the future. It was destructive. As his therapist always said: Think positively and you can make it happen.

Brian slipped out of her. "I'll get something to clean us up with."

He trotted to the bathroom, wondering how much of Jillian's attraction to him came from her tiger and how much was her actually liking him? Doubt was like a cancer that should be avoided at all cost, but he couldn't help it. The facts kept stacking up. She was a lawyer for God's sake, living in a big city, and Brian was a wannabe carpenter with only a few tools to his name. Sure, he'd saved his money over the years, but it wasn't a fortune by any means.

He'd grown up in a fairly rural area in Ohio. What if she changed her mind and decided not to move out here because she missed LA so much? If she asked him to go back with her, would he be able to cope? And what would happen with Elana? Brian had already fallen in love with Aiden even though he'd only seen his nephew a few times. Having family close was what had helped him heal this much in the first place. He needed to stop worrying about something that might not occur.

"Brian?" she called.

"Sorry." He'd been standing in front of the sink. He nabbed a clean towel, wet it, and returned. He gently cleaned her up, and then wiped off. As much as he wanted to sit and talk about her needs and desires, from the way she was looking off to the side, that madman had returned to the forefront of her mind.

In silence, they both dressed. "Let me get my keys and I'll follow you home," he said.

Her shoulders sagged. "You don't have to."

Really? "Jillian, I want to. If that crazy man is out there, what better time to harm you than on a dark road at night?"

She held up her hands. "You're right. I can't be too careful. You need to be aware of your surroundings too. If he shifts and attacks, you wouldn't survive."

"I'll look before I move about."

She sidled up to him and pressed against him. "You're too good to me. First the beautiful box, then the amazing sex, and now you want to protect me." She lifted her head and kissed him tenderly. "Thank you."

"You're welcome, but don't worry. I understand my limits. I'd ask you to stay here, but Dalton can protect you better." He kissed her back, fearing that if he delved into her sweetness again, he wouldn't be able to stop.

She nodded. "True."

He helped her on with her coat and then escorted her downstairs. This time Jillian insisted on poking her head out first, claiming she could sense if Frank Whitlaw was near. When she signaled it was safe, Brian walked her to her car then jumped into his.

All through the drive back to Dalton's house, he kept his gaze on the rear view mirror. As he considered Jillian's situation, he realized there might be worse things in life than having bad parents—such as someone who wanted to kill you.

Once he'd come to grips with the fact that he was part bear, he wondered if as a child he had been a nightmare. His human side could have been fighting his inner bear, creating a child no parent could control. Add in the fact that his parents were totally human and his mother was embarrassed by her indiscretion, and it was a disaster waiting to happen.

WHEN JILLIAN ENTERED Dalton's house, he was on the phone with his back to the entrance. She set Brian's present on the dining room table then slipped off her coat.

"When did he arrive?" Dalton asked the caller.

He didn't seem to hear that she'd come in, so she softly called to him. "Hi, I'm home."

Her brother waved a hand then paced in front of the kitchen island, his gaze on some far away place on the floor. "I think Kip should keep an eye on Jillian. Whitlaw will think he's some ordinary man and won't give him a second glance."

Jillian's stomach tumbled. Did Dalton just say a bodyguard was necessary? While she didn't know what kind of shifter Whitlaw was, she had mad skills of her own. Her tiger was not only powerful, she was fast. Hell, Whitlaw would never know what hit him if she attacked.

Regret swamped her. She should have charged Whitlaw the moment he came out of her house and put an end to his miserable life. Then again, explaining how a man died from a tiger bite that close to the city would have raised an insane number of questions.

Dalton turned around and nodded to her. "I can drive her over tomorrow. Yes, I agree. See you at nine."

Dalton disconnected and faced her. "That was Connor."

She was having a hard time keeping up with everyone. "Who is he?"

"He runs McKinnon and Associates. You were right; Whitlaw is here. He boarded a plane out of Los Angeles two days ago and rented a car in Knoxville. None of the hotels have a man by the name of Frank Whitlaw staying with them, but he's probably using an alias."

And here Dalton thought he wasn't that smart. "I heard you mention Teagan's mate, Kip. So he'll be my bodyguard?"

"Yes."

"What can he do to stop Whitlaw?"

"Remember when I was telling you about the incredible retrieval of Kip's brother's powers?"

"That was him? The one who zapped a few guards and cut the electricity to the bunker?"

"Yes."

Okay, maybe he would make a good bodyguard. "I trust Kip will keep his distance. I want Whitlaw to make his move, so I can fight him. I'm going to take great satisfaction in killing him."

"Whoa. You will not engage with him. Who's to say he doesn't have some Wendayan powers of his own?"

Shit. She hadn't thought of that. "Fine, but I make no promises. I need to be ready if he attacks me."

"We'll make certain that doesn't happen."

"If you say so."

"Jilly, don't be that way." He came up to her and gave her a hug. "You're my sister. My only sister. It would kill Mom if anything happened to you."

"Only mom? You wouldn't shed a tear?"

He smiled. "You know better. Oh, by the way, Mom called."

"What did she say?" Her pulse sped up.

"She was worried about you. She stopped by your house two days in a row, and of course, you weren't there."

"Did you tell her about Whitlaw?" Their mom would freak, but she wouldn't try to take the law into her own hands. She understood the system too well.

"Yes. I wanted her to be on her guard. She said she would be careful."

"I'll call her later—using your phone."

"Perfect. On a different note, Connor wants us to stop over at the office tomorrow to go over a plan. We all need to be on the same page when Whitlaw makes his move."

For the first time since she'd taken off from California, she felt as if that ass would finally be caught and thrown in jail. Or even better—killed.

Chapter Seventeen

JILLIAN, DALTON, AND Connor sat across from Kalan, Jackson, and Kip at a large table in the McKinnon and Associates office. Dalton had said that both Connor's and Jackson's dads were building a new office for them, but she didn't see the need. This place was already up-to-date, if the projection system and Smart Board on the wall were any indication. Hell, even the entrance was nice. It had comfortable looking sofas and chairs, and the pictures of the Smokey Mountains on both walls gave off a serene vibe.

The main room was more practical. It was divided into two sections. Near the back of the room, across from the coffee station, sat a table surrounded by cushioned chairs. Off to the side was a sofa and two lounge chairs. According to Dalton, the doors across from the coffee machine led to private offices. The front half of the room had a table positioned parallel to the wall along with eight chairs facing it. It was where they were now seated. Apparently, Jackson needed to set up his computer that was now displaying a large picture of Frank Whitlaw. Damn but those eyes seemed to be mocking her.

"I found this photo on the LAPD's website," Jackson said. "Jillian, would you say this one is fairly current?"

She studied her father's killer once more. "He's a bit older now. I'm guessing he was probably twenty-five when he killed our dad, which puts him at about fifty."

Using a red laser, Jackson circled the scar on Whitlaw's face and addressed the rest of the group. "This is his most recognizable marking. Judging from some pictures I found of him standing with others, he's probably six feet." He looked over at her and she nodded. "Whitlaw rented a gray Ford Taurus at the Knoxville Airport, but there is no guarantee he didn't stash it somewhere and steal someone else's car. I've asked Kalan to check for any reported stolen vehicles within a hundred mile radius."

"On my to-do list," Kalan assured them.

Jackson passed around a piece of paper to each of them. "Here are some contact numbers. Communication is key." He looked straight at her. "Jillian, this is especially critical for you. When you're not with Dalton, please let Kip know if you need to go anywhere."

"Okay. I should give you Brian's number, since I'm often with him."

"His number is on there," Jackson said.

Jillian glanced down and spotted it. Heat raced up her face. "That's good."

Connor picked up his mug and took a long drink. "I'll be making a list of times we each need to either be looking for Whitlaw or following him should his location be discovered. I don't need to remind you that if he spots a tail, he may abort his mission. While we don't like that he's after Jillian, we do want him to attempt something so this nightmare can be ended."

Everyone nodded. "How are you going to find him?" Jillian asked. "If he's been able to avoid being caught for twenty-five years, he has skills."

"Don't worry," Connor said. "We have our ways. For starters, there are a lot of shifters and Wendayans in our community. They will be our eyes and ears. From what Dalton told us, you're either at Blooms of Hope or at his house. Whitlaw will have to be close to one of those two places. When he is, we'll make sure he doesn't leave our sight. As difficult as this may be, when you want to see Brian, I suggest you remain at his place or Dalton's."

"I agree. When Whitlaw found me the first time, Brian and I were at the Carnival. I believe being surrounded by so many people helped keep him at bay." She glanced around to each of them. Their serious demeanor and determined looks gave her confidence that this nightmare would be over soon. "Thank you all for everything. I've been a nervous wreck ever since he murdered my friend."

"Just so you know, we won't be able to apprehend him until he does something illegal," Connor said.

"I understand." It was all she could ask for.

Dalton stood. "I'll take my sister home now."

She turned toward him. "I need to go back to the store."

"It's Sunday," Dalton said.

"We're open today and closed on Monday. Even if Frank Whitlaw didn't exist, I'd go in to work. I don't want to leave Anna alone. The weekends are our busiest time."

Kip stood. "I guess that means I'm up. I'll head into town and find a spot to watch you from."

She tried to smile, but her lips wouldn't cooperate. "It's scary knowing I'm a target, but having all of you helping gives me peace of mind."

The rest of the group stood. Dalton placed a hand on her shoulder then led her out. During the ride home, her brother thankfully didn't lecture her or try to convince her to remain locked up in his house. He must have realized he couldn't change her mind.

Once he arrived at his place, she moved from his car to hers then headed into work. Dalton followed her at a discreet distance. Once she parked in back of the shop, Jillian waved to him then went inside. Dalton said he wouldn't leave the lot until she'd closed the back door.

Anna was in the front helping a customer and smiled as soon as Jillian came in. While she waited for her to finish up, Jillian kept an eye on the road in front of the store. A minute later, she spotted Dalton's car. Jillian was tempted to rush out the door and wave to let him know she was safe, that Whitlaw wasn't inside, but she knew the goal was to keep everything looking normal.

Because there was only one customer, and Anna was taking care of her, Jillian went into the back room to straighten up. Having order helped calm her. While she cleaned, Jillian listened for footsteps above her, but she didn't detect any. She thought Brian had said he'd be home today, and that tomorrow he was doing a double shift, but perhaps she had it backwards. She certainly hadn't been her sharpest since leaving Los Angeles.

Jillian had to chuckle at Brian when he said he'd asked to work longer hours. Now that she'd put the bug in his ear about possibly having a shop of his own, he said he needed to earn as much as he could to finance his dream. He assured her that he wasn't trying to avoid her. Until Frank Whitlaw was brought to justice, he agreed with Dalton that Jillian would be better off under her brother's watchful eye.

For the rest of the morning, she and Anna kept busy with customers, but Jillian still managed to sneak some peaks outside, trying to spot either Kip or Whitlaw. When both remained out of sight, she eventually began to relax.

Close to twelve, the flow of customers had basically stopped. Anna emerged from the back. "Would you mind if I take an hour to visit Elana? I'll go through the drive through on the way back so that I'm not gone too long."

"Unless anyone asks for a special order, I'm good." Jillian's breath caught, remembering she needed to warn Anna. "I need to tell you that Whitlaw is in town."

"Who?"

"Frank Whitlaw, the cop who killed my friend back in Los Angeles."

"Oh, shit. I'll stay. I'm not leaving you."

If Whitlaw showed up, Jillian wasn't sure how having Anna there would help anyway. "Don't be silly. Go see Elana. Dalton hired a bodyguard to watch the store, but you still need to be careful whenever you go out."

"Why? Are you saying he might come after me because I'm your friend?"

Jillian shrugged. "He's already killed one of my friends, though it was possible he thought Dalia was me. I'm not discounting the possibility that he wants me to know that if I talk, he's capable of killing someone else I care about."

"Oh."

"Just be careful. I just don't want you to get caught in the cross-fire."

"Then I'll be extra aware of my surroundings at all times." She patted her purse. "Plus, I have my gun in here. Besides, I'm only driving three miles."

Jillian gave Anna her most reassuring smile. "You'll be fine. Give Aiden a kiss and Elana a hug for me."

She smiled. "Will do."

Once Anna left, Jillian felt oddly vulnerable, despite knowing that if Whitlaw had entered the store when Anna was there, her friend would have been more of a liability. Jillian debated texting Kip to make sure he still had an eye on everything, but then swallowed her worry. Let the bastard walk into her shop. If he shifted, she'd shift, and he'd be dead in minutes. Even if he remained a human and attacked her, she'd be on the other side of the room before he could even blink.

Hell, she wished he tried something.

When the bell above the door dinged, her heart almost stopped. It was Kip.

"Hey," he said, looking around. "I saw your friend leave. Everything okay?"

He had been watching. "Yes. She's off to visit Elana. I'm here just waiting for Whitlaw to make his move."

"We all are. Finding him first would take a load off my mind."

"Me too."

Kip walked over to the cooler containing the flowers. "I thought I'd pick up something for Teagan. What do you suggest?"

Most likely he wanted to make his visit look legit. She scanned the options. It might have been because Jillian was so fond of daisies that she pulled out a vase full of them that were interspersed with zinnias. "What do you think of this one?"

He smiled, pulled out his wallet, and handed her his credit card. "Teagan will love them."

"Awesome." She rang up the purchase. "Say hi to Teagan for me. I'm sorry we didn't get to spend much time together at your party."

He nodded. "We have Aiden Murdoch to blame for that."

Jillian chuckled. "That we do. When this mess is over, I'd like to get to know her better. I've never even spoken with another Wendayan that I know of before coming here—other than my mother of course."

His brows rose. "Seriously?"

"If any existed in Los Angeles, they weren't seeking me out."

"I'm sure the community here will welcome you." He picked up the vase. "Text me if you see anything suspicious."

"I will, and thank you."

As soon as Kip left, Jillian took the opportunity to clean the glass cooler doors. No other customers came in, but she suspected the overcast skies might have caused people to think of staying inside where it was warm. To her, it was the dreary days that demanded something cheery—like flowers.

For the next hour, Jillian moved between the back room and the front, twice checking that the back door was locked. The only way anyone could get in would be if someone had the code.

I am not paranoid, she told her tiger who mocked her with each door check. Her animal really wanted a piece of Whitlaw.

Around two, Jillian began to wonder what was taking Anna so long. She said she'd be gone no longer than an hour. Most likely she and Elana got to chatting and time ran away from them. Once three o'clock rolled around, and Anna still hadn't returned, Jillian pulled out the sheet with the phone numbers on it, hoping Jackson had included Elana's number. Sure enough, hers was there, as was their Alpha's number next to Izzy's. Given her talents, Jillian could see why someone might want to contact her.

Jillian dialed Elana. When she answered, the baby was crying in the background. "Hello, Elana, this is Jillian."

"Oh, Jillian. Is everything okay?"

That was an odd response. "I hope so. Has Anna left?"

"Anna?"

Hadn't Jillian spoken clearly? "Anna left at noon to visit you. Oh shit. Didn't she arrive?"

"No. Oh, my goddess. Did you try her cell?"

When Jillian and Anna had been at McKinnon's Pub, they'd exchanged numbers, but Jillian had scribbled it on a napkin and hadn't put it in her cell yet. She wasn't sure what she'd done with the paper. "No. Can you give me the number?"

"It's 459-5555. Call me back and let me know what you find out."

"Will do." As soon as she hung up, she dialed Anna, but her cell went to voicemail. Damn. "Anna, it's Jillian. I hope you're okay. Call me when you get this message."

If she'd broken down somewhere, she would have called the shop number to let Jillian know what happened. A sinking feeling swirled in her gut. Jillian should call Kip and asked him to check on Anna's whereabouts, but he'd say his job was to watch her, so she called the next best person—Dalton.

"Did you see him?" her brother asked as soon as he picked up his phone.

"No." She explained that Anna was supposed to be visiting Elana but she never showed up. "I tried calling her cell, but it went to voicemail. I'm hoping she just broke down on her way to Elana's."

"Let's hope. I'll retrace her steps and call you back as soon as I can."

"Thank you."

Jillian's hands shook. Was this Frank Whitlaw's doing? If he wanted to mess with her mind, he was doing a good job.

While she waited for her brother to call back, she futzed around in the back room. Because the store would close in an hour anyway, she figured it would be okay to put the Closed sign out and lock the front door. She didn't need anyone walking in when she was in the back—and by anyone, she meant Frank Whitlaw.

Her cell rang, jumpstarting her heart. "Hello?"

"Any news on Anna," Elana asked.

Jillian let out a huge breath and leaned against the large table in back. "No. I couldn't reach her so I called Dalton. He's checking the roads now. I promise to call if I find out anything."

"Thanks."

No sooner had she disconnected than her cell buzzed again. Jillian checked the caller ID but all it said was Private Caller. It wasn't Dalton.

Her underarms began to sweat. *Answer it.* Jillian swiped her cell. "Hello?"

"Jillian, it's Camille. I wanted to see how you were."

Once more, she sagged against the table. "I'd be lying if I said I was good. Whitlaw is here. In Silver Lake."

"Shit. What are you going to do?"

"Wait it out. I now have a bodyguard." She explained that a group of professionals were searching for him. Given what a sneaky bastard he was, Jillian hoped he hadn't bugged Camille's phone, though if he had, it might work in Jillian's favor. If he thought he was a wanted man, he might leave her alone.

Dream on.

"Frank told his partner that his mother was ill and that he wasn't sure when he'd be back."

Jillian shook her head. "What a douchebag. You didn't let on that you knew anything, did you?'

"No, but if he contacts Maria or anyone else asking for information, I'll let you know." Someone in the background called Camille's name. "Hey, I gotta go. Keep in touch and be safe."

"Will do." Relief filled her just knowing so many people had her back.

It wasn't until close to five that Dalton called. "Yes? Did you find Anna?"

"I found Anna's car. It looks as if she was run off the road."

Her chest squeezed tight. "Where's Anna?"

"I don't know. I called Jackson and Connor. They're both checking the road to the hospital in case she headed that way."

"If she were injured, she'd have called 911. Where's her purse?" The one with the gun in it.

"Let me check if it's inside." A car door opened. "Got it. It was on the floor in the front seat."

"Look inside and see if her cell phone or her gun are there."

A moment later he answered. "No to either."

Her heart broke. "Shit. That means Whitlaw might have her."

Chapter Eighteen

"JILLIAN?" BRIAN CALLED a second after the back door to the building clicked close.

She spun around and ran into his arms. "I'm so glad you're here."

He leaned back. "I saw the Closed sign on the door when I drove by. What's happened? Did Whitlaw try to get in?"

"No." She told him about Anna and her car wreck. "I think Whitlaw has her."

Brian stroked her face. "You can't be sure of that."

Jillian sniffled. "I know, but Anna's purse was still in the car. She'd never leave without it."

"Will Dalton come here to follow you home?"

"Yes, but I think he's still at the accident scene."

Brian wrapped an arm around her waist. "How about coming upstairs then? You can call him from there and tell him where you are."

She was happy someone with a clear head was near. "Okay."

Jillian gathered her jacket and purse and followed him up the stairs. This time when Brian closed the door, he threw the deadbolt. "There. You're safe."

She fished out her cell and checked to see if by some miracle, Anna had texted her. Nothing. Jillian tried to think what she'd do if she'd been in an accident. She'd call 911 and wait.

Jillian swiped her phone and pressed Dalton's number. He answered on the first ring.

"You okay?"

"Yes. Brian's back, and I'm at his apartment. I was wondering if you had called the hospital to see if they'd received a 911 call from Anna."

"Jillian. Please. Let me handle this." *Let me handle this,* she mocked back. Anna was her friend. "It was one of the first things I did after checking the area. The hospital said they hadn't received a call from her, but Jackson is checking her cell records now in case she called someone else."

"Was there any blood in the car?" She wanted to know if Anna had been severely injured in the crash.

"No. I did, however, find one set of footprints that were rather large next to the car that had been kicked and scuffed as if to disguise them. They could possibly belong to Whitlaw."

Damn. "What do you need me to do?"

"Stay where you are. I should be there in a bit. I'll call when I'm at the back door."

"What about Kip? He doesn't need to stay."

"He'll stay until you're with me. I'll text him where you are."

She'd never heard such tension in Dalton's voice before. "Okay."

As soon as she disconnected, Brian handed her a glass of wine. "Thought you could use this." He sat next to her with his beer. "Why would Whitlaw take Anna?"

"Your guess is as good as mine, but it has to be to lure me someplace."

He tipped back his beer. "If he's been following you, he has to know you'll bring backup."

"I'm not sure what he knows other than you're with me and my brother is a cop. He might have a plan to take the three of us out if we show up."

"So now what?"

"We wait." It was one of Jillian's worst traits. "If I didn't think my brother would kill me himself, I'd give Kip the slip and hunt

Whitlaw since I know what he smells like."

Brian ran a comforting hand down her arm. "How close do you need to be to detect him?"

"Too close." She slunk back against the sofa arm. "I feel so helpless."

He leaned over and kissed her cheek. "We'll get him."

She hoped so. Her cell rang and she jerked. "Hey. Are you downstairs?"

"I'm close. How about asking Brian to pack a bag and stay the night at my place? I don't want Whitlaw to get any ideas. Rye McKinnon rounded up a few men to watch the shop in case Whitlaw tries anything."

Hoped surged through her. "That would be great. Thank you. I'll ask him."

"Meet me in the back when you're ready."

"You're the best brother ever."

"Keep thinking that." His chuckle was brief.

She swiped off the phone and faced Brian. "You've been invited to spend the night at Dalton's."

His brows rose. "In your bed?"

"It's only a double bed, but I'm sure we can make do. If it is too cramped, I can always shift and sleep on the floor. That way, if anything happens I'll be ready."

"Can I pet you?"

"Only if you behave." Jillian winked and stood. "Get packing. Dalton will be waiting out back."

DALTON TOSSED THE keys on the kitchen counter. "Brian, you can sleep in my room."

Jillian was thirty-two and didn't need her brother dictating who she slept with. "You have to know we've already slept together."

Dalton faced her. "This isn't about sex. It's about the fact that I plan to sleep on the sofa in case anyone tries to get to you. I don't know what kind of shifter Whitlaw is, but I suspect I could take down a bear if need be. I know for a fact I can handle a wolf."

"I'm sorry. I didn't mean to snipe at you, but I've been stressing out ever since Anna's accident."

One side of his mouth lifted up. "I understand. I'm on edge too. Don't forget, he was my father too."

Now she felt like a heel. "I know."

Brian wrapped an arm around her shoulder, providing some much-needed comfort. "I'm good sleeping in Dalton's room. It's probably better if we're not together. You need to keep your wits about you."

"You're right." If she and Brian shared the bed, they'd be distracted in seconds.

"Now that that's settled," Dalton said, "I need to rustle up some food."

"Rustle up some food?" That almost made her chuckle. "So Tennessee is the Wild West now?"

"I'm just trying to blend in with the locals." Dalton winked then slipped into the kitchen. He opened the fridge and pulled out a dozen eggs along with a package of bacon.

She wanted to shake him. "Why are we just sitting here when Anna is out there?"

"Because Whitlaw wants you to go after her. When you do, he'll pounce."

"That would be hard since I don't know where she is."

He pulled a frying pan out of the cabinet and set it on the stove. "For your sake, that might be a good thing. I can't be sure, but I bet he wants Anna alive to use as bait. Remember, he's after you."

"I haven't forgotten. So, he's just going to call and invite me to his place? Wherever that is?"

Dalton shrugged. "He might. He has Anna's cell. Does she have your number programmed?"

"Most likely. I wrote it on a napkin when we were having drinks."

"Make sure your cell is on and charged then."

"Good thinking." Jillian checked her purse and made sure it was turned on. "I guess all we can do is wait."

Dalton stopped what he was doing. "I know you think no one is doing anything, but on my way over to Blooms of Hope, I called Connor. He said Rye was rounding up the wolves. Some will keep watch over the shop, while others plan to shift and scour the area for both of them."

That was more than she thought anyone was doing. "Do you know if Kalan learned of any stolen vehicles?" Knowing the make and model of Whitlaw's vehicle would help.

"I haven't spoken with him, but if he learned anything, he'd tell Connor and the rest of the team. Right now, they need us to stay put. The last thing anyone needs is to have two women snatched."

He dumped some butter in the pan and then turned on the burner. After locating a bowl, he cracked a dozen eggs into it and then added milk. Next he whipped them so hard she bet they'd become pure air.

"Will they call if they find anything?" she asked, her patience having run out a while ago.

Dalton inhaled and looked at her for a few seconds before answering. "Connor promised to keep me in the loop. If they find where Whitlaw's keeping Anna, they might send Ainsley in to check out the place."

"Ainsley?" Brian asked. "She's just a slip of a woman."

Dalton poured the egg mixture into the pan. "Ainsley has a special Wendayan talent."

"What's that?" Jillian asked.

Brian lifted a finger. "I remember. Ainsley can disappear and move about without notice."

She looked at Brian and then glanced over at her brother who nodded. "I wish I could do that," Jillian said.

"Me too." Dalton placed the bacon on a tray, covered it with a paper towel, and shoved it in the microwave. He stirred the eggs, and when they were done cooking, he placed them on three plates. The microwave oven dinged just as her cell chimed.

She had a message, and every muscle froze. When she saw Anna's name on the message her hope soared. Brian leaned close as she tapped the screen. "It's a video."

Heart in her throat, she pressed the arrow. "As you can see, Ms. Garner, your friend is still alive, but barely. Meet me in fifteen minutes or she dies. And come alone. Take Pine Avenue to Crandall Boulevard and head left. I'll find you."

The video continued for another few seconds, but the only sounds were Anna's whimpers. Jillian's need to kill soared.

Dalton stepped next to her. A strong light was shining on her friend who was gagged and tied to a chair. Her left eye was swollen shut, her lip was cut and bleeding, and her cheek bruised. Jillian grabbed her stomach, needing to vomit. She looked up at Brian and then at Dalton. "I have to go."

Brian squeezed her shoulder. "You can't. This is what he wants."

"I will not have another friend's death on my hands," she said between gritted teeth.

Dalton held out his hand and wiggled his fingers for her phone. "I want to send this to Connor. He might be able to figure out where this is."

"Whitlaw put a white sheet behind her to disguise the location."

"You'd be surprised what those guys can figure out."

Jillian handed him the phone. "I need to go."

"I'm coming with you," Brian said.

She loved that he wanted to protect her, but she had to do this alone. "I don't want to lose you too."

"Brian, Jilly's right. We'll follow behind discreetly," Dalton said. "I promise he won't suspect a thing. I've been trained to be invisible."

Someone having her back made her feel better. "If you're sure he won't know."

"He won't." He handed her phone back to her. "Message sent."

Dalton walked around the counter and hugged her. "Be careful."

"I will."

Brian hugged her and whispered in her ear. "I can't lose you."

"You won't."

Even though her heart was slamming against her chest and her stomach was threatening to upheave, she had to do this for Dalia, for her dad, and for Anna. *Please let Whitlaw be a wolf.*

Dalton gave her brief instructions on how to reach Pine Avenue. "You can't miss Crandall. Pine Avenue dead ends at it."

Once Brian helped her on with her jacket, she grabbed her purse and keys. "Wish me luck."

"Luck." His chin wobbled. Brian then grabbed her to his chest again and pressed his cheek against hers. "I'm scared."

"Me too."

His hold tightened as he dipped his head and inhaled. "This can't be goodbye. You have to promise me."

Jillian sniffled and leaned her head back. She tried to give him a confident smile, but the corners of her lips refused to hold the pose. "I promise. You're my mate and mates never leave each other."

His eyes watered as he slanted his lips over hers. Her tiger rose to the surface to greet him as he deepened the kiss.

"Jillian," Dalton said. "You don't want to be late."

They broke the kiss. "You're right."

She looked deep into Brian's eyes and the love she saw gave her courage. As much as she wanted to tell him that she loved him, her heart wasn't strong enough right now.

Brian stroked her cheek with his knuckle. "Be safe."

Before she broke down, Jillian twisted around and rushed out the door. Cold air met her as she dashed out of the house.

I can do this.

Hell, yeah you can. I can't wait to claw the bastard's throat out, her suddenly vicious tiger warned.

We have to be patient. We need to find Anna first.

Leaving Brian had been so hard, but it was what she had to do.

Because her hands shook so much, it took her a few tries to fit the key into the door lock, and then two more attempts before the engine turned over. Once on the road, she found Pine Avenue easily. As much as she wanted to speed so that she could reach Anna faster, she wanted to give Dalton and Brian time to follow her. At least they knew where she was headed.

Not only did she glance at the clock to make sure she wouldn't be late, she kept looking in the rear view mirror trying to spot Dalton and Brian. The sun had set, making it dark enough to detect headlights, but she couldn't see any. Either they hadn't left the house yet, or her brother was one stealthy cop.

By the time she reached Crandall Avenue, her stomach was in a thousand knots. She shouldn't be nervous. Her tiger was strong. Unless Whitlaw shot her multiple times, she'd survive. The chances of him even having time to raise his weapon though were slim. The second he went for his gun, she'd shift and attack. Being able to move almost instantaneously would assure that she would succeed.

Her headlights illuminated the road's end. She came to a stop at the intersection then checked both ways. No cars were on the road in either direction. Following Whitlaw's instruction, Jillian turned left but didn't see him. What kind of game was he playing?

About a quarter of a mile down the road, a car pulled out from the berm and turned into the road to face her. The bright lights nearly blinded her. Unless she drove around him, she had to stop. Not wanting to block traffic should anyone come her way, she edged over onto the berm.

Now what?

Chapter Nineteen

THE TEMPTATION TO jump out and shift was strong, but Jillian had to think of Anna.

Whitlaw opened his car door, and when the light illuminated his face, acid burned in her gut at his image. Her nails extended and her bones cracked. She wanted to take him down so fucking bad.

Head slightly forward, he marched toward her car. Oh, shit. Because she didn't know if he wanted her to follow him or what, she stayed where she was.

Whitlaw yanked open her door. "Get out."

Jillian slipped her keys into her purse. As she slung the strap over her shoulder, he yanked on her arm. "Leave your purse and keys." His arrogant command grated on every one of her nerves. Asshat.

Dalton would not be pleased. He'd added an app to her burner phone that would allow him to trace her location. Now, he'd be blind.

"Mind if I move my car completely off the road? I doubt you want the police to investigate an abandoned car blocking traffic."

He huffed out a laugh. "Those incompetents couldn't find a rock if it hit them in the face."

The urge to defend Dalton and his friends was strong, but she bit back the words. Let Whitlaw think he was invincible. He tugged on her arm again. If she hadn't been able to stick her leg out for balance, she would have fallen. Drawing on her animal strength, she tried to jerk out of his grasp, but he held on.

Once she managed to stand, she glanced back toward Pine Avenue, wondering where Dalton and Brian were. Hopefully, they'd stopped at Pine Avenue, and were waiting there before continuing. She had no doubt that they'd find her car, but they wouldn't know where she'd gone.

With long strides, Whitlaw half dragged her back to his car. He jerked open the passenger side and shoved her. "Get in."

Jillian debated running for it, but she needed to do what he said for Anna's sake. Whitlaw slid into the driver's seat. Sitting so close to him had her heart pounding hard and her mouth turning as dry as sandpaper. Jillian wasn't sure if she could even look at the vile man, but she didn't want the bastard to think she feared him.

"We meet once more," Whitlaw said with too much glee.

She ground her teeth together. "You killed my father." She hadn't meant to blurt that out, but it had been burning inside her for way too long to keep it contained.

"You're direct, aren't you. I like a woman with spunk."

She didn't give a fuck what he liked. "Why did you kill him? He was a fellow officer."

"Tsk, tsk. Such an idealist. If you must know, your father threatened to turn me in to Internal Affairs."

She swiveled toward him, needing more information. As if his confession meant little to him, he smoothly pulled onto the road and headed back toward Pine Avenue. As they neared the 3-way intersection, a white SUV turned left onto Crandall Boulevard. She fisted her hands. That was Dalton. She released her grip, not needing Whitlaw to know they had company.

Dalton would see her car and might assume they would continue heading west. Hope drained out of her. *Focus*, her tiger urged.

"So that's why Dad wanted to turn you in. You were a dirty cop."

"*Dirty* is such a nasty word. I was helping myself to what would otherwise sit in the evidence locker for years and rot. So many of the unused weapons would never be used again, and the drugs were destined to be burned. That was such a waste of money. Hell, I was doing the station a favor by getting rid of some of that stuff, but your father didn't share in my beliefs. When he suspected I was the thief, he said he was going to turn me in. I couldn't let that happen."

So her father died because he was doing his duty. Life wasn't fair. "And Dalia? What did she ever do to you?"

He sighed. "That was an unfortunate error on my part." Whitlaw glanced over at her. "I thought it was you, though now I suspect I went to the guest room instead of the master."

Jillian's heart ached for her friend. If Jillian had been in the house, she would have sensed the bastard and killed him then and there. "Where's Anna?"

"Someplace safe. You'll see her shortly. Oh, how I'm going to take great pleasure torturing her in front of your eyes."

"That so?" *Shut up.*

"Don't worry. I'll let you die a noble death right next to her."

Jillian grabbed the door handle. "I'd like to see you try."

"THAT'S JILLIAN'S CAR," Brian said pointing to the blue vehicle off to the side of the road.

"Which means she's in Whitlaw's car." Dalton slapped the wheel then pulled over.

"Why are you stopping?" They needed to go after Jillian. Unfortunately, he didn't know where that was.

"I need to think. Didn't you see the gray sedan head in the opposite direction just now?"

"You think that was him?"

"It looked like the car he'd rented." Dalton put his SUV in drive and did a U-turn. Just then his cell rang. He picked up his phone and glanced at the screen. "It's Connor," he told Brian. He placed the cell to his ear. "What did you find out?" He listened for what seemed like a full minute. "You're sure? Okay, okay. We'll meet you there." He disconnected.

"What did he say?"

"Connor didn't explain how they figured it out, other than Jackson's drone was involved, but they found Anna. She's being held at the site where Jackson's and Connor's fathers are building the new office."

"Really? It's almost like Whitlaw wanted her to be found."

"I doubt Whitlaw knows who owns it."

Being a cop, Whitlaw had means and skills to break in. "Didn't you say it was mostly finished?"

Dalton shrugged. "There are walls and a roof, but not much else. We're meeting the team there."

"What's the plan?" Brian hoped it involved taking down Whitlaw as soon as he arrived. "Did Connor and his men free Anna?"

"We'll find out when we get there." When they reached Pine Avenue, instead of keeping straight, Dalton hung a right.

"Where are you going?"

"Taking a short cut," Dalton said as calm as could be.

Five minutes later, he pulled into a lot about a block away from the building. His cell rang again. "Yes? They are? What do you want us to do? Okay?" Dalton turned to Brian. "Whitlaw's been spotted. He'll be here in less than a minute."

Brian wanted to rush over to him and kill the bastard, but he understood if Whitlaw shifted, Brian would be dead in a matter of seconds. That caused his hatred for the man to fester even further. With the overhead car light turned off, they eased out of Dalton's SUV and then kept to the shadows. As the gray car came to a stop, Dalton squatted and Brian followed suit. The passenger side door opened, and when Jillian eased out some of the tension in Brian's muscles released. She was safe, for now.

All of a sudden, gravel spewed and some of the rocks pinged against the car. Brian blinked and then Jillian was gone. What the hell? One of the doors to the building banged open. Holy shit. Was that Jillian? She'd said she was fast, but he had never imagined she could be that speedy.

Whitlaw smacked his hand against the car hood and took off toward the building. Brian expected the team to appear en masse and charge after him, but other than Whitlaw shouting at Jillian and his feet smacking against the cement, the area was bathed in silence.

What was everyone waiting for? The woman Brian loved was being chased by a man who'd killed at least two other people and had beaten a third. These men were doing nothing! If any harm came to her, he'd make them all pay.

Go after her, his inner voice counseled.

Fucking A, I will.

Brian jumped up, and just as he was about to charge, a shot rang out from inside the building. His bear went crazy.

Not waiting for Dalton or any of the other men to do something, Brian darted into the open, heading toward Jillian. Footsteps echoed from behind and to the right of him. Now they acted? They better not be trying to stop him.

Jillian screamed, but he couldn't be certain if it was from outrage or pain. All Brian could think of was saving her. As he tore open the door to rush into the dark, his bones cracked, and his vision blurred.

What the hell? Pain seared his gut and mouth, and he swore his face had been set on fire. As he crashed into the large room, his hands met the cement floor—or rather his furry paws met the floor. Holy hell. He'd shifted. As much as he wanted to celebrate this miracle, he didn't have time.

A lone flashlight pointed upward, barely illuminating the exposed beamed ceiling, but it was enough to see blood pouring from Jillian's side. He froze. Next to her, Anna was hunched over in a chair. Whitlaw was fifteen feet from the women with a gun raised, aimed at Jillian.

As if a power from above sent a charge through him, Brian rushed Whitlaw. A deep throaty roar emitted from Brian's mouth, startling him as well as his enemy. Whitlaw whipped toward him, the gun clasped in both hands.

The sound of the shot echoed off the cement floor as a white-hot ember burned his front left leg, slicing his skin. Brian's heart hitched at the attack, but a bullet wasn't going to slow him down. Nothing could stop him now that Jillian was hurt.

Brian's new mission was to end this man's life. Suddenly, fur flew and a wolf appeared before him with bared teeth.

The animal howled. He was close enough that when Brian reached out, his front paw swatted the wolf across his snout, sending him backward. The animal shook his head and then immediately righted himself. Body low to the ground, he charged.

Brian dropped onto all fours, ready to do battle. Out of the corner of his eye, white fur flew. A moment later, Jillian was in her gorgeous tiger form. Except for the blood covering her belly, she looked fierce. He expected her to charge, but all she was able to do was stagger toward them, and his protective instincts shot into a higher gear. His moment of distraction cost him. Whitlaw's wolf managed to land on Brian's shoulder, and he clamped down hard with sharp teeth. Damn it. As much as he wanted to make sure Jillian was okay, he had to fend off this ferocious mangy wolf first.

Brian twisted his head and bit down on the animal's flank, causing the feral animal to squeal. Blood squirted out of Whitlaw's side, and though the coppery taste was unpleasant, Brian would eat the damn wolf if that was what it took to make him die.

Jillian had finally crawled close enough and reached out with her paw, digging her nails into Whitlaw's head. The wolf let go of Brian and fell to the ground, but then quickly jumped back up, acting as if he was fit for another round.

News flash, buddy. Not with that hole in your side, you aren't. All of a sudden, Whitlaw's wolf staggered, and Jillian growled. As much as Brian wanted to finish him off, he knew Jillian needed to do this for closure.

Voices sounded off to the side as two men—one being Dalton— rushed to Anna's side and untied her. Dalton glanced over at them before returning his attention to the injured, captive woman. He must have believed Jillian would be okay or he would have entered into the fray.

Jillian suddenly yelped, and Brian moved forward, ready to help her. She had slammed the wolf into the ground, and had sunk her teeth into his neck. With him firmly in her grasp, she tossed the animal right and left. Wanting another chance to end this miserable man's life, Brian took a bite out of the animal too, until the small wolf body went limp. Jillian moved back and so did Brian. What was once an animal transformed back into a man—and a very dead one at that. Holy crap.

Brian turned to Jillian ready to comfort her, but because he was still in his bear form, he was afraid to hug her. Just as he attempted to shift, she looked up at him with eyes that were glazed over. Her rear dropped to the ground and then the rest of her body followed.

Oh, shit. Brian roared, hoping to attract the attention of the others. When no one rushed in, he had to do something. Needing to return to his human form, Brian closed his eyes and concentrated. Pain ricocheted through him more intense than the first time, but that could have been because he'd been shot. His body twisted and spun and for a few seconds, he couldn't see anything.

The next thing he knew, he was on his knees next to Jillian in his human form. He glanced down at his naked body. His chest was covered in blood. Some was probably his, but he suspected most belonged to Frank Whitlaw. Brian reached out and touched her shoulder. "Jillian. Are you okay?"

When she didn't respond, his heart dropped to his stomach.

Chapter Twenty

B RIAN WAS DEVASTATED that Jillian had been injured. If he'd
run in faster, he might have been able to prevent her from
being shot.

Don't be so hard on yourself, the voice in his head said.

Only now did Brian realize that inner voice had been his bear
talking to him all along. If only he'd introduced himself years ago,
his life would have gone a little smoother.

Connor and Kip checked out Jillian, who was still in her tiger
form. She was lucky. The bullet had been a through-and-through.

"We'll carry her," Connor said. "You shouldn't be using that
arm."

As much as Brian wanted to argue, he and Kip could handle her.
He bet Dalton would have been there had he known his sister had
been injured, but he'd already left with Anna when Jillian had been
in the middle of fighting Whitlaw.

"We can take her to the office or back to Dalton's place," Connor said. "We have a room where she can recover. Which do you
prefer?" he asked, deferring to Brian.

"She'd be more comfortable at Dalton's, but why not take her to
a vet or the hospital?"

Connor sighed. "Because a human is inside her body. We can't
let anyone find out about our kind. Don't worry, as a shifter she will
heal on her own."

"If you say so."

"Dalton's it is," Connor said. "Stay here for a minute. Once we put Jillian in the car, I'll bring you a spare set of clothes."

"Appreciate it." He could handle the cold, but someone might call the cops on him if they saw him naked.

Once he changed and slid into the back with Jillian, Connor took off. When they arrived at her brother's house, Dalton wasn't there, which meant Connor had to use his lock picking tools to get inside. Kip and Connor carried her to the bed.

"Do you want us to stay?" Kip asked.

Brian looked down at Jillian who was out cold but breathing evenly. From what he could tell, Kip didn't have any medical skills. "You go on ahead. I'll call if she takes a turn for the worse."

Once the men left, Brian stroked Jillian's fur. His own wound hurt like hell, but he wanted to make sure Jillian would be okay before shifting back into his bear form to heal.

A woman by the name of Missy showed up about a half hour later, saying Rye had called her. She explained that she was a Wendayan with healing powers and that she wanted to perform her magic on Jillian. Brian was all for it.

Between the lit candles, the crystals, and some herbs she placed under Jillian's head, Missy said she would wake up soon and shift back. She also explained that when Rye had been stabbed, he'd slept a long time too, but after he had woken, he was mostly healed.

Jillian should be so lucky. Once Brian was alone with her, he shifted into his bear form and rested on the floor for the next few hours. He'd just woken up, shifted back into his human form, and tossed on clean clothes when Dalton stepped into the room. "Why don't you shower and get some sleep. I can watch her."

Brian appreciated his concern, but he wanted to believe that Jillian would heal faster with him by her side. "Give me a little bit more time with her."

"Sure. I'll be in the living room."

"How's Anna?" Brian asked.

"She's resting in the hospital. Her face is swollen, but she'll heal.

The doctors expect she'll be good enough to go home tomorrow.

"I'm glad she'll be okay."

Dalton nodded and left. Now that Whitlaw was dead, Brian should return to his apartment, but he didn't want to leave Jillian just yet. She moaned, and he leaned closer. "That's it, Jillian. Wake up so we can run in the woods together and splash in the rivers. Hell, the next time it snows we can roll around in it and maybe even slide down a hill on our butts."

Keeping his hand on her side, he sat back and let his mind wander. "Can you imagine what our kids will look like? If one's a bear, I bet he'll be more tan than brown, and if one is a tiger, she'll have creamy fur with dark brown stripes." As if Jillian was imagining the same thing, her body shook. He hoped that meant she was trying to come out of her healing stupor. "I don't think I ever told you that I love you, but I do. Please, Jillian, come back to me," he whispered in her ear as a tear trickled down his cheek.

She probably had no idea how much she meant to him. Besides Elana, Jillian was the first person to see the real him and accept him for who he was. She never laughed when he was weak or when he needed to take his pills. He had no doubt that Jillian Garner was one of a kind, and he loved her.

Her paws twitched, giving him hope she'd be okay. When her eyes opened, he nearly jumped up and shouted. As if she was aware she was in her tiger form, she shook, swirled, and transformed before his eyes. His gaze shot to where she'd been wounded. All that remained was a small scar, surrounded by some redness.

Jillian's eyes widened. "Brian?" She glanced down at her body then touched her tender wound. "That bastard Whitlaw shot me. He's dead, right?"

She must have blacked out right before he died. "Yes."

She hissed in a breath and clasped his hand. "Are you okay? He shot you too."

"It was a scratch. My bear took care of it already." Resting in his bear form had done wonders.

She ran a finger along the back of his hand. "Is that your blood?"

"I imagine it's a combination of all of ours, but I suspect what' on my hand is mostly yours." He really needed to wash.

She lifted up on her elbow. "What happened to Anna? How is she?"

"She's in the hospital. Dalton and Rye took her. Your brother seemed quite concerned, but he said she should be released tomorrow. Speaking of Anna's rescue, Dalton and I arrived at the same time you and Whitlaw did. I saw that trick you pulled. I was quite impressed."

"Trick?"

"Your talent to move fast."

Jillian looked off to the side, her lips pressed together as if she was reliving the event. "Yeah, I needed to beat him inside. I figured I only had a few seconds to find Anna. Since it was so dark inside, I nearly tripped getting past all the framing."

"Me too."

Jillian glanced at the ceiling. "When I saw Anna tied up in that chair, I lost it." She faced Brian. "He told me in the car that he planned to torture her in front of me before taking me out. I had to set her free, but all I managed to do before Whitlaw came in was to rip off the gag and undo about half of the rope that held her hands together."

"How was he able to shoot you? I would have thought you would have been on him and taken the gun away before he had the chance to pull the trigger."

She ran a hand down his arm, sending his thoughts in the wrong direction. "I guess I didn't believe he'd shoot me. I thought we'd fight wolf to tiger. My trick, as you called it, must have unhinged him. When he ran in and saw me with Anna, he must have decided I needed to die right then. I saw him raise his arm, and I waited a split second too long before rushing him. He shot me just before I reached him."

Brian's gut twisted. "He shot you at close range?"

She pressed her hand to her side, as if she was reliving the pain. "Yes."

Brian could barely keep from throwing something against the wall. Frank Whitlaw didn't deserve such a quick death. "I guess that's when I burst in."

"Yes." She smiled. "When I saw you, you were still in your human form, and I wanted to shout at you to leave, that he would kill you, but then you shifted into your bear. The look on Whitlaw's face was priceless. He was fucking scared."

Brian replayed that moment in his mind's eyes. "He did seem surprised."

"Oh, Brian, seeing you in your bear form—finally—made me so happy. I know how much you've wanted to shift."

"Yes, but at that moment, all I wanted was to shift so that I could protect you."

Jillian sat up, her breasts perky. "Thank you. You did awesome."

He was no hero. "While I was the one to bite him first, you finished him off."

"I wouldn't have survived the fight in my condition if you hadn't weakened him."

Jillian seemed determined to rewrite history. For now, he'd let her. "Let's agree that we work well as a team."

She grinned. "We do." A knock sounded on the door and Jillian grabbed her sheet to cover herself. "Come in."

Dalton entered with a grin on his face. "I thought I heard voices. How are you feeling?" He sat down on the edge of the bed.

"Surprisingly good. I'm a little sore where the bullet went through, but otherwise my tiger did an excellent job of healing me."

"You were lucky."

"I know. What would you have done if the bullet had lodged inside me? I was too out of it to shift into human form."

"I would have called Chelsea McKinnon. She's a vet tech, though I don't know if she's ever done surgery."

Hadn't Brian suggested that to Connor? His idea wasn't stupid after all.

"You should ask Rye what the protocol is in cases like this—for future reference," she said.

"I will to that," Dalton said.

"Did you find out how Connor and the team located Anna?" Brian asked.

He nodded. "Connor figured it out. When Whitlaw videoed Anna, he had her phone in one hand and a flashlight in the other. While he'd carefully placed the sheet behind her, it was evident that the material had been nailed to the studs in a wall. What gave it away was when he moved the camera for a second, it exposed the pink batting behind the sheet."

"How did Connor know it was his building? I'm sure there are several places around town that are under construction," she said.

"There are. That's where the drone came in. Jackson flew it over all of the sites that are still being built, and only one had a heat signature inside."

McKinnon and Associates had more tricks than Brian ever imagined. "That was clever."

Jillian glanced between them. "Brian said you and he arrived just as we did, but what about Jackson and Connor?"

"They were there with Kip. Rye came as soon as Connor told him they'd found Anna."

"Why didn't they take him out when they had the chance?"

Dalton stabbed a hand through his hair. "They wanted to be sure they had enough evidence to arrest Whitlaw. For all we knew, you willingly got into his car. Legally, he hadn't done anything yet."

"Other than beat up Anna," she said.

"It would have been her word against his. Remember, he was a man of the law. You know better than anyone."

Jillian sank back against the bed. "Sadly, I do."

Dalton stood. "I'll leave you two lovebirds alone. I'm glad you're both okay."

Jillian reached out and grabbed Dalton's arm. "By the way,

Whitlaw confessed he killed Dad."

"Did he say why?" Dalton eased back down.

She explained that Whitlaw was a dirty cop, and their dad planned to turn him in. "It sucks, I know."

"You got that right."

"I'm surprised you didn't want to take your turn at him. When I heard you come in, you went straight to Anna," she said.

Dalton glanced away. "Between you and Brian, I figured you two could handle him." He patted Brian on the shoulder, and that one action did more to boost his confidence than anything had. He'd earned Dalton's respect and that meant a lot to him.

"Luckily we were able to," Brian said.

"At the time, I didn't realize you both had been injured or I would have stayed to help."

She smiled. "It turned out okay in the end, and that's all that matters."

"Amen." Her brother stood. "Now that you're awake, you might want to consider taking a shower. You stink." He turned to Brian. "You ain't no sweet smelling rose either."

"You suck, bro," Jillian yelled at Dalton as he closed the door, leaving the two of them alone. She laughed heartily, the happy sound sending a flood of hormones straight through Brian's body. The love between brother and sister was so special.

Testing Dalton's theory, Brian lifted his arm and took a whiff. He definitely smelled rank. "Dalton's right. If you'll excuse me, I need to shower."

Jillian threw off the covers. "I'm joining you."

"You need to rest."

"Rest? What do you think I've been doing?"

He held out his hand. "Okay then. Let's go shower." His bear roared in approval.

JILLIAN STOOD AND when a wave of dizziness assaulted her, she stilled in order to regain her balance. If she mentioned she was less than one hundred percent, Brian wouldn't let her out of bed for a week. All she needed was a hot shower to perk her up. Sharing said shower with her mate-to-be would be an added bonus.

Her tiger had healed her quite well. Cuts and bruises cleared up in minutes, but a bullet was a different matter. In just a few hours though, she was almost as good as new.

Not wanting to walk down the hall naked, she pawed through her suitcase and tossed on an oversized shirt. "We'll use Dalton's shower in the master bedroom. It has two showerheads."

"That right?" His eyes lit up, and then his cock pressed against his fly, telegraphing his desire.

The thought of being with Brian had her tiger ecstatic. "Let's go see if I can get your bear to roar."

He halted, concern written all over his face. "It's too soon."

"We'll see about that."

Once inside the bathroom, she whipped off her shirt and then turned on both faucets. She faced Brian, concerned for his well-being. He needed a shave, his hair was mussed, and gray smudges resided under his eyes. "Have you slept?"

"I shifted into my bear for a few hours to heal."

"You should be good them. Take off your clothes. I want to check out your wound."

When she reached out, he swatted away her hands. "I know your game. You just want to get your hands on me, but I need to clean up first."

Damn. Brian knew her too well. "I was merely going to lift your shirt and check you out."

"Uh-huh." He slipped off his pants. Crossing his wrists, he grabbed the hem of his shirt and lifted it off in one fluid motion.

Jillian stepped closer and dragged a finger down his side. "You are a dried bloody mess."

"Never you mind, missy." He nodded toward the shower. "Let's go. You can play doctor in a minute."

Yes! They both stepped into the shower. The two heads were side by side, each with a built-in shelf in the wall to hold the soap and shampoo. Since this was a rental with fuddy-duddy furniture, she'd never expected such a nice bathroom. Jillian stuck her head under the spray of water, and the heat was divine. "That feels so freaking good." Brian reached around her, brushing her shoulder. "Brian? Be good."

"I just need the soap."

A spare bar was on the other side too. Hmm. Come to think of it, why did her brother have two bars of soap in his shower anyway? From his emails and phone calls, all he ever did here in Silver Lake was work, work, work. She didn't remember him mentioning he even dated any woman. That probably meant he had a different one every week.

As Brian soaped up, she checked over his body for his wound. "Where did you say you were shot?"

He grinned. "Why don't you look for it?"

"Smart ass. I need to wash my hair." It was fun playing hard to get, though she bet her eyes had changed colors numerous times already. Now that Brian had shifted, his body must be going crazy with need. A quick glance downward confirmed her suspicion. Jillian shampooed and rinsed her hair, and then dragged the soap over her body, wanting to wash away all the dried blood.

Brian slipped the bar from her fingers. "Let me. I don't want you to tire yourself out."

She cracked up. "You are so full of shit. You just want to touch me."

Brian stepped closer and turned her to the side. "Is there anything wrong with two mates wanting to be together?"

"We aren't mates yet." *Please say you want to be with me forever.*

"That can be easily rectified, right?"

She shrugged. "Depends on whether you can turn me on."

Brian dragged the soap over one breast, and her tiger woke up. Blue sparks shot off her body. Darn. So much for pretending indifference.

"Is that so?" he asked.

She grabbed his cock. "I guess we can't hide our feelings from each other."

Brian leaned in closer. "Do you want to?"

Her stomach summersaulted. Jillian had spent her life hiding—hiding her tiger and hiding her feelings. The guilt at not having done something about her father's death sooner had eaten away at her for years. Now she'd found closure and a man to love. "Not anymore."

She wrapped her arms around his neck and kissed him, recognizing that this was the first day of their new life together. The steam swirled around them as they plunged and explored each other's mouths. Brian tasted fresh, like he'd recently brushed, sending her hormones into overdrive. More sparks flew and she pressed against him, needing him more than ever. Suddenly, the water stopped.

"You were right," he said with half closed lids. "Now that my bear has been released, he's yelling at me to possess you. I keep telling him I don't need him to urge me on anymore. I want you all on my own."

"Same here."

Brian elbowed open the glass shower door, swept her up in his arms, and then stepped onto the bathroom mat. Once he wiped his feet, he headed to the door.

"Brian? Where are we going? We're all wet," she said.

"Open the door." He lowered his head, his mouth inches from hers.

As if she'd been hypnotized, she did as he asked. All during the short walk down the hallway, she hoped her brother didn't investigate what was happening. After Brian eased her through the bedroom doorway, he kicked it closed with his heel, his gaze never leaving her face. "I want us to be together. Forever. My bear and your tiger."

"I want that too."

Brian placed her on the bed. "I hope you're ready for some loving 'cause I'm not sure I can go slow."

Jillian raised her arms to welcome him. Hopefully today she would finally get her mate.

Chapter Twenty-One

B RIAN WAS OVERWHELMED with desire. He hadn't been able to keep his thoughts off Jillian before the shift. After his change, it was worse in part because her scent was constantly electrifying his senses. More so than ever, he wanted to fully mate with her.

At first, he thought the mating ritual was barbaric, but now he was willing to give it a try, especially if it meant the two of them would be bonded forever. The whole idea still kind of scared the shit out of him, but Brian wanted to go through with it. His need for Jillian was like no other.

Brian knelt on the bed and stroked her long, blonde hair. "You are so beautiful."

"You're pretty hot yourself," she said as she latched onto his stiff member. His breathing suddenly increased. Jillian pumped her fist up and down one time, and he came close to losing it. He chastised his inner bear, but it didn't seem to work, so he closed his eyes for a moment and enjoyed the ride.

A man could only take so much stimulation, however. "I need to taste you."

"Please do."

Easing out of her grasp, he slid down between her legs, ready to feast on his woman. The first lick had her blue aura pulsing, adding to his excitement, and her sweet taste had his bear clawing at him. Brian needed to stay in control for a little bit longer.

Wanting to see her aura glow even brighter, he slipped two

fingers inside her. Jillian bucked her hips up and wadded the bedspread. "Brian, please. I need you."

He needed her too, but he didn't want to rush. In the years to come, he wanted Jillian to remember this moment, how they'd grown more and more desperate until their bodies threatened to shift if they didn't mate.

As he wiggled his fingers and licked her tiny pearl nub, her moans intensified, causing the hair on the back of his hands to sprout and his teeth to sharpen. Holy shit. Shifting now would ruin everything.

Jillian clasped the top of his head and held on tight. With each suck and wiggle, her body pulsed a beautiful cobalt blue. Her delicate cooing sounds made his bear claw his insides for release.

Brian couldn't take it any longer. Releasing his hold, he stretched out on top of her. Her luscious tits drew him in, but he yearned to taste her lips too. *Decisions. Decisions.*

Tits first then lips, his bear urged.

"Brian, touch me, please!"

JILLIAN HADN'T MEANT to sound so desperate, but...well, she was. When Brian withdrew his fingers and stopped licking her, she wanted to throttle him. The pressure had been divine. Then when he crawled on top of her and just stared at her chest without doing anything, her patience ran out.

After her plea, he palmed one breast and licked the other nipple. It was as if he'd plugged her in, and judging by her blue glow, she was putting out some serious wattage.

"I love your breasts," he said.

"I'm glad you enjoy them."

He smiled then drew one nipple taut, sending a different kind of spark straight to her core. She lifted her hips and pressed hard against his cock. When she wiggled, his growl brought so much satisfaction.

"Kiss me," she pleaded. As wonderful as it was for him to suck on her breasts, she wanted his lips and cock more.

Brian kissed the hollow of her throat and then tugged on the shell of her ear. She dug her nails into his shoulders and tried to pull him upward, but he seemed intent on feasting on every part of her body. Didn't he know how hard it was for her to hold back her climax right now? He too had a powerful aura radiating from him, so he must want her just as bad.

Finally, he lifted his head, and when he captured her lips, bolts of joy skipped down her spine. She widened her legs to accept him, and he didn't disappoint. In one thrust, he entered her, and the friction set her on fire. She planted her feet on the bed and met the next plunge with equal force, her glow intensifying with each encounter. Their breaths mixed, and it was as if they were becoming one, a molecule at a time. On the next thrust, he hit every nerve in her body, and her blue glow increased and grew until both of them were encased in a bubble.

He must have recognized what that meant, because he broke the kiss and lowered his head, his teeth scraping the tender part of her neck. "I love you, Jillian Garner. And that's not just my bear talking."

His love soothed every emotional ache in her body, and the tears leaking out of her eyes were from pure joy. "I love you too, Brian Stanley. I want you forever."

As if they had rehearsed this, they each sunk their sharp animal teeth into the other's neck. Her climax swooped in with the force of the strongest tornado, and carried her to a safe and wonderful place.

Brian then lifted his head and kissed her. When their tongues touched, his cock detonated, pummeling his hot seed into her. He held her tight, and when his breathing slowed, he rolled over, taking her with him. Still connected, she rested her head on his rather furry chest, content beyond all belief.

"Maybe I should thank Frank Whitlaw," she mumbled.

Brian tightened his hold. "Whatever for?"

"For escalating the time of our meeting."

He kissed the top of her head. "I hope I'm worth it. You've been through a lot of pain, losing your dad like that and then your friend."

Brian was so sweet. "You had it worse. You lost your parents and a sister for thirty-eight years."

"But I found you and that makes up for everything."

Aw. Jillian was one lucky woman.

THE NEXT WEEK was bittersweet for both of them. Brian asked Jillian to move into his apartment, and she'd agreed. That was the good part. Now that they'd mated, their need to be with each other was growing stronger every day, which meant the pain of separation while they were at work, intensified with each hour. Keeping busy helped—somewhat. Because Anna was still recuperating, Elana had come into work. Kalan's mom had been thrilled to take care of her only grandchild.

"So what are your plans now?" Elana asked.

Jillian and Brian had spent hours discussing what needed to happen next. "Once Anna returns, I'm going to head back to California."

Her brows pinched. "What about Brian? This will crush him if you leave."

Jillian waved a hand. "I'm not moving back. I've already called my boss and given my notice, but I need to clean out my office and put my house up for sale."

"Brian didn't say anything about going with you."

"We talked about that also, but he has responsibilities at work and didn't think it would be wise to ask for a few weeks off. He'll stay here."

Elana rubbed her arm. "That will be hard. I remember when Kalan and I first mated, we could barely go a few hours without each other."

Jillian smiled. "We're the same way, but this has to be done. Besides, the sooner I leave, the sooner I can return and look for a job." Elana didn't need two employees.

"You've done such a great job here. I really appreciate you helping out."

"I'm not sure Anna feels the same way. Whitlaw wouldn't have targeted her if I hadn't been here."

"She doesn't blame you."

Jillian hoped that was true. "Speaking of which, have you talked to her today?"

"I called her this morning, and she's feeling better. Now it's a matter of letting the stitches dissolve and the bruising to go away," Elana said. "However, she said she wanted to come into work tomorrow, but that she'd stay in the back room and help with the arrangements." Elana finished placing the roses in the vase. "Anna also said that your brother has called a few times to check up on her."

"Really?" He hadn't mentioned it. Then again, Dalton was closed mouthed when it came to women.

"She couldn't believe that he rushed into the building and saved her when you'd been injured."

Jillian hoped Anna wasn't developing a crush on Dalton. He might be more handsome than any man deserved to be, but he was a workaholic. "Dalton said he didn't know I'd been injured at the time."

Elana placed the flowers in the cooler. "Now that Anna will be returning tomorrow, when do you think you'll leave?"

"I guess I can go anytime. I'll see if I can get a flight tomorrow."

Elana hugged her. "I can't thank you enough for everything you've done here."

"It was my pleasure. I would have died of boredom if I hadn't worked. If you hear of a law firm in need of a lawyer, let me know."

"I will."

When five o'clock rolled around, Jillian was sad to say goodbye to Blooms of Hope and Elana and Anna. Jillian loved the fragrance of the flowers and the peaceful setting, but she had to tie up her own affairs.

She trudged up the stairs, already missing this place, this town, these people. Brian had today and tomorrow off, and as soon as she walked into the apartment, he came over with a glass of wine for her. "How was your day?"

She kissed him then took the proffered drink. "Good. Anna will be back tomorrow."

He glanced away, the energy he'd emitted seconds before diminished. "I guess that means you're leaving?"

She set her glass down and wrapped her arms around his neck. "Leaving, yes, but only for a short period of time. I've already hired movers to come in and pack up everything. I won't be gone for that long."

He held her tight. "A day is too long."

"I know."

"You sure you won't realize how wonderful Los Angeles is and want to stay?"

Brian was being silly. She pulled his head down and kissed him. Out of the corner of her eye, she spotted her sparks streaming off her body. When their tongues touched, she absorbed all of his goodness. "Does that answer your question? You can always come with me, you know. I'll warn you now, it will be boring."

"I really wish I could."

He was so dedicated. She understood that he hadn't experienced much success in his life and wanted to turn things around.

"I understand."

He stroked her face. "I guess tonight will have to be something special then. I don't want you to forget me."

She laughed. "Never in a million years." Jillian ran her hands down his back and lifted up his shirt. "Turn around."

"Why?"

"I want to look at your marking again. I want to be certain that our incredible mating wasn't a figment of my imagination."

He turned his back to her. "Still there?"

She ran her finger around the symbol of their union. "Yes. Your bear paw seems to be darkening every day. The vine looks good behind it."

He faced her. "And yours?"

Jillian smiled. "It's the same as yours."

"Show me." Brian grinned. The oven timer dinged and he stepped back. "Crap. Bad Timing. Hold that thought."

She sniffed and detected the heavenly scent of sugar. "What are you baking?"

"Chocolate chip cookies."

She'd told him that was her favorite food and that she missed her mom's home-cooked ones. "You made me cookies?"

He grinned. "Just for you."

She loved him even more. Brian headed into the kitchen and Jillian dropped down on the sofa to enjoy her wine. She'd taken one sip when her cell rang. "It's Dalton," she called to Brian then returned her attention to the call. "Hey, what's up?"

"I wanted you to know that Whitlaw's body was autopsied by Dr. Williams."

"Meaning what?"

"Our shifting identities are safe. We could have shipped the body directly to Los Angeles, but we wanted one of our own to perform the autopsy. We don't need anyone to realize that a bear and a tiger killed him."

"Good point, but wasn't Dr. Williams suspicious?"

"He's a shifter, and cleverly put the cause of death as blood loss due to a stab wound."

"That's an understatement. Let's hope the LAPD doesn't question his results," she said. "They'd know he'd faked them."

"From what I could tell, he had no next of kin, so maybe we'll be in the clear."

She sipped more of her wine. "Do you think I can tell Dalia's parents that he confessed to murdering their daughter?"

"Let's hold off on that. It might be hard to explain how you learned about it. I'm not sure we want to say that Whitlaw came after you and that you managed to overpower and kill him."

Dalton always was so logical. "True. While I'm happy Whitlaw is dead, I would have enjoyed seeing him brought to trial and convicted. His cellmates would have had a ball with a cop."

"Jillian, we need to be content knowing he can't hurt anyone anymore."

Dalton was right. "I agree. By the way, I'm going to see if I can get a flight tomorrow for LA."

"What about Brian?"

"We'll Skype or call." Sure, he'd suffer with her gone, but she'd be in just as much pain.

"Stop by tomorrow before you go."

"Will do."

As soon as she disconnected, Brian brought over two cookies and the tin. "I didn't want you to spoil your dinner. I'd like to take you to the Lake Steakhouse."

She smiled. "This will be a night to remember."

Chapter Twenty-Two

B RIAN TOSSED BACK his second scotch. It had been nineteen days and counting since he'd been with Jillian. That was nineteen days too many. He looked around and absorbed the sights and sounds. There was something soothing about McKinnon's Pub and Pool. It might be because this was the first place he'd stopped at when he'd visited his parents so many months ago that made it almost feel like home.

Finn McKinnon wiped the bar in front of him. "I take it you're missing Jillian?"

"Missing is an understatement. Wait until you find your mate."

He laughed. "Ain't going to happen for a long ass time. I'm twenty-five and have a lot of enjoyment to look forward to first."

Brian didn't need to be lecturing this young pup about how much enjoyment he and Jillian had found, especially after they mated. Of course the sex was off the charts amazing, but that one night when they'd gone out for a run had been fantastic. Freeing. Exhilarating. Mind-expanding. When she returned for good, he wanted to romp and play every night. Thank goodness, she wasn't some tiny wolf or he might end up hurting her by mistake. He still hadn't learned how much damage a swipe could inflict. While Jillian was almost as powerful as he was, she was much faster.

"Now that you've seen my brother in action at McKinnon and Associates, are you tempted to join them?" Finn asked.

Brian polished off his glass. "No, thank you. Killing isn't my style, though I was highly impressed with their operation. Besides, my technical skills are definitely not up to speed. That drone of theirs is something else."

Finn puffed out his chest. "Connor does run a pretty sweet operation. I could have joined him in the family business, but I like working here. Hell, I probably know more secrets about this community than anyone. I pay attention to everything that goes on."

What he said was true. If it hadn't been for Finn vouching for Brian's whereabouts the night of his parents' murders, no telling where he might be right now. "Do you think you'll be manager someday?"

Finn shrugged. "I'm hoping, but I'm happy stocking the bar and waiting on customers. The pay's great and the hours are decent." He looked up and nodded. "Mr. Murdoch! Fancy seeing you here."

Daniel Murdoch, Kalan and Jackson's dad, slid onto the seat next to Brian. "I'll have an ale," he told Finn. He faced Brian. "Elana tells me you want to have a place to start a woodworking shop."

He'd called Mr. Murdoch and asked for an appointment with him. "I do. I'll keep my job for as long as need be, but someday I'd like to make custom furniture."

Finn delivered the ale and then moved to the end of the bar to serve some other customers.

"How can I help you?" Daniel asked.

Brian inhaled. "Elana said you have a small cabin not too far from here that you don't use much anymore. I was wondering if you'd be interested in selling it?" He held onto his drink with both hands. Asking for favors never sat well with him.

"I might. Let's talk about it."

"WEREN'T YOU SCARED?" Camille asked as she stuffed a piece of chicken in her mouth.

"Absolutely, but I knew I had to save my friend Anna," Jillian said.

They were sitting at the small kitchen table at Camille's house. Jillian had picked up some Chicken Cacciatore from her favorite restaurant, along with a few bottles of wine. They had a lot of catching up to do.

"What was it like to kill the scumwad?"

She chuckled at Camille's name for him. "Brian had wounded him severely already. I merely delivered the fatal blow, but I did enjoy tearing out his throat."

"Gross."

"Yeah, well, that's the fastest way to kill a wolf shifter. I wish I'd had the strength to really go head-to-head with him. Whitlaw was so freaking self-confident. His death was too swift." Jillian took a bite of the spaghetti. The sauce was divine. "What's going to happen to Dalia's case? He confessed that he killed her."

Camille shrugged. "You know better than anyone that hearsay like that won't count in court."

"I know."

"Marie's taking over the case, but I doubt she'll get very far, especially since Whitlaw told you he tampered with all the evidence."

"Yes. I know Dalia's parents want closure, but that would mean finding some proof that Whitlaw killed her."

"Unless you're willing to reveal that shifters exist, they'll always have to wonder." Camille tossed back more of her wine. "So you're really moving back to Tennessee?"

Jillian nodded. "Yes. Brian wouldn't be happy if he moved here. Besides, those few weeks have shown me how much I enjoy being around Dalton. I was always so focused on work that we never spent quality time together."

"Do you have a job lined up?"

"No, but I have enough money saved that I can afford to take my time looking. When I sell the house, I'll be in good shape for a while."

"Your mom's going to miss you. How is she dealing with this?"

That had been a hard conversation. "She understands. She's

happy I've found someone and that I will be close to Dalton."

"She can always move to Tennessee."

Jillian chuckled. "I don't think she could get used to the small town."

Camille sighed, reached out, and clasped her hand. "I'll miss you, girlfriend."

"You can always Skype me. Or better yet, if the rat race gets to you, I bet the Silver Lake Sheriff's department could always use a top notch officer."

She laughed. "I think I'd freak knowing that half the town's people were really shifters in disguise."

"It's not like they walk down the street in their animal form. Remember, humans still don't know we exist."

"If I decide to leave the department, you'll be the first person I call." Camille lifted her glass, and they toasted. "So tell me, what's it like to be a person's mate?"

"Oh, boy. Where do I begin?"

AFTER THREE VERY long weeks of running around getting her house ready to sell, putting her possessions in a storage unit that she could ship to Tennessee, and saying goodbye to her good friends at the law office, Jillian was exhausted. It was worth it if it meant she could return to Brian for good. Would she miss Los Angeles? Sure—at least part of it—but she was looking forward to starting a new life. She'd never really explored her animal side, and with Brian by her side, she'd be able to.

Once she boarded the plane to Knoxville, she texted Brian to make sure he'd pick her up when she arrived. Jillian couldn't wait to be with him. They'd finally be able to live without the heavy cloud of Whitlaw hanging over them.

While she enjoyed Brian's cozy one-bedroom apartment, even he'd said he would enjoy something bigger. It would be fun to house hunt—something with a couple of bedrooms, along with an office for her and a large workspace for Brian. He had such talented hands.

Don't I know it, her tiger chimed in.

She swallowed a laugh. Her poor tiger had been so depressed these last few weeks. She'd begged Jillian to find a place where she could run free, but that wasn't going to happen in a crowded city.

The flight seemed to take forever, probably because she was so anxious to see Brian again. While they would Skype and text almost every night, it wasn't the same as when she could taste and touch him.

Many long hours later, the plane landed, and she eased her way to the front. Once in the main terminal, she rushed down the walkway and exited the restricted area, but she couldn't find Brian. Instead, she spotted Dalton and immediately feared the worst.

"Welcome, home." He hugged her. "Did everything go okay?"

Dalton and she had talked, but not as extensively as she had with Brian. "Yes, the house is on the market. Where's Brian?"

Dalton walked her outside. "He said he didn't think he could keep his hands to himself if he drove you home."

She laughed. "For real?"

Dalton shrugged. "I didn't ask for details, but your mate has been rather anxious since you left."

She didn't like knowing she'd caused him more pain. "Has he been okay?"

"I haven't seen him much."

That didn't sound good either, but hopefully her brother was merely in the dark. "How's Anna doing?"

"Good." He looked away.

"Have you seen her?" From his short response, Jillian wondered if there might be a budding relationship between them. Nah, Dalton was too straight-laced for the likes of her.

"I stopped by the flower shop once, and I was pleased that I couldn't see any evidence of the fight."

"I'm happy to hear that." The lack of physical scars, however, was only part of the issue. Jillian worried more about her mental state. "Did she ask about shifters? It had to have been quite the shock to see me human one minute and an animal the next."

"No, she didn't bring it up."

And he didn't think to question her? Something was going on, but even if she asked him, he wouldn't tell her. During the ride home, he told her that he'd finally met Aiden and what a cute little baby he was. He then updated her on the new building for McKinnon and Associates as well as a case he was working on. She noted how he avoided anything to do with Anna.

An hour later, they finally arrived in town. To her disappointment, Dalton drove right passed Blooms of Hope. "Ah, did you forget where I live?"

"No."

She blew out a breath. After arriving at the airport two hours in advance then sitting on a plane for hours, she wasn't in the mood for this mystery stuff. "Where are we going? I'm tired."

"You'll see."

When Dalton turned into the shifter compound, she feared he'd drive them to Elana and Kalan's house for some kind of surprise party. Not that she didn't want to see her friends again—she did, just not tonight. For days she'd dreamed of being with Brian.

When he drove past their street, Jillian became more confused. "What's going on?"

Instead of answering, Dalton pulled down a long, unpaved driveway that needed some serious repair work done on it. At the end of the drive sat Brian's red pickup truck, and her pulse sped up. No sooner had Dalton put the car in gear than Brian came out of the lovely one-story log cabin. Exhaustion must have clouded the logical part of her brain because she couldn't figure why out he was there.

"Go," Dalton said. "Brian has a surprise for you."

Her head swam. Jillian rushed out of the car and charged up to him. While she wanted to ask him what he was doing at this person's house, that question would have to come later. Right now she needed to absorb everything about him—his scent, what he looked like, and how he felt in her arms. She hugged him then kissed his lips, nose, eyes, and then returned her attention to his lips.

Dalton came up behind her. "Here's your suitcase. I'll set it on the porch. Talk to you later."

She lifted a hand and waved goodbye. Jillian would thank him properly later—once she stopped kissing the man she loved.

"I can't tell you how much I've missed you," Brian said after breaking the kiss. His lustful gaze drank in all of her. "Come on in."

When she stepped inside, she pretended interest in the all-wood interior so as not to appear rude. She noted a cute kitchen sat to the right with a dining room table in front of it. A comfy sofa and chair faced a lit fireplace, and off to the side was a mattress. "This is nice."

Brian slipped off her jacket and let it fall to the floor. "You're nicer. Oh, Jillian I've been going crazy without you."

"Me too." Keeping her gaze on him, she kicked off her shoes then began to unbutton his flannel shirt. While she was fumbling to undo it, Brian unzipped her jeans and then dragged them down her hips.

As the seconds passed, their movements turned more frantic. Finally, he stepped back. "I can't wait any longer. I'm sorry. I know how much you love foreplay, but I've been dreaming of this for weeks."

"So have I." Jillian was happy he didn't want to spend a half hour kissing and touching and driving her crazy. Her tiger for sure would have emerged.

Once they were both naked, Brian growled and swept her up in his arms. The skin-to-skin contact made her crazy with need. She dragged her nails down his chest, loving the texture of his hair on top of his muscles. He rushed them over to the mattress that was next to the fireplace.

Dropping to his knees, Brian set her down then crawled on top of her. "I don't know where to start," he said. "My bear is beating and kicking me inside. I don't think he'll ever be satisfied now, no matter what I do."

She smiled. "That makes two of us. Now shut up and kiss me some more."

And kiss her he did. Resting on his elbows, he lowered his body on top of her with the perfect amount of pressure. The first dip of her tongue into his mouth had her blue glow nearly overpowering the yellow hue from the flames in the fireplace. Brian sprouted some facial hair and his teeth sharpened. If he didn't watch out, he'd shift first.

Their kiss intensified. It was as if she'd been deprived of fresh air for days and she'd finally been given an oxygen mask that was cranked up to high. She cupped his face and held him still, never wanting to let him go. When one of their bones began to crack, they broke apart.

"I'm sorry," Brian said. "I want you too much."

"Don't ever be sorry for wanting me."

As if he was a bit peeved at himself for almost losing control, he slid lower and captured her nipple between his rather sharp teeth. The brief shot of pain morphed into delicious desire, and each tug and pull made her nails grow longer and her bones crack. "Lower," she pleaded.

Brian lifted her legs over his shoulders and supported her butt as he licked her. Dear goddess in heaven, but what he was doing tantalized her beyond belief. He flicked, sucked, and flicked her clit over and over again, causing her moans to come out louder and louder. Trying to connect more deeply with him, she dug her nails into his shoulders.

He looked up at her. "You taste so fucking good."

"Then take me, please."

Chapter Twenty-Three

B RIAN EASED OUT from under her legs, and flipped Jillian over onto her elbows and knees—a vulnerable position that excited her. Leaning over her back, he cupped her tits and massaged them while twisting her nipples. Not only did sparks shoot through her and then jump off her body, her tiger purred. As much as she loved the attention, she didn't understand why he was taking his time. Her need was escalating to epic proportions with each pinch and pull.

His cock edged close to her entrance, and she pressed her hips back.

"Easy, Jillian. I'm really working hard to keep my control."

She totally understood how difficult it was to stay in human form, but shit, that was why he needed to take her. "Bri-an!"

His hands slipped to her waist and when he plowed in, it was as if she'd been set free for the first time in her life. Every hormone flooded her body, and her blue glow intensified. The fire crackled and lights flickered, but she couldn't be sure it wasn't her mind playing tricks on her or if her desire really was that high. Jillian lowered her head and forced in a big breath. He slowly withdrew then drove right back in, heating her to the core.

Brian kissed her shoulder and then trailed his lips up to her neck. "Jillian, Jillian, Jillian."

Excitement sizzled at his words as he pounded into her over and over again. Each time he hit her back wall, she edged closer to her climax. This time she feared that when she came, her tiger would burst forth.

He ran his hands up the side of her body, and the feel of the calluses on his palms nearly did her in. His scent invaded her cells, and his cock totally possessed her. When he growled and then sunk his teeth into her neck, her release shook her so hard, that she nearly collapsed. His hot seed spewed, claiming her fully.

He held her tight, while it took a few minutes for his cock to stop pulsing. By then, her limbs had weakened. Brian must have sensed her inability to remain upright for he wrapped his arms around her waist and rolled them to the side, his chest to her back.

"I love you, Jillian, more than you can know. You are my everything," he whispered as he kissed the back of her head.

Tears leaked from her eyes, and she wiped them away before he could see them. "I love you too."

"Are you crying?" Brian slipped out of her, rolled her toward him, and then lifted her chin. "Tell me what's wrong."

"Nothing is wrong. Absolutely nothing. I'm so happy I can't stand it."

He smiled. "Really? I guess I have a lot to learn about you."

She cupped his cheek. "Just keep being as wonderful as you've been and you'll have nothing to worry about."

"I can do that."

Jillian lifted up on her elbow, loving that she was back with Brian. "Care to explain why you're in this cabin?"

"Do you like it?"

"It's incredibly charming. Did you rent it for my homecoming?"

Brian looked pleased with himself. "Nope. I bought it from Kalan's dad."

The words took a few minutes to sink it. "You bought this place?"

Brian sat up. "I did. I saved my money and wanted a nice home for us."

"That's wonderful, but I thought we'd find something together."

His face fell. "Oh, shit. I wasn't thinking."

"It's okay. Maybe if you give me a tour, I can figure out where everything will fit."

"Yeah, about that. Except for a small loft upstairs, this is it, but don't worry, I plan to expand. I was hoping you could help me redesign the place."

Jillian sat up as excitement raced through her. "Seriously? How big are we talking about?"

"At least three more bedrooms and a workshop for me."

She clasped his hands. "When I sell my house, I'll be happy to pay for the expansion."

"You don't have to do that."

Brian didn't get it. "We're a team now. Fifty-fifty. I want to do this."

"Really?" She nodded. "In that case, I'll give you free reign to replace anything you want."

She envisioned her California furniture in this space, but somehow the white sofa and chairs, as well as the glass table, didn't seem to work in a rustic cabin in Tennessee. "Maybe we should keep this stuff for now."

"Or we can buy new furniture—whatever you want."

"We have plenty of time to think about it."

He grinned. "That calls for a celebration, and I have an idea."

"What's that?"

"You up for an evening run? I believe it's a full moon, and you can't get any more romantic than that."

Jillian stood. "What are you waiting for?"

THE FIELD WHERE Brian had first tried to shift was only a short walk from Silver Lake. He parked near the field, and they walked in together holding hands.

"Awesome. I'm so ready for a run," Jillian said rubbing her hands up and down her arms.

The weather had warmed significantly, but she'd just returned from California, so it made sense she'd be chilly here. "Let's head near the lake. Those boulders should block the wind as we undress."

They trotted down the path until they reached a cozy area where they could change. As quickly as they could, they disrobed, folded their clothes, and placed them on top of the rock. Brrr. It was bitter cold even for him.

"I'm shifting," she said a second before her beautiful tiger form appeared. He loved her sleek body as well as the intricate patterns on her fur.

As soon as Brian shifted, he stood on his hind legs and roared, pretending he was the Alpha. If Jillian had been in her human form, she'd be laughing.

"Cute."

He froze. Her words seemed to manifest itself in his head. *"Did you just say cute?"* He nudged her head with his snout.

"Oh my goodness. It worked. It really worked!"

His heart pounded against his ribcage. His view of the world kept being altered. *"How is it possible that we can talk to each other with our minds?"*

"It's because we've mated."

That didn't explain anything, but he wasn't going to argue about it now. Brian just wanted to enjoy the experience. *"Race you to the field,"* he telepathed.

"Seriously?"

During the time she'd been away, Brian had gone on many runs. With each one, he found he was able to move faster and faster. When he'd mated with Jillian, he'd inherited some of her Wendayan genes—or so Finn had told him. At first, he thought he was imagining things, but then he reminded himself that nothing was what it seemed around Silver Lake, Tennessee.

"Take it easy on me," he communicated to her. *"How about we aim for the far side of the field?"*

"You're on."

Knowing she could move faster than the eye could track, he took off, but when he emerged from the forest, she was already at the designated spot. Damn.

"Brian? You moved really fast."

"I'm part Wendayan now too, remember?"

"I was told you might inherit my talent, but I didn't know you'd be so good at it."

He opened his mouth in the hopes it looked like a smile. *"Lucky, I guess."*

Wanting to return to normal speed, he took off across the field, and Jillian followed behind him. A second later, she landed on his back, surprising the hell out of him. She nipped his neck. Wanting to spend time playing with her, he stopped then rolled to his side. She jumped off and licked his face. That almost made him want to shift into his human form and make love with her, but she'd never go for it. When it came to living in the cold, Jillian Garner was a light-weight.

Using his big bear paw, he stroked her front leg. Once she began to purr, he wanted them to stay in their animal forms forever and just play. She reached out and ran her paw down his face. Even though she was a beautiful white tiger, he could see the expression of love on her face.

While he wanted to continue petting and licking her, it was time to take a romantic walk around the lake. He'd spoken with Dalton about what their next step could be, but the man hadn't offered any advice. He just said that once two shifters mated, that was it. Well, Brian wanted more. The problem wasn't with other shifters; it was with the rest of the world. He wanted everyone in Silver Lake to know that Jillian and he would be together forever.

Brian lumbered onto all fours and headed back to the path. Jillian appeared in front of him.

"Slow poke," she teased.

Using his ability to move fast, he was beside her in a flash. He wasn't sure which was more fun—shifting or moving fast. When they reached the rock area, they shifted back into their human form, and quickly donned their clothes.

"As much as it's fun to communicate with you just by directing my thoughts, I rather enjoy talking to you."

She hugged him. "I like talking too, but sometimes I like to communicate in a third way."

"Oh, no you don't. It is too cold to be making love outside."

She stepped back. "Silly. I wasn't talking about now."

He was. "Come on then. There's something I want to show you." Actually, there was something he wanted to ask her.

He led her down the path to the lake. With the moon at its fullest, the light made the water glow, almost from below.

"It's beautiful," she said.

He turned toward her. "As I've said before, not as beautiful as you."

Jillian wrapped her arms around his neck. "You always say the sweetest things."

"Let's hope the next thing I say goes over as well." He dug his hand into his pocket and extracted the ring. He stepped back and clasped Jillian's left hand. "I know this might be silly for two shifters, but remember I grew up thinking I was human." He inhaled, but the deep breath failed to slow his rapidly firing heart.

"Nothing is silly when it's about love."

He opened his palm to expose a ring that contained a white diamond next to a chocolate one. "Will you, Jillian Garner, marry me?" He swallowed hard.

She took the ring from his palm and slipped it onto her ring finger. "It's incredibly beautiful." Jillian sniffed. "Yes, I'd love to marry you."

He couldn't believe it. Okay, he figured she'd say yes if only to appease him, but he could actually feel her awe and excitement. Not only could he understand her thoughts, their emotions seemed to compound each other's.

She drew his face to hers, and when she kissed him, the cold air turned warm and the lake's waves beating against the shore ceased to exist. It was as if they were the only two people on earth. He would have continued to explore this wonderful woman had it not been for the glow off to the side that distracted him.

He broke the kiss. "Ah, Jillian?" He turned her around. "We have company."

The glow faded, and all of a sudden, a woman with shimmery long white hair in a light-colored long dress appeared twenty feet in front of them. She moved toward them as if she were floating on air. When the apparition came closer, she transformed into something fully human.

"Hello," she said. "I'm Naliana."

Jillian grabbed his hand and did a small curtsey. Not knowing the protocol of being in front of a goddess, he cast his gaze downward and bowed the upper half of his body.

"You don't need to bow," the goddess said. "I wanted to meet you two in person."

Really? "Thank you for all you've done."

"I love happy endings, and both of you suffered when you were young. If anyone could understand best what you each had been through, it would be each other."

Brian looked down at Jillian, truly seeing her strength. He could only hope he would be as strong one day. "Is that why you paired us?" he asked Naliana.

The goddess smiled. "I'm not sure why or how I pick who belongs together. I just go with my gut." She patted her stomach. "I came tonight to warn you, Brian."

"Me?" Was someone out to harm Jillian again?

"In time, your new hormones will make you whole in every way, but in the meantime, be careful of your newfound abilities. You will grow stronger with each new moon."

"Stronger?"

"Yes."

He wasn't sure he understood, but if she'd want him to know more, she'd have been more explicit. "I'll be careful."

Naliana nodded. "I must go. I have so little time on earth, and what time I do have, I want to spend with James. And congratulations on your engagement."

How did she know? Of course, she was a goddess. "Thank you again."

That might have been a dumb thing to say, but right now, he was rather tongue-tied, and he didn't think Jillian had even blinked the whole time the goddess was in front of them.

Naliana turned and floated back down the path and then slowly faded into the night. He faced Jillian. "Can you believe that?"

"No. I mean, it was hard enough to believe James was an immortal, but to meet a goddess was beyond my wildest dreams." She faced him. "Though in reality, meeting you was even more amazing."

Her words meant the world to him. "That so? How about we head on home and you can show me just how wonderful it is?"

"Race you to the car!"

He laughed. "You're on."

The End

Don't forget to sign up for my newsletter to receive three free books, as well as up-to-date information on my stories. If you prefer to only receive notices regarding my releases, follow me on BookBub
http://smarturl.it/o4cz93?IQid=MLite

I hope you enjoyed Brian and Jillian's story. Up next is FREEING HIS TIGER. It's Dalton and Anna's story. Here is a sneak peak of the first chapter.

Chapter One

OFFICER DALTON GARNER leaned back in his office chair, worried about Anna Fairchild, the woman who smelled of warm honey kissed by the summer sun. She'd said her therapy was going well, but even after three months of meeting with James, she still seemed skittish—not that he was keeping tabs on her or anything.

Dalton couldn't blame her for always looking over her shoulder. Hell, if someone had driven him off the road and then dragged him somewhere, tied him up, and beat him, he'd have had a hard time recovering too. Of course, that could never happen since Dalton was too fast to be caught. Being a shifter and a Wendayan had its advantages.

Mine, mate, his tiger growled.

Stop it, he told the persistent animal. So what if he'd had been the one to carry Anna out after her abduction. It didn't mean she was his—yet. *Anna's not ready* he told his tiger.

That was an understatement. Anna had only learned shifters existed that fateful night because his sister had altered her form right in front of her. It didn't matter the act was needed to kill the man who'd kidnapped her. The shock alone of learning his kind existed would be enough to make Anna scared to be around him and everyone else.

Damn. Dalton wished there was something he could do to help her get over the trauma, but any move on his part might scare her more.

When are you going to tell Anna she's your mate? his tiger asked.

Dalton didn't respond this time.

"Garner!" Phil Smythe, his boss at the sheriff's department, shouted Dalton's name as he rounded the corner from the hallway containing the department offices. He barreled toward him, his face contorted. The man was as military as they came with his short hair, ramrod posture, and booming voice. Dalton's partner, Kalan Murdoch, was right behind him, appearing equally serious despite his light brown hair flying behind him.

Dalton sat up straighter. "Yes sir?"

He tossed a piece of paper on his desk. "Crystal Wedgewood was murdered in her home tonight. I want you and Kalan to take the lead. Paramedics responded to the call by the husband, but she was already dead when they arrived. The coroner is there now and I've dispatched the crime scene unit. If you hurry, you'll beat them there."

Typical Smythe. His discourse was always to the point and with a minimum number of words. Good thing they'd switched shifts with Brant Thompson and Drew Compton. Otherwise, Kalan and he wouldn't have been given the case.

Dalton stood and then had to rush after his partner who was charging toward the exit, acting as if he'd been told his mate was in trouble. Kalan had lived in Silver Lake his whole life and must have known the victim.

Kalan strode to his vehicle that was parked in front of the building, jumped in, and slammed his door shut before Dalton reached the squad car. He managed to slip into the front seat just as Kalan took off.

"I take it you know the vic?" Dalton asked.

"Yes. She owns the Silver Lake Bookstore," he answered. From the way, Kalan's knuckles were clenched on the wheel, he knew her quite well.

"What kind of person would kill a lover of books?"

"Someone with a grudge, I guess. It's not like she was in the wrong place at the wrong time. She was murdered in her own house for goddess's sake." He slapped the wheel.

Violating the sanctity of one's own home was the worst. "Could be she didn't stock some sexy romance novel the killer wanted," Dalton said trying to lighten the tense mood, but the moment his words escaped, he regretted his inappropriate response. Kalan cared for this woman and Dalton had trivialized his concern. The fact his partner didn't even glance his way proved it.

"Whatever the reason," Kalan announced, "I'm going to do my damnedest to find out who killed her."

Dalton wisely kept quiet. They reached Elkwood Lane six minutes later and didn't need to check the numbers on the houses because the flashing ambulance lights led them straight to the door. At the end of the drive, Kalan stopped and jammed the vehicle in park, leaving his lights flashing. "How about you talk to the husband while I check the back for a possible entry point?" Kalan asked.

"Can do." Speaking with a grieving spouse was the worst part of his job, but it might be more difficult for Kalan, especially if he was a friend of the husband.

The neighborhood looked upscale with most homes sitting on at least an acre lot. All were manicured and had long driveways and mature trees. The Wedgewood's home was a two-story brick mansion with tall pillars at the entranceway, and was possibly the nicest place on the block.

As soon as Dalton entered the foyer, the paramedics were on their way out with their gear. Dalton stopped Trevor Harden, one of the paramedics he played pool with. "What can you tell me?" Dalton asked. He didn't expect to learn much from them, but paramedics were trained to check their surroundings.

"The wife was dead when we arrived, and the husband is pretty shaken up. Dr. Williams is in there now. He'll be able to tell you more. Whoever did this was a damned fine shot. The bullet hit her squarely in the chest."

"Or else he stood close."

"Always possible. The doc will have to give you that information."

"Thanks."

Dalton stepped into the living room and was surprised by the opulence. From the fact Mrs. Wedgewood owned a bookstore, he'd pictured flowered curtains, brown recliners surrounding a wooden coffee table, and antiques crammed onto shelves—kind of like his old fashioned rental. This place couldn't be farther from his image nor could it be any colder. That might be because Dalton wasn't a fan of modern. About the only things that weren't black or white were the beige curtains and a throw rug that had a few splotches of red woven in it.

The coroner and his assistant were working on the body while a man of about forty-five was on the sofa with his head leaned back and his eyes shut. Before speaking with the husband, Dalton glanced around hoping to find a weapon conveniently sitting on a table, but luck wasn't pointing his way today.

He returned his focus to Mr. Wedgewood. Most middle-aged women would call him handsome in a square-jaw kind of way. His tailored suit looked expensive as did his shoes and silk tie.

Dalton moved closer. "Mr. Wedgewood?"

The man looked up then swiped a hand over his eyes and down his jaw. "Yes?"

"I'm Dalton Garner from the sheriff's department. I'd like to ask you a few questions."

"Of course. I'll tell you what I can. I want my wife's killer found."

Even though he sounded sincere, it didn't mean the man wasn't guilty. Dalton always asked questions based on the assumption that this person could be the killer. Tonight would be no exception. "We'll do our best. If you don't mind, I'd like to record our conversation." Dalton pulled out his phone.

"Sure, but I don't know much."

Husbands were a wealth of information whether they believed it or not. "Can you walk me through what happened?"

Mr. Wedgewood pulled a monogrammed handkerchief from his

pocket and blew his nose. "Crystal's shop closes at six on Mondays. She owns the Silver Lake Bookstore." Dalton nodded. "I usually arrive home before her, but tonight I had to stay late. I was working on a client's portfolio and didn't leave until six thirty. When I walked in, I found Crystal…like that." He swallowed hard.

"Do you own a gun?"

A tic appeared around his left eye. "Yes, but it was stolen about a month ago."

He'd heard that story a hundred times. "Did you report it?"

"Yes."

Dalton made a mental note to check that out. "You have blood on your shirt. How did that happen?"

Mr. Wedgewood looked down at the red smears than glanced off to the side. He sniffled. "When I came home and saw Crystal, I thought she might still be alive, so I cradled her in my arms, hoping my body heat would help revive her. When she didn't moan or respond in any way, I called 911."

That explained the blood—assuming his story was true. Kalan came in through the front door but didn't indicate what if anything he'd found. Instead of joining him, Kalan made a beeline toward the coroner and his assistant.

"Does your wife have any enemies?" Dalton asked.

"No. Everyone loved her."

Someone didn't. "Do you think one of her employees could have been angry over something? Like not getting a raise or a promotion?"

"I couldn't say. I really didn't know them very well. Crystal ran her business and I ran mine."

How sad. Not that he believed he'd end up with Anna, despite her being his mate, but if he did, he'd want to know everything about her job like how many customers came in that day and who was nice and who wasn't. At least he knew Anna's boss well since Elana was Kalan's mate.

"I realize this is overwhelming, but I'll need you to come down to the precinct."

"What? Why? I didn't kill my wife." His grief was replaced with disbelief tinged with anger.

Dalton held up his hands. "I'm not accusing you of anything. We need to process your clothes."

"Why? I told you my wife's blood is on my suit." He acted as if he couldn't believe someone would accuse him of any wrong doing.

"I understand, but it's procedure." They'd need to test for gunshot residue too, but he had no intention of telling that to Mr. Wedgewood.

Just then two policemen arrived along with the crime scene unit. Dalton nodded to Will Mathers, one of his coworkers. "Can you help Mr. Wedgewood pack for a few days?"

Wedgewood jumped up, his jaw tight and his hands clenched. "What, so now I can't even stay in my own home?"

The man was losing it. "Mr. Wedgewood. It will take a day or two to process the scene, which means you can't be here. Is there anyone you can stay with? A friend, a coworker, or a family member perhaps?"

His breathing calmed as he tried to figure out his options. "Yeah, sure."

As soon as Will Mathers escorted the husband down the hallway, Kalan joined Dalton. "What did you learn?" Dalton asked.

"Forced entry in the back. I'll have CSU dust for prints. Doc Williams confirmed she died about an hour ago. The bullet hit her in the chest, but he won't know how far back the shooter was standing until he gets her to the lab. You?"

"The husband has blood on his shirt. He said he found her on the floor and picked her up in his arms. We'll take him down to the station and have his clothes and hands processed for gunshot residue."

"Does he look good for it?"

Dalton shrugged. "He said he was at work until right before he called 911."

Kalan nodded. "We can follow up on that later. Come on. Let's let the CSU do their job. We don't need to be contaminating anything else."

EVEN THOUGH ANNA told her therapist she didn't need to have weekly sessions anymore, James insisted she return one more time. As far as she was concerned, no amount of talking or counseling could erase what happened to her. One thing he said rang true. Her future was up to her. Either she could walk around in fear or embrace the challenges of life and move forward. Anna's whole life had been one battle after another, and moving forward had always been her motto. First, her parents had given her up at birth, and then her first foster home failed to take care of her properly, putting her back into the system until she was adopted at the age of six. Unfortunately, her new parents were only supportive when it suited them. All in all, she'd been dealt a raw hand. Until a few years ago, she'd allowed self-pity to guide her decisions. If nothing else, James had shown her there was a lot of good in the world, and it was there for the taking— if she had the courage to grab it.

Her thoughts shot to Dalton who personified good. He'd been there for her when she needed him, which was more than she could say for anyone else in her life—except for maybe Elana and Jillian. When she questioned James about Dalton, he just shrugged, claiming he didn't feel comfortable telling her about another person. James was after all a therapist whose role it was to respect a person's privacy.

It didn't matter. She wasn't in therapy to discuss her lack of a love life anyway. She was there because Frank Whitlaw had kidnapped her. With much work, James had finally convinced her that involvement with the man had been a fluke. Not only had James helped her put the trauma in perspective, he'd been a font of information, especially when it came to what she'd seen the night of her capture. Anna hadn't wanted to believe that her friend had shifted from a human into a white tiger, or that her boss's brother

Brian had transformed into a bear right in front of her eyes, but apparently they had. For weeks Anna had been positive she'd lost her mind, but James had explained she had been mistaken.

Apparently, people who could shift from an animal into a human were appropriately called shifters. He even went on to say that Silver Lake was full of these shifter-like creatures. Now that was scary. Every time someone came into the flower shop where she worked, she tried to decide if they might be one. Of course, she was unable to detect if they were, but it was interesting to guess nonetheless.

After a week of deep reflection on the topic, Anna dredged up the courage to ask James for more info on shifters. He seemed happy to oblige and explained such concepts as a shifter's mate, and then what happens after a shifter bites the human he was destined to be with. The whole idea of a fated mate still freaked her out though she did like the concept that when a shifter found his fated mate, he would protect her at all cost and would be totally devoted to her. Now that she could get used to.

Sadly, who was paired with who was not up to the shifter or the person he was mated with. The gods decided it—or rather one goddess in particular did. Talk about another paradigm shift! Because of being in the system, she wasn't brought up with a religious background. Still, the idea of gods and goddesses was hard to get used to. According to James, she had no control over this part of her destiny. She might be mated with a shifter or she might not.

Regardless of whether she had any control over her fate, she still dreamed of Dalton. Then the underdeveloped rational side of her brain told her the gods wouldn't be that cruel. They'd never pit someone who was so straight-laced and uptight with someone like her. He'd balk for sure. Anna loved art and all things relating to nature, and she bet Dalton feasted on spreadsheets and logic.

It was silly to even dream about something like that since she wasn't buying the concept of a destined mate. However, no harm ever came from a little make believe.

Just in case she was wrong, at the next session she asked James how someone could tell if two people were destined to be together. All he would say was that the answer would be in the shifter's eyes.

Great. The whole window of his soul thing didn't help her at all.

Bottom line, she needed to push the whole idea aside and let nature take its course. Truth was, the whole biting stuff scared her, despite having the end result worth it. If a shifter bit his human mate, she'd become a shifter too. Having power like that would go a long way in being able to protect herself.

James did stress that the shifters and Wendayans worked together in Silver Lake, and that the shifters protected their fellow witches. In the end, it didn't matter if her mate turned out to be a shifter or not. Someone would be there to protect her. Anna got great comfort from that fact.

For weeks after that talk, her head didn't stop spinning from all the information James had so casually tossed out at her. But weird shit like that wasn't all they discussed. James and she talked about her life growing up as well as her need to find her birth parents. She'd always believed that knowing why they'd given her up might help heal her belief that she'd somehow been unlovable. James told her that she personally had nothing to do with her parents' decision. Circumstances might have dictated that they give her up. While probably true, she'd come this far in her search and would like to learn their identities.

So here she was at his house for the last time. Anna had finally put to rest what had happened to her, yet a bit of melancholy had seeped in. She liked talking to the old man. Not only was he was wise and so sure of himself, he possessed an aura of pure knowledge. What she wouldn't give to unlock what made him tick.

Anna smiled thinking back to the first time she'd arrived at the ancient looking stone house. It had given her the creeps for sure with its dark interior, but after a few weeks she began to feel safe inside. It might have been because James didn't judge her or because he was the only person she'd never been able to get any kind of reading from when she touched him. No, that wasn't true. She hadn't been able to get a reading off of Dalton either. Both of them seemed to be able to block her talents. While she'd never asked James, she wouldn't be surprised if he too was some kind of Wendayan like Dalton.

Anna knocked on his door and James answered quickly. "Anna, nice to see you again. Please come in."

The smell of freshly baked cookies caused her stomach to grumble. As soon as she entered the main room, she spotted a plate filled with chocolate chip cookies on the table.

"My wife baked them," he said answering her unasked question.

"She did?" Anna had assumed the woman had passed. Never once had she been around when Anna visited, though it was possible she worked the night shift at a hospital or perhaps was a waitress at an all night diner.

"Yes, last night, but Naliana had to leave today. Otherwise, the two of you could have met." She didn't need to touch his arm to feel his pain.

"I'm sorry."

He smiled but the joy didn't reach his eyes. "Thank you. She'll return in a month."

"A month? That must be tough to be separated for so long."

"Indeed. Shall we begin?"

PACK WARS (Paranormal)
Training Their Mate (book 1)
Claiming Their Mate (book 2)
Rescuing Their Virgin Mate (book 3)
Box Set (books 1-3)
Loving Their Vixen Mate (book 4)
Fighting For Their Mate (book 5)
Enticing Their Mate (book 6)

MONTANA PROMISES (Full length contemporary)
Promises of Mercy (book 1)
Foundations For Three (book 2)
Montana Fire (book 3)
Hart To Hart (book 4)
Burning Seduction (book 5)
Montana Promises Box Set (books 1-3)

ROCK HARD, MONTANA (contemporary novellas)
Montana Desire (book 1)
Awakening Passions (book 2)

HIDDEN HILLS SHIFTERS (Paranormal)
An Unexpected Diversion (book 1) – FREE
Bare Instincts (book 2)
Shifting Destinies (book 3)
Embracing Fate (book 4)
Promises Unbroken (book 5)

SOUTHERN SHIFTERS KINDLE WORLDS
Bear 'N Dirty

WERES & WITCHES OF SILVER LAKE
A Magical Shift (book 1)
Catching Her Bear (book 2)
A Surge of Magic (book 3)
The Bear's Forbidden Wolf (book 4)
Her Reluctant Bear (book 5)

Author Bio

Want 3 FREE books? Sign up for my newsletter.

COPY AND PASTE INTO YOUR BROWSER:
http://smarturl.it/o4cz93?IQid=MLite

Check out my latest interview on You Tube:
youtube.com/watch?v=sQo5pyyVMDI

Not only do I love to read, write, and dream, I'm an extrovert. I enjoy being around people and am always trying to understand what makes them tick. Not only must my books have a happily ever after, I need characters I can relate to. My men are wonderful, dynamic, smart, strong, and the best lovers in the world (of course).

You'll find me most days on my chaise lounge with my laptop and my iced tea(unsweetened!) on the side table. I love to sleep in late and write into the wee hours. I also love FB, so you'll find me on there, too!

I believe I am the luckiest woman. I do what I love and I have a wonderful, supportive husband, who happens to be hot!

Fun facts about me

(1) I'm a math nerd who loves spreadsheets. Give me numbers and I'll find a pattern.

(2) I'm addicted to taking pictures (I taught high school photo for 30 years). I plan to periodically post some of my favorites on my newsletter [so sign up!].

(3) I also like to exercise. Yes, I know I'm odd. Not only do I walk with different women each week, I teach Pilates twice a week at a local rec center, and lift weights the other days.

I love hearing from readers either on FB or via email (hint, hint).

Social Media Sites

Website:
www.velladay.com

FB:
www.facebook.com/vella.day.90

Twitter:
@velladay4

Gmail:
velladayauthor@gmail.com

Google:
plus.google.com/u/0/116041077486216602121/posts

Tsu:
www.tsu.co/velladay

www.ingramcontent.com/pod-product-compliance
Lightning Source LLC
Chambersburg PA
CBHW022010170626
46808CB00001B/353